I0633808

Finding Dolly

BECKI LEE

LITERARY ESCAPES PRESS

Copyright © 2023 by Becki Lee

Finding Dolly

Becki Lee

www.beckileeauthor.com

becki@beckileeauthor.com

Published 2023 by Literary Escapes Press

Edited by Rachel Shipp Editing

Cover design and formatting by Chris Kridler, Sky Diary Productions

All rights reserved.

No part of this book may be reproduced in any form by any electronic or mechanical means, including photocopying, recording, scanning, information storage and retrieval systems, without permission in writing from the author. The only exception is a reviewer, who may quote short excerpts in a review.

This book is a work of fiction. All names, characters, places, organizations, events, and incidents are either products of the author's imagination or are used fictitiously. Any resemblance to actual events, locales, organizations, or persons living or dead, is entirely coincidental and beyond the intent of either the author or the publisher.

First Printing: June 2023

Literary Escapes Press

Paperback ISBN: 978-1-960969-01-9

Contents

For Dolly Parton
Thank you for living a life full of color, class, and
courage.

Chapter 1

GRACE

"When someone shows me their true colors, I believe them."

Dolly Parton

GRACE PARSON PACED THE parking lot of the Landmon Funeral Home. She didn't want to be talking to her boyfriend on the phone. She wanted him here. By her side. On the toughest day of her life.

"Drake, where are you? Bree and I are about to go in."

"I'm sorry, babe. I got called out of town. I really wish I could be there to give you a hug."

"You're going out of town? Today? How could you, Drake? I need you here." Grace couldn't believe what she was hearing. How could his company send him out of town today, of all days?

"I tried to fight it, babe. But apparently, no one else is able to make it today. I'm really sorry."

"Well...safe travels, I guess. At least Bree is here. I'll talk to you later." Grace hung up, feeling dejected, and walked to the door where Breena, her best friend, waited.

Grace dreaded opening that door. Her life would never be the same once she did.

Why wasn't today gloomy or raining? Orlando's gift of a bright beautiful October morning mocked her.

She smoothed down her black dress and rubbed her bright yellow heels against her tights to shine them up a bit. Finally, clutching Breena's hand for support, Grace pulled open the funeral home's heavy oak door.

It was time to say goodbye to her mother.

Grace tentatively stepped into the tastefully decorated room but halted with her first look at the dais. Despite the room's low light, the casket holding her mother was a beacon directly in front of her.

"Bree!" Grace's emphatic whisper held a note of shock. "What the heck is Mama wearing?"

Grace wasn't surprised to find her best friend's shoulders shaking. Laughing.

They'd come to the funeral home early to have some time alone with her mother before the funeral started. And now she was glad. It was wildly inappropriate to laugh at the outfit her mother had chosen to be buried in—well, costume might be a more apropos word. But Grace knew if they weren't laughing, they'd be crying.

Of course Mama had probably anticipated that when she'd chosen her burial outfit. She would have wanted her girls to have something to smile about.

Grace grabbed Breena's hand as they moved toward the coffin to say their goodbyes and to take in a close-up view of the outfit before the doors opened for the service. She shook her head, gazing down at her mother, unable to keep the grin off her face.

Marilyn Parson had been laid to rest in a bright pink jumpsuit—no doubt inspired by her hero, Dolly Parton—that sparkled and shined all over. Silver fringe lined her arms and legs, and the neckline proudly displayed a bedazzled collar that reflected the light shining down on her. At her waist was a similarly glittery belt, and while the bottom third of the coffin was closed, Grace was sure her mother had chosen the silver boots she'd worn to school pick up, so often embarrassing Grace. Grace's mother sure knew how to go out in style, so to speak.

"Well." Breena grinned, her eyes shining with tears. "She still knows how to make a statement."

Grace's grin widened. "When the funeral director told me Mama had already picked her burial outfit, I guess I should have been suspicious. I suppose we can be grateful she didn't want to wear a pole-dancing outfit." She laughed, despite the threatening tears. "She does look good though, doesn't she?"

"Your mother always looked good." Breena put her arm around Grace's waist and squeezed.

"Bye, Mama," Grace whispered, then leaned down to kiss her mother's rouged cheek. She closed her eyes for a moment as she caught the light floral-and-citrus scent her mother had worn every day. Estée Lauder Beautiful. A tear rolled down her cheek as she realized that, with her mother's passing, she was officially an orphan.

People started to arrive as she and Breena drifted to the front row to claim their reserved seats.

Breena leaned over. "Should we save a seat for Drake?"

"No. Just you and me. He had to go out of town for work today so isn't able to come."

While Breena didn't say anything, Grace noticed her frown. It mirrored Grace's own disappointment.

One hour and a box of tissues later, after saying thank you and goodbye to almost everyone who had come to pay their respects or support her, Grace groaned as she fell into a chair at the back of the room. It was only then she noticed two people still there—a hospice nurse, Nancy, was making her way to them, and an older man still by the coffin.

"Grace honey, Breena, I'm so sorry for your loss. Your mother was a treasure." Nancy sat down next to Grace and rummaged through her purse. "I have a note for you from your mama. Somewhere in here."

Grace exchanged a confused look with Breena before the nurse handed her a pink envelope.

"She asked me to write a few things down for her the day before she fell into her coma. Some of it didn't make sense, but I wrote down everything I could understand. I'm so sorry I forgot about this."

"No problem, Nancy. Thank you for coming today, and thank you for all your help and compassion with Mama." Grace stood and gave her a hug, then watched as she left the room.

Grace nodded her head toward the casket. "I wonder who he is?"

"Yeah, I was wondering too," Breena said softly. "He seems pretty broken up about your mother's death. He's been up there for some time now."

Just then the man turned around and strode toward them, stopping in front of Grace. "I am so sorry for your loss. Marilyn was a wonderful woman." He held out his hand. "I'm Edward Pillingham. Your mother and I were friends for three decades."

Grace shook his hand. "It's nice to meet you, Mr. Pillingham. You knew my mother for so long, I'm surprised I don't know you."

He smiled. "I live in Nashville. I just happened to be in Florida when I was alerted to your mother's passing. I am so thankful I was able to make it here for her service. You probably wouldn't remember me from your father's service. I had to leave shortly after it finished and was unable to meet you then."

Grace studied the man in front of her. About her mother's age, mid- to late-sixties. Which meant they were in their thirties when they met. His full head of white hair was perfectly cut and combed, his charcoal gray suit looked made to fit him. He was a handsome man. She wondered how her father fit into all of this.

"I...uh, no. I don't remember." Grace knew her confusion must have shown on her face.

"May I?" He gestured to the seat in front of the two women. At her nod, he turned the chair around to face them and settled into it. "I was your mother's lawyer. Like I said, we met over thirty years ago. Your father and I were good friends, and I met Marilyn through him. She was pregnant with you when we met, actually."

"Oh." Grace wasn't sure what to make of this new information. She didn't know much about her parents' past, but this was a lot to take in. Especially today. At her mother's funeral.

"You'll be heading to Nashville at some point?" Mr. Pillingham asked.

"I hadn't planned on it." Grace was confused.

Mr. Pillingham didn't say anything for a moment. "Your mother kept her apartment up there. She didn't mention it?"

"Oh. No, she didn't. I didn't find any paperwork in her things, so I thought she must have sold it before moving here."

Mr. Pillingham shook his head. "No, she wanted to save it for you. She was actually very insistent."

"Well, I guess I'll need to plan a trip to Nashville. We can probably go in a couple of weeks or so." Grace looked at Breena for confirmation.

This was one of the many times Grace was thankful to be her own boss. She was able to take time off without putting in for leave or worrying about how many days she had left. Of course, because she was her own boss, she also didn't get paid until she secured her next client. Her dwindling savings account had been feeling the squeeze lately.

"I'll have my secretary call to set something up at your convenience. I'll be back up there in about two weeks, so the timing should work well."

"I...um..." Grace sagged back in her chair. She was having a hard time focusing. It had been not only a long day but a long several weeks. Heck, a long couple of years. "I have the address, but I don't have the key."

He smiled kindly. "I have those at the office. I'll have my secretary call Brian to let him know to expect you." At her blank look, he continued, "Brian is the doorman at Marilyn's building. He can help you until I get back and get the keys to you." He stood and spoke to both of them. "Again, I'm very sorry for your loss."

"I guess we'll see you in a few weeks then. Thank you, Mr. Pillingham."

As she watched him walk away, Grace felt her life was headed down a completely new path. One she wasn't prepared for.

The scary part was, she had no idea what direction she was supposed to go.

"That was nice of Drake to give us a ride," Breena said as they arrived at their gate.

Grace and Breena were both exhausted, so when Drake offered to give them a ride to the Orlando airport, Grace gratefully accepted. After two weeks of cleaning the townhouse, sorting through her mother's belongings, and preparing for the next chapter, it felt good to settle into the hard, uncomfortable plastic chairs with nothing to do except wait for their flight to Nashville to be announced.

She looked at the woman who had been her true friend through thick and thin for so many years. Breena O'Malley was lovely. Even in middle school, she'd been lovely. No awkward phase for her. Soft, curly, dark red hair that fell just past her shoulders, bright green eyes, and the creamy pale skin many Irish women are blessed with—though Breena certainly didn't see it that way.

Grace kept her smile inside. "Yes, it was nice, wasn't it? He's been very attentive since Mama passed away."

She knew Breena didn't like Drake, so she appreciated the comment. Grace smiled a little, thinking of her beau. Drake was beautiful—dark brown hair, always perfectly cut and coiffed, startlingly light blue eyes, a Hollywood smile he used to charm everyone. It was one of the reasons he was successful in his sales position. That and the fact he always looked like he'd just stepped off the pages of *GQ* magazine. *And for some reason*, she thought, *he chose me*.

They'd met briefly at a charity auction and ran into each other in the parking garage at his office building after she'd just finished a frustrating meeting with a fundraising committee. She had a talent for running fundraisers, but all too often, she let others run over her and change what she knew was a good plan, resulting in a fundraiser that was rarely as good as it could have been. That day, coming out of the meeting to find her Toyota wouldn't start had added to her bad mood.

Drake had walked out behind her, saw her car troubles, and offered her a ride home. He seemed surprised and impressed by her address in one of the nicer, older neighborhoods in Orlando. She was grateful she'd been able to live in the townhouse she grew up in after her mother moved out several years before.

Since then, he'd been courting her, to use an old-fashioned term. But it felt kind of old-fashioned to Grace. He wasn't pushy or forward with her, which she appreciated. He showed a proper amount of interest without scaring her away.

He regularly sent flowers and made it known he was her boyfriend when she had meetings in his building...not that she had hordes of men lining up or anything. Besides, she didn't really have the time or emotional capacity for an all-in relationship right then. Drake made it easy, and somehow, he'd slid into her life.

"He's been talking about the future," Grace hesitantly added. "That maybe we should get married."

She hadn't mentioned this to Breena before because she wasn't sure how she felt about it. Could she picture being with Drake for the rest of her life? He was certainly nice, considerate, handsome, but was that enough? She'd always dreamed of someone who made her stomach flutter, of a kiss that made her forget where she was. Maybe that kind of thing wasn't real, just fairy tales and romance novels. Maybe what she had with Drake was as good as it got.

Breena looked over at her, startled, opening her mouth, then closing it again. "And how do you feel about that?" she finally asked diplomatically.

Before Grace could answer, her phone pinged. Confused, she pulled up the security app to see what was going on in her townhouse.

"Hang on a sec while I check the house. The alarm must be malfunctioning...you and I are the only ones with keys." Even as she said it, she remembered a day last week when her purse had been lost for a few hours. Drake had found it tucked away somewhere. She wondered now if someone had copied her keys.

Her mouth hung open as the app's video feed revealed someone in her house.

"Hey, everything okay?" Breena's voice was laced with concern.

Grace held the phone so her friend could see the video as well. They watched as two people walked around her living room before moving in close together. Whispering? And then they kissed, which was extraordinarily odd if they were there to rob her house.

"What the...?" Grace and Breena looked at each other, confused.

The couple, hand in hand, went from the living room to Grace's bedroom. It was clear they were not there to rob her. Drake's face came into focus.

Grace flinched as if she'd been slapped across the face; her heart hammered. An internal war between hurt and anger waged inside her.

"That bastard!" Grace said through clenched teeth.

Breena rubbed her back. "Who's the woman?"

She took a deep breath. "Deanna. I worked with her on my last project. I can't believe he's with her."

The phone slipped from her fingers. Her hand automatically went to her throat, only to find it bare. She hadn't been able to find her necklace when she dressed that morning.

Grace ground out, "Will you call the cops for me?"

"Absolutely." Breena's Irish temper simmered.

Grace watched as Breena talked to the operator at 911, pacing in a tight circle with her right arm wildly gesticulating, causing a few passengers to move further away.

Grace, her anger giving way to nausea, took a few screenshots of a shirtless Drake and Deanna, then turned off her phone and stuck it in her purse. Closing her eyes, she furiously wiped away the traitorous tear running down her cheek. *He doesn't deserve my tears,* she scolded herself.

Grace wished her mother were here to give her a hug. Grief lanced through her heart once again; sadness for the moments that would never be gripped her. Grace remembered something her mother used to say all the time. "Honey, if someone shows you who they really are, believe them."

Well, Mama, I guess I know who Drake really is now, don't I?

With the cops alerted and on their way to her apartment, Grace wondered what she had done to make Drake cheat on her. Maybe if she'd been more attentive or more available...

But that had been impossible. Between caring for her mother and running her own business, her time had been limited. She let out a long, frustrated breath. She was ready to get the heck out of Florida. She needed a fresh start; maybe Nashville would offer one, at least for a little bit. Did she even have a reason to come back to Florida? She had no family here, no job since her last contract finished before her mother passed away. And now no boyfriend.

Oh sure, she had a townhouse she would have to figure out, but Florida seemed to be handing her one heartbreak after another lately.

When the gate agent called their row, Grace and Breena moved to the back of the line. Grace stuck her hands in the pockets of the long black cardigan she'd jokingly thrown on to "dress up" her black leggings and white T-shirt. She felt the stiff edge of a piece of paper in her pocket. Curious, she pulled it out.

"Whatcha got there?" Breena asked, looking at the envelope in Grace's hand.

Grace was holding the pink envelope the hospice nurse had given her at her mother's funeral. "How could I have forgotten about this?"

"Excuse me, ma'am." The gate agent held her hand out for their boarding passes.

Grace quickly stuck the note back in her pocket, scanned her boarding pass, and headed onto the jetway.

Several moments later, buckled into seat 24B, she pulled the note back out.

Sitting next to her, Breena leaned over. "Do you want to talk about Drake?"

"I really don't." Grace shook her head. She didn't have the emotional capacity to think about him at the moment.

Breena nodded, understanding. "Let's have a look at your note then."

Grace slid the paper from the envelope and unfolded it. She held the pale pink paper to her heart and inhaled deeply. A wave of memories rolled over her along with her mother's scent. She thought of her mother dropping her off for her first day of kindergarten. The Christmas the two of them had worn matching pink-and-green dresses with white boots for a party. The day her father died when she and her mother hugged so tightly, sharing their grief. The day she graduated from college—her mother was definitely the loudest in the arena, but Grace hadn't cared.

"What's it say?"

Grace smiled a little as the memories faded. She held the note under Breena's nose and watched as she inhaled and smiled too. Grace thought Breena probably had her own mental movie of memories playing through her mind.

She unfolded the letter and laid it on Breena's tray table. With their heads together, they read the short note from her mother.

My Darling Grace,

There's something on my mind I really need to share with you.

It's very important!

After I pass away, I want you to find Dolly.

It's so important.

Find Dolly!

(Marilyn was very emphatic about this.)

Grace smiled at Nancy's commentary before reading the rest of the note.

My past was in Nashville.

Your future is there.

Find Eddie and Carl in Nashville, they can help you.

I love you, baby girl.

Mama

Grace looked at Breena, whose furrowed brows mirrored her own confusion.

"Find Dolly?" Grace questioned. "Why would Mama ask me to find Dolly? Dolly who?"

"Is she asking you to find *the* Dolly? As in Dolly Parton?"

Grace felt her eyes go wide. "She wouldn't ask that...would she?"

"Of course she would." Breena snickered. "And Eddie and Carl? Who the heck are they? Are they more country music superstars you'll never be able to find?"

They talked through it for a bit longer, but it made no sense. Breena announced she was going to take a nap before curling into the window, and within minutes, she was breathing deeply.

But Grace, never able to sleep on a plane, thought through her mother's note. What had she meant *her past had been in Nashville*? Sure, her mother did live there for a few years before she came back to Florida, but that could hardly be considered a *past*, could it? Then she thought about the man she'd met at her mother's funeral. Mr. Pillingham. He said they'd known each other for thirty years. And he lived in Nashville.

So many questions.

As for her own future, Grace had no idea where it was headed. She just knew it wasn't with Drake. But Nashville? She had no reason to think her future was there.

And then there were Eddie and Carl.

Who were they? And why would her mother think she'd want to find them?

Grace recalled that when her mother had first moved back with her, she'd often talked about a man named Carl. From her mother's stories, Grace had the impression Carl was a kind, older man who was a little lonely. If she remembered correctly, he was her mother's contractor. She couldn't recall her mother mentioning Eddie at all.

"Would you like a drink or snack?" A flight attendant stood in the aisle with the clunky cart in front of her.

Grace glanced at Breena, still sleeping peacefully, her head leaning awkwardly against the window. She shook her head. "No thanks."

Grace looked back at Breena, envious of how her friend could sleep pretty much anywhere, anytime. Her gaze wandered back to the note and journal in her lap.

The message from her mother was confusing. Why would her mother send her on a mission to find Dolly? As far as Grace was concerned, she only needed to go to Nashville to get her mother's condo ready to sell and to see a little of the city.

Why had her mother left her this crazy mission?

Grace's time in Nashville was going to be busy, and she needed to get her thoughts organized. The best way to organize was always to write it all down.

Pulling down the tray table, she opened her journal and decided the best place to start was to write down what she knew right now.

Finding Dolly Project:
Here's what I know so far...

1. I rediscovered the note Nancy gave me at Mama's funeral today. It was in the pocket of my cardigan. The days after the funeral were so busy, I completely forgot about it. In the note, Mama gave me a mission. A mission to find Dolly. I'm headed to Nashville now, so maybe I'll run into her at the grocery store, LOL. I'm curious what Mama had in mind. Why she'd want me to find Dolly, and how she thought that might happen? Nancy said Mama gave her the message the day before she fell into a coma. Maybe Mama wasn't thinking right. After all, she had dementia, and it was pretty bad by then. Who knows what she was thinking?

What I do know is Mama really enjoyed and respected Dolly Parton. When I was growing up, Dolly influenced Mama's wardrobe, and for a while, mine too. Mama always loved the bright, sparkly, and outlandish, and was disappointed when I turned away from it.

Bright and sparkly suited Mama though. It was just who she was. She was bright and sparkly herself, so it very much worked for her to wear all those fun and crazy outfits. I remember when Mama came to live with me, we watched so many Dolly movies during those three years. Her favorite was Steel Magnolias.

I know Dolly is a country music superstar.

I'm pretty sure she's from Tennessee and lives some-where near Nashville.

I know Mama loved her music, her movies, and her clothing.

2. Mama thinks my future is in Nashville. While that's a little crazy for her to think since my whole life has been in Florida, it's even crazier to learn Mama's past was connected to Nashville. Especially since she'd just bought her apartment there six years ago. When Mr. Pillingham told me he had known Mama for thir-ty years, I didn't know what to think. Thirty years! And he and Daddy had been friends too?

So many questions...but both Mama and Daddy are gone, and I can't get any answers. Maybe Mr. Pillingham will have some. I'll meet with him in a week, so hopefully, I can learn something.

Chapter 2

CARL

*"Don't get so busy making a living that
you forget to make a life."*
Dolly Parton

STANDING IN HIS OFFICE on the outskirts of east
Nashville, Carl Montgomery was in his zone. At
thirty-five, he was proud of the business he'd built over
the past decade and a half. He could say, without a
doubt, he had one of the best restoration contract-
ing businesses in Nashville. Maybe even in all of Tennessee.

Midway through a proposal to renovate an old
barn for a newlywed couple, they were all startled by
the familiar opening notes of Dolly Parton's *Nine to
Five*. Everyone looked around, trying to figure out

who had the audacity to not silence their phone for this meeting.

Carl looked sternly at each person until he realized it was *his* phone merrily chirping away.

His face heated, and he fumbled to turn off the ringer. Why would *his* phone be ringing? And with that song? He'd only ever used that particular song for one caller, Marilyn.

Marilyn!

The realization of what the call must have meant struck Carl, and a big grin split his handsome, boyish face. Three years ago, he'd left his number with Brian, the doorman at Marilyn's building, to call when he heard any word about her. Carl had been waiting ever since. He barely resisted the urge to return the call immediately, but this was an important meeting. He wanted this job for the challenge and for his crew.

He looked forward to listening to Brian's message after work, but for now, Carl needed to finish the meeting.

He ran his hand through his reddish brown hair and realized he needed a haircut. A fact his mom was bound to point out when he saw her in a couple of hours.

"Sorry," he said sheepishly before looking at the young couple across from him and pushing on. "Let's get back to business."

With revived enthusiasm, he explained the plans to convert the barn on her family's property. He loved projects like this, and his enthusiasm came through in his presentation.

An hour later, with the contract signed, he shook hands with the couple and the architect, then locked up the office. He was thrilled he'd be able to leave his mark on this couple's beautiful old building, and he relished the challenge of converting it into a home, making it something new and fresh while respecting its history and lines.

But now, as much as he wanted to stay in his office planning the next several months with this new project, he needed to head across town to his parents' for Sunday dinner...on this Friday afternoon. His mouth already salivated in anticipation of his mom's pot roast.

Carl leaned back in his chair—the one he'd used since he was a child—at his parents' dining room table. Everyone was still in their same seat—Dad at the head of the table, Mom to his left, and Carl and his sister, Jillian, next to each other on the right.

"Have some more potatoes, Carl honey."

Carl groaned and rubbed his full belly. "Mom, I've had three servings already. I know you think I don't eat when I'm not here, but I do." He laughed and ran his fingers through his hair, a little surprised he hadn't yet heard about needing a haircut. Even at thirty-five years old, dinner with his family was one of his favorite things. And he made time each month to fit it into his schedule.

As always, his mom's pot roast was delicious. She was technically his stepmother, but he thought of her as just Mom. And because he'd lived with her for most of his life, he knew where this conversation was headed.

He wasn't looking forward to it.

"Well, with you not having a wife, I just worry." She heaved a dramatic sigh. "I don't know when you have time to eat. You're always so busy."

This was a familiar complaint. He could feel a headache starting behind his eyelids. He loved his mother, but dang, he wished she weren't so intent on him getting married.

"Mom, I don't need a wife to make sure I have dinner each night. Believe it or not, I do manage to eat, even on my own. Besides, it would be easier to hire a cook than to worry about a wife...or even a girlfriend." He thought for a minute. "Actually, that's not a bad idea. Maybe I'll hire a housekeeper who can cook some meals. Thanks, Mom."

"That is neither what I said nor what I intended, and you know it, Carl James." She gave him the piercing look he knew from childhood. "And no hanky-panky with the housekeeper."

His father choked on his water, and Jillian started laughing.

"Ooh, you got the middle name. You're in trouble," she taunted.

He poked her in the ribs with his elbow. "Nobody asked you, Jilly." But he was laughing along with her.

No one could deny they were siblings. They looked so much alike with thick, wavy auburn hair that always looked a little out of control, the same smile and dimples. But where his eyes were green, hers matched their dad's deep blue.

He looked at his mom. "I appreciate your concern, Mom, but I'm good. Actually, I'm really good. My business is doing very well, I've got some great friends, and...well, I don't want or need a wife—or any woman—in my life right now." He looked over at his dad, silently pleading for help, but just got a grin and a twinkle in those deep blue eyes.

"Honey, you need more balance. There's more to life than work, you know."

It grated a bit that his mom couldn't accept that his life was good the way it was.

"Oh lighten up, Shell. Our boy's doing great." Doug Montgomery looked at his wife, Michelle, his eyes still twinkling. "But I do agree with your mom on one point." He looked at Carl with a mock-stern expression, finger pointed for effect. "No hanky-panky with the help."

Carl could feel his face heat up. How was it his parents could still embarrass him? "Why aren't you picking on Jilly? She's not married either."

He was whining and he knew it. Throwing his sister under the bus wasn't his usual tactic, but she seemed to handle it better than he did. Maybe because she was a cop.

Jillian elbowed him back. "Hey, don't drag me into this. I just bought a house. I don't need a guy in my life. I've got enough to deal with."

His dad finally took pity on him. "So tell me what's going on with your business."

Grateful for the shift in conversation and always happy to talk about his work, Carl told them about the contract he'd closed a couple of hours earlier. He had worked hard to build his company's reputation, and now he was pretty much able to pick and choose which projects to accept. And this barn renovation was one he'd desperately wanted.

"Glad to hear business is going so well," his dad said.

"When Mr. Kline ended our work on his house a few months ago, I was concerned we might have to lay off a few of the guys, but we've actually had to hire a few more to keep everything on the schedule. Jim's complaining he's too busy." Carl chuckled.

His foreman, Jim, relished the challenge of multiple projects almost as much as he enjoyed complaining about them. Since Jim was one of his best friends as well as the best at what he does, Carl long ago decided to just let him complain.

"I'm really proud of the business you've built, son."

Carl could hear the pride in his father's voice. He found it difficult to speak around the lump in his throat. He smiled, nodded, and somehow got a "thanks" out.

Hearing those words from his father meant the world to him. *This is why I work so hard*. He wanted his parents to be proud of the life and business he'd created. That was probably why his mom's comments about a wife bothered him so much. Why couldn't she just be proud of who he was and what he'd built without a woman in his life?

Driving home after dinner, Carl smiled as he thought about his parents. If he could have what they had, he might consider getting married. It hadn't come easy for them, but they were the real deal. His experiences with women had shown him just how rare their relationship was. His pattern was to date once or twice then leave before it got too serious.

First thing tomorrow morning, he was going to check his current inventory, order any needed supplies, create his timeline, and update Jim and the customer. But for now, he had an open Friday evening to look forward to and a new contract to celebrate.

And time to think about the fact that Brian had finally called after three years of silence. He wondered what exactly it meant. He knew that before going to Florida, Marilyn had been in and out of the hospital a few times, but she'd never shared what the problem was despite his concern.

When she left, all she told him was she was going to visit her daughter and asked him to watch her cat while she was gone. She'd failed to mention how long that would be. If he'd known it was going to be long-term, he probably wouldn't have agreed to take Miss Kitty. *Of course*, he grinned to himself, *Marilyn had probably known that.*

And now, Brian had called; Marilyn was home.

He supposed he'd have to give Miss Kitty back, even though they had long since made peace with one another.

Carl fondly recalled the day he first met Marilyn about five years ago. She'd just purchased one of the penthouse apartments at The Athenian just off Demonbruen Street and inquired with him about some updates and changes she'd like to make.

The Athenian—playing off Nashville's nickname *The Athens of the South*—was one of the best locations in the city. It was a gorgeous historic high-rise, about a hundred years old, near the Cumberland River. It was pretty much perfect for him to work on. He loved old buildings. His specialty was restoring and updating the old, making it amazing again.

But when he heard the kind of changes Marilyn had wanted, it'd just about killed him to decline the job. He thought she was just another eccentric, rich client who wanted to destroy a beautiful building, and he wanted no part in that. Marilyn had some really unique and out-there ideas for her home. *I mean, who puts a pole—as in pole dancing!—in their living room?*

Marilyn, however, wouldn't take no for an answer. They worked together to develop a plan which would meet Carl's need to preserve the beautiful apartment but would also satisfy Marilyn's need for a quirky atmosphere.

He adored her, and working with her was one of the best experiences of his career, if not his life.

His life had been in a weird place when he met Marilyn. He had pretty much isolated himself from everyone who cared about him.

She—the infamous *she* whose name he still didn't like to say out loud—had left him hurt and bitter. The lesson he'd learned from that experience: *if you don't trust or love rich people, especially clients, you won't get hurt*. Deep down, he knew it wasn't logical, but he'd been following the personal maxim for so long, it was just how he lived now.

Marilyn had been the exception to his rule. While working together, she'd become one of his best friends. Not a mother figure...or even a grandmother figure, though she was probably the right age. Carl guessed she was a good forty years older than him. No, she was much more of a friend. A friend he didn't realize he so desperately needed.

She used to get on him about working too hard. "Carl," she'd say in her soft southern drawl. "Don't get so busy making a living, you don't have a life. You're much too young and too good-looking to be workin' all the time." She sounded an awful lot like his mom in those moments.

He wondered what she'd make of his life now. He was looking forward to hearing about it.

But as much as he wanted to rush right over to Marilyn's, Carl knew he needed to put in a couple of hours on admin tasks before he'd have time for a proper visit.

Chapter 3

GRACE

"The way I see it, if you want the rainbow,
you gotta put up with the rain."
Dolly Parton

G RACE AND BREENA GAPED at the tall, beautiful building where her mother had lived. The low sun bathed the building in a golden glow.

The Athenian.

It was beautiful. At least twenty-five stories high, with light stone on the lower three stories and glass for the rest of the building. Each apartment had a balcony overlooking either the city or the mountains, depending on which direction the unit faced.

All the way up on the top floor, a row of windows sparkled in the sunshine. *The view from those windows must be stunning*, Grace thought. When her mother told her she lived in an apartment in downtown Nashville, Grace hadn't pictured this.

As she flew in, Grace had loved seeing the mountains and how different everything looked from her home state of Florida. A river wound through the city, and now she could see it ribboning past the apartment building. Being a map nerd, she knew she'd look it up as soon as they were settled in.

As they approached the front doors of the building, a man who looked more like a football player than a doorman pulled the tall glass door open for them. He looked to be in his early forties, military-cut dark hair, dressed in a red jacket and black pants. "Good afternoon, ladies. How may I help y'all today?"

"Hi. I'm Grace Parson, and this is my friend, Breena O'Malley. My mother has a condo here, Unit 2501. I...um, I'm hoping you can tell us how to find it."

His face lit up with pleasure. "Ms. Parson, Ms. O'Malley, it's a pleasure to meet y'all. I'm Brian."

His soft southern accent elicited smiles from Grace and Breena, who were immediately charmed.

"Mr. Pillingham's office called about your arrival. I'm real sorry for the loss of your mama. Marilyn was a special woman."

It shouldn't have surprised Grace the doorman remembered her mother's name after three years; after all, her mother *was* memorable. "Thank you, Brian."

Smoothly switching back to business, Brian asked, "Do you have a vehicle?" At their nod, he gave directions to the parking garage. "Come back in through the door closest to the parking space, and I'll be waiting to take you up."

It took a few minutes to make their way back to their rental, then to find the entrance to the garage.

"Ooh, careful you don't hit that sexy little red car next to you when you open your door," Breena said as she pulled into the parking space. "Sorry it's so close. The guy on this side is super close to the line."

Grace slid out of the car with the door only partially open, careful not to hit the shiny sports car. They dragged their luggage out of the trunk, then paused, trying to figure out how to get it all to the door where they were meeting Brian.

Breena looked at the sports car. "What a sweet ride. Can you imagine driving it through the mountains with the top down?"

Grace smiled at her friend. She found convertibles impractical, but Breena had always wanted one. They stared at the little car for another moment, then grabbed their huge suitcases and lugged them to the doorway.

After struggling to open the door for a moment, Grace startled when Brian swung it open, teetering backward and stumbling over the two suitcases behind her. Brian's strong hand reached out and grabbed her arm while Breena stabilized her from behind.

"Whoa. You okay there?" Brian held onto her until she straightened back up.

"Yikes! Thanks for the helping hands!"

"Here, let me grab these bags for you." He reached for the two huge suitcases.

"Actually..." Breena looked sheepishly at Brian. "These are both mine."

"Oh." He looked at Grace and her small carry-on. "That's all you have?"

"No," Grace grumbled. "The airline lost my luggage. Hopefully, I'll get it later today, otherwise you'll see this outfit a lot."

Brian laughed. "Sorry to hear. I'll keep an eye out for the airport shuttle and let you know when it arrives."

"You might be seeing a lot of Grace's black leggings and white T-shirt over the next couple of weeks." Breena laughed. "I'd be happy to share some of all this"—she waved to her two huge suitcases—"but they won't fit you. You're too tall and skinny."

Grace also laughed and playfully hit her on the arm, then followed Brian into the elevator wheeling her small bag, Breena stepping in behind her. Once the doors closed, Brian slid a card into a slot and pushed the P1 button.

"After you get the key from Mr. Pillingham, you'll be able to use it. In the meantime, this is a temporary card that'll get you in without needing me every time." He handed Grace a plastic card. "Once it's inserted, you'll be able to push the P1 button for Marilyn's penthouse."

"W-what? Mama lived in the penthouse?" Grace's chest felt tight. She glanced at Breena, who seemed just as surprised. How was it her mother never mentioned living in a penthouse? She was just full of surprises.

Brian grinned. "She'd been looking at another unit in the building when the penthouse became available, which thrilled her. She immediately jumped on it and made an offer. A slew of people were in and out during the remodel—painters, carpenters, furniture, all kinds of people. She had a great time making it her own."

His crooked smile made Grace wonder just what kind of changes her mother had made to the apartment.

The elevator came to a silent stop and the doors slid open. Grace stepped into the small off-white entryway. Her stunned face reflected at her from a large mirror facing the elevator. The jewel-toned glass tiles along its edged sparkled in the light. On the mirror, in what appeared to be lipstick, was written *Smile* in her mother's handwriting.

Her mother's handwriting was both comforting and heart-wrenching.

A turquoise table centered beneath the mirror held a small stack of books, each with a different color spine. A purple coat rack stood in the corner, her mother's pink rain slicker draped from the top. A floral umbrella leaned against the wall nearby. Grace smiled at the whole space; it was the perfect reflection of who her mother was—colorful, fun, and bright.

Walking further into the apartment—well *penthouse*—Grace and Breena stood aghast, mouths open, looking around.

Then they burst out laughing.

"Of course she has a pole in the middle of the living room." Grace rolled her eyes.

Breena ran to it, reached high, and spun around, giggling. "I can't wait to see if I remember our lessons."

Grace grinned. "I might have to try it out too."

Smiling, Brian shook his head. "Ladies, let me know if you need anything. I'm always happy to help." He slipped back into the elevator, and the doors silently closed behind him.

They wandered through the apartment to see what the rest of it looked like, starting in the living room. The far wall featured a fireplace with floor-to-ceiling windows on either side offering an amazing view of the city. To the left of the entryway, a wall of colorful glass blocks with a doorway led to a small home office that opened, in turn, to the master bedroom.

"Oh my gosh, Bree. Look at all these clothes." Grace stared into her mother's closet, filled end to end with clothes.

"Wow!" Breena came up next to her. "Well, at least now you don't have to live in your leggings for the next two weeks."

Grace let out a big breath. "Yeah. But geesh...she's so colorful."

Breena put her arm around Grace's shoulder and laughed. "It'll be okay. A little color won't kill you."

Grace shook her head and headed back to the office. This was going to be a bigger challenge than she had imagined. She wandered over to a huge map of Nashville that took up one entire wall of the office and smiled at the yellow You Are Here sticker. Her finger traced the river she'd seen from the air. It was only a block or so away.

The Cumberland River.

Grace had always loved maps. They grounded her. She felt anchored when she knew where she was in the world. She wondered at the other markers on the map and made a mental note to check them out in her future explorations of the city.

"I wonder if your mother left all her records here?"

Grace turned around to see Breena pointing to a filing cabinet next to the desk. She walked over to check out what was left on the desk. "Hey, look at these." Grace gestured to the bulletin board above the desk with three business cards tacked to it. One for a Carl Montgomery, Contractor. The second for Edward Pillingham, Esq., Estate Planning Attorney.

The third card was the one that caught her attention. Her own business card. It made her smile but also tugged at her tender heart.

"I wonder if these are the Carl and Eddie Mama mentioned in her note to me?"

"Could be," Breena said. "I can't picture Mr. Pillingham as Eddie, though. Can you?"

Grace shook her head. "He certainly didn't look like an Eddie. I wonder just what their relationship was? Then again, maybe I don't want to know."

With her mother, anything was a possibility.

Later that evening, long after Breena had gone to bed, Grace curled up under the soft pink duvet on her mother's king-size bed. She loved her mother's bedroom. It had surprised her with its soft, feminine feel. It was calm and soothing while the rest of the apartment buzzed with energy and color. The contrast fit her mother. Loud and bold on the outside, sweet and serene on the inside.

How Grace missed her.

Grace's mother bought the condo just a few years before she suffered a series of ministrokes. Transient ischemic attacks, or TIAs, her mother's doctor called them. Due to their frequency, they'd thought it best her mother move back to Florida to be closer to Grace. She realized now how hard it must have been for her mother to leave this beautiful space.

Grace had known living with her mother again would be challenging, but she hadn't wanted to put her in a facility if she didn't have to. She'd hoped to better understand her mother in her final years, maybe hear a few of her growing-up stories. But with the dementia that resulted from the TIAs, those conversations never happened. Vascular dementia, they had said. In the end, those ministrokes made way for a much bigger one. One that took her mother much too soon.

She thought about some of the odd conversations they'd had. Her mother talked about her time in Las Vegas or New York City or running from the mob. Grace was never quite sure what was real and what her mother's muddled mind made up.

When her mother moved in three years ago, Grace reached out to Breena, who was, without a doubt, an angel walking around on Earth.

Grace and Breena had grown up together in Central Florida, meeting in elementary school when Grace popped a boy in the nose for laughing at Breena's red hair. From that moment on, they were fast friends. When Breena went into the foster system in fifth grade, Grace's mother had done everything necessary for Breena to stay in their home. They'd basically lived as sisters from middle school on.

As a traveling nurse, Breena had been between assignments and waiting to hear where her next placement would be when Graced called her. Grace was grateful Breena had been willing to put her career on hold to help with Mama. The last three years had brought them all even closer together. Breena felt the loss as much as Grace did.

Grace was grateful Breena joined her on this trip to Nashville. She needed her best friend's support, and she wanted to support Breena as well. It would be fun to explore the city with her friend, and in the process, maybe learn a little more about her mother. It threw her off to learn just how much she didn't know, and she was nervously wondering what other surprises Mama might have in store.

She remembered her mother trying to get her to come for a visit. She had wanted to play match-maker, but the timing was always off. At least now she didn't have to worry about Mama fixing her up with some man.

The last thing Grace wanted right now was a relationship. She was done with men. After the de-bacle with John, her college sweetheart, and now Drake's betrayal, she was happy to be single. At least she didn't have to worry about her mother's friends, Carl and Eddie, being who her mother had wanted to set her up with. She'd thank them for being Mama's friends, and that would be that.

Absently, Grace reached up to her neck, once again devastated it was missing. At her sixteenth birth-day party, her father had pulled her aside to give her her first real piece of jewelry—a silver chain with a diamond-framed butterfly pendant. She loved the way it sparkled when she moved. It was one of the few things she had from her father. She treasured it. And now it was missing.

Looking down at her lap, Grace grabbed her leather journal and added to the notes she'd made on the plane.

Finding Dolly Project:
Here's what I know so far...

3. We made it to Mama's place. I thought Mama's condo up here was small. Boy was I wrong! Mama has a penthouse apartment. Right in the midst of downtown Nashville. It's beautiful! While I have no idea how she afforded this place, I can certainly understand why she wanted it. I'm guessing there is a lot about Mama I don't know. Which, if I'm being honest with myself, scares me. I might need to change some of my stories about her. There's a quote hanging in the living room—a Dolly quote of course—that says something about how you have to have the rain if you want the rainbow. I feel like getting to know Mama is my rainbow, but it will be a little stormy getting there.

If my future is in Nashville, I certainly won't mind with the view out these windows. I can see the filtered colors of the city from here on the bed. It was fun watching the sky get darker while the lights from below got brighter. Nashville looks very different at night, especially from this height.

The apartment is colorful but not in an overwhelming way. I think the living room is my favorite space. There are shelves on one wall, filled with all kinds of books. The seating, while colorful, is quite comfortable. I spent time in there tonight, curled up in her squishy red chair with a book and a fire. It was perfect!

I love having Breena here to experience this with. We can see the river from the living room windows, and there's a screened balcony off the dining room looking out over the mountains. I might sit in that space with coffee one morning, see what a sunrise over the Smokies looks like.

When we first learned about Mama's condo up here, I thought we'd be in Nashville for a few days cleaning out a small space and putting it on the market. But wow, was I wrong. This is turning out to be quite the unexpected adventure.

I still don't know what she meant by "finding Dolly," but I think I might be finding Mama too.

Chapter 4

CARL

"I still close my eyes and go home—I can always draw from that."
Dolly Parton

THE NEXT MORNING, STANDING at the sink, waiting for the coffee to brew, Carl looked out over the nature preserve behind his house. He watched a mother deer and her two babies eat at the edge of his property. This is why he had chosen this particular piece of land. It reminded him of family camping trips when he was young. He'd always loved being outdoors.

His thoughts were interrupted when Miss Kitty wound her way through his legs, ready for her breakfast.

After feeding the cat, drinking a cup of coffee, and a quick run on the path through the preserve, Carl cleaned up and headed across the yard to his office with Miss Kitty. He needed to put in two or three hours to organize plans for the week.

Then, he could go see Marilyn. He would find the biggest bouquet in the most vibrant colors he could to welcome his friend home. The thought of having to give the cat back to Marilyn tugged at his heart more than he cared to admit, even to himself.

He watched the cat make herself at home under his desk. He smiled as he remembered first agreeing to watch her. He was *not* thrilled. He had never really considered himself a "cat person." At first, he left the cat in Marilyn's apartment and fed her there each day. But when it became clear Marilyn wasn't coming back, at least not anytime soon, he bundled up the black fluff ball and brought her home.

Initially, neither of them was very happy about the arrangement. But surprisingly quickly, he found he looked forward to coming home to a warm, vocal body. She was always happy to see him...or at least he pretended that was why she meowed. And now, on days when he didn't have clients, he would bring her over to the office with him. He'd built a carpeted jungle gym, spanning a couple of the walls, for her to walk around on. But she usually just sat in the spot over his desk and looked out the window while he worked.

The arrangement seemed to work pretty well for both of them, and it saddened him to know he might have to give her up. He wasn't sure how he felt about that.

He decided to leave Miss Kitty at home for this visit to Marilyn's. He would figure out when to bring her back to her owner based on what she wanted.

As soon as he finished what he needed to do, Carl drove his large SUV to his local flower shop, Flower Power. The bell over the door tinkled at his arrival. It had been a while since he'd been in. Taking flowers to Marilyn had once been a regular part of their routine, and then when she left for Florida, he started taking them to his mom, though not as often. He looked around the small shop, enjoying the colorful displays of flowers and plants and knick-knacks. He took a deep breath, savoring the floral scents surrounding him.

"As I live and breathe, Carl Montgomery." An older woman came out of the back room and walked around the counter to envelop him in a hug.

"Mrs. Snowden, how are you? I've missed your hugs." He smiled down at her. He hadn't been in for a couple of months, and it was always a pleasure to catch up with her.

"And who, might I ask, is the lucky lady today?" she asked, a twinkle in her dark brown eyes that matched her smooth brown skin.

"Well, I'm headin' over to Marilyn's place. Brian called yesterday, so I thought I'd show up with her favorites. I know you can help me."

At that moment, Carl realized he still hadn't listened to Brian's message. He felt a twinge of unease that he might be wrong about what it said. *But why else would he be calling?*

He chatted with her about family, the weather, and local events while she moved purposefully around the shop, putting together a huge, colorful bouquet. After paying and saying a lengthy goodbye, he headed to Marilyn's.

It was a short drive along the Cumberland River toward downtown, only about fifteen minutes. He took advantage of the beautiful October day by parking on the stadium side of the river and walking across the pedestrian bridge about a block from Marilyn's building. It was always a little crazy driving downtown, so it was nice to avoid it when possible.

Stepping into The Athenian after so long was a balm on his weary heart. He looked around the tastefully decorated lobby, and it hit him just how much he'd missed coming here.

"Good morning, Mr. Montgomery." Brian shook his hand. "I see you got my message. Would you like me to call up and let the ladies know you're here?"

Ladies?

"Sure." Carl's smile wavered a bit. "Go ahead and give the heads-up. Do you mind if I grab the elevator?"

Brian nodded and picked up the house phone to call upstairs while Carl headed down the short hallway to the elevator.

Ladies, he thought again. He wondered if Brian had made a mistake or if there was something else going on.

Or *someone* else?

His heart beat a little faster. Surely, the burly doorman would have said something if there were a problem...right? Of course, Brian probably assumed Carl had listened to his message. His stomach sank a little, but not from the elevator ride. He worried a bit about why he was avoiding Brian's message.

He didn't want to hear anything except that Marilyn was back.

All worries disappeared when the doors to the elevator opened. His smile was reflected in the mirror as he stepped out. A heart-pounding bass assaulted him, though he couldn't identify the song. Walking out of the entryway and into the living space, Carl froze in his tracks, the bouquet hanging limply at his side, his brain incapable of any thought except *Wow*!

There, on the pole he'd installed for Marilyn, was a woman. She was dressed like his friend in bright pink shorts and a lime green sports bra. But this woman was definitely not Marilyn. She looked to be thirty at most, had a slight build with well-defined muscles and long legs he couldn't look away from.

She hung upside down with her legs somehow holding her in place on the pole, her dark blonde hair partially covering her face.

His pulse thrummed to the beat as he stood transfixed, watching the woman do some fancy move, unwrapping her legs, holding herself with her arms this time, and doing what he supposed were upside-down splits in the air. His blood made a hasty journey south, leaving him feeling lightheaded.

If he weren't so jaded, he'd say it was love at first sight...or at the very least, lust.

And then she noticed him and the moment was broken.

The startled look on her face revealed that not only had she just noticed him, but she'd lost her concentration and her grip.

In the next split second, several things happened in quick succession.

The woman propelled dangerously down the pole.

Carl lunged forward.

She struggled to re-establish her grip, sliding closer and closer to the ground.

Instead of gallantly plucking her out of the air and into his arms as he'd pictured in his mind, he found himself flat on his back, gasping for breath.

But it wasn't all bad; the scantily clad woman was safe and sprawled on top of him.

Chapter 5

GRACE

I'm flashy, and I'm flamboyant. Had I not been a girl, I definitely would have been a drag queen.

Dolly Parton

GRATEFUL FOR THE LANDING pad—albeit a stranger's body—Grace did a quick internal assessment. With her face smushed against what felt like a jean jacket, she decided not only was she alive but nothing appeared to be broken. No small miracle to her mind. Stunned from having her breath knocked out of her, she lay still for just a second longer with her eyes closed, even though she was nose to chest with a stranger. She noted the strangest mix of rose, carnation, and sandalwood.

"Ahem."

The music had abruptly stopped, and Grace's eyes popped open at the sound of Breena clearing her throat. *Oops, not nose to chest. More like nose to button-fly. Yikes!*

Very ungracefully, with limbs going in all directions, Grace tried to get to her feet. There was a loud *thwack*; her foot had made contact with some part of him as she scrambled off.

Maybe that'll teach him to not come into someone's house uninvited!

In fairness, he did save her from a broken bone.

Then again, she wouldn't have needed saving if he hadn't been in her apartment.

Scrambling to distance herself from his very fit, warm body, she rushed over to Breena, standing in the entryway by a boombox. Grace thrust her arms into a sweatshirt, covering the lime green sports bra she'd found in her mother's dresser.

"Ow! Fudge!" The stranger groaned.

Breena gave her a questioning look, and she shrugged her shoulders in response. She had no idea who this guy was. Or why he was here. Leaning over, hands on her knees, Grace took a couple of deep breaths, trying to slow her breathing and heart rate while Breena hurried to the kitchen.

Grace peered at the man sprawled on the floor. His dark green eyes pierced hers. An involuntary thrill ran down her spine.

Even with blood all over his face, Grace could tell he was handsome. His wavy reddish brown hair looked soft and was just a tad too long in the back.

Not that she was interested. *Just noticing*, she assured herself.

She also noticed the large bouquet of smashed flowers spread out all over his jeans. *He'd brought flowers?* Why did he bring flowers to a stranger's home?

She blushed a bit, thinking about his flower-strewn jeans.

Breena, ever the caregiver, arrived back on the scene with a kitchen towel to clean up the blood still gushing from his nose. He looked like he could use a little care at the moment, and Breena, being a nurse, was just the one to give it.

But Breena was no fool, so she'd also grabbed a heavy frying pan. Grace took the pan and stood watch over him. They didn't know who this man was or why he was in their house, and they weren't taking any chances.

He sat up gingerly as Breena reached him. He looked at the very squished flowers in his lap, and his shoulders seemed to sag a bit.

Breena gazed down at him with steely eyes, one hand clamped on his shoulder while she pressed the towel to his nose. "You just stay right where you are. I'm not sure why you're in my friend's apartment or how you got in here, but you need to explain yourself once we get you cleaned up."

He nodded once to indicate he understood.

Grace watched as Breena stanched the blood flow and cleaned up his face with practiced skill and speed. Once she was finished, they moved into the dining room to the table where they waited for some answers.

"I...my name is Carl," he started, gingerly touching his nose and wincing. It was starting to swell, and there was still a little dried blood. Not an attractive look.

"C-Carl?" Grace stammered, a very confused look on her face. She looked at Breena, who looked equally confused. "My mother...um, Marilyn's friend, Carl?"

He nodded, looking around, as if searching for her mother.

"That's not possible." Grace's voice was clipped. "Carl's an older man...and you, obviously, are not older."

"Wait, what? Marilyn said I was old?" He looked bewildered, and maybe a little insulted, by her comment.

Breena, standing behind Carl with the frying pan and watching the exchange, spoke up. "You know, Grace, I'm not sure your mother ever actually mentioned Carl's age."

Grace reached over, took the frying pan from Breena, and set it on the table. Carl with his gorgeous green eyes and battered nose seemed to relax a bit. Breena smirked before walking around the table to sit next to her.

Grace tried to remember if her mother had ever described her friend or mentioned an age. Why had she assumed he was older? Was it just because her mother was older? And they were friends, so she had guessed Carl must be about the same age?

"Tell me, Carl." Grace plastered on a fake smile and pulled the frying pan a little closer. "How exactly did you know Marilyn?" She knew she was being snarky, but it tempered the other emotions rolling around inside her. "And why the heck did you think it was okay to just walk into this apartment? How'd you even get in?"

"I'm sorry about that." His sheepish look seemed sincere. "Brian said he would call up to make sure it was okay. I guess with the music going, he didn't get through, and I didn't wait to find out. Again, I apologize. As for how I know Marilyn, she hired me to remodel this apartment. This was back...five years ago now, I suppose. I'm a contractor and work on older homes and buildings." He paused. "I originally declined the job. She wasn't looking to restore it to its former glory." His eyes twinkled at the memory, and he looked at the pole in the living room.

Grace raised an eyebrow. "Did you install that pole, Carl?" She had been curious about how it came to be in her mother's living room.

"She somehow managed to talk me into working for her, dancer pole and all. She has a way of getting what she wanted." He chuckled and waved a hand toward the pole Grace had just slid down. "I can see you have your mother's colorful style...um, I'm assuming you're Marilyn's daughter? Is she not here?"

Grace watched Breena go to the kitchen to make a pot of coffee. This would be a tough conversation, and she appreciated that Breena must have figured it out too.

"Yes, I'm Marilyn's daughter. I'm Grace. And this is my friend, Breena." Grace gestured toward Breena in the kitchen. She was avoiding the real conversation, but she needed to delay it for just a little longer. "Mama did mention you. Actually, she talked about you often. I guess she never actually said you were her age. I just thought you were because you hung out together a lot."

Carl grinned and seemed to understand the mistaken assumption.

"And no," she added a little too stiffly. "I don't have my mother's style. Though, I suppose I do for the moment. The airline lost my luggage. Fortunately, I inherited Mama's build so I can wear some of her clothes until mine show up. I'm surprised at how much she left here when she moved to Florida."

Carl looked a little sad. "Marilyn never told me she was moving, just that she was going to visit you. When she asked me to keep an eye on things while she was gone, she gave me a key." He placed it on the table and slid it to Grace.

Breena reappeared with a tray bearing three cups of coffee, creamer, sugar, a few muffins, and an ice pack for Carl. He nodded his thanks, and they all took some time getting their coffees.

If Grace had thought she could just pop into Nashville, sell her mother's apartment, and head back out of town without getting emotional or confused, she had most assuredly been wrong. Her mother had been part of this community, and her loss affected them all.

The energy in the room had shifted. It felt heavier, as if it knew the conversation was coming.

"So is Marilyn not here?" he repeated softly, as if afraid to ask.

Grace shook her head slowly. "No. Mama passed away about a month ago." She paused, a little confused. "She didn't tell you what was going on?"

Carl shook his head, and a tear rolled down his cheek.

Surprised by his grief, Grace laid her hand over his, jerking a little at the electric shock running through her fingers, up her arm. His head snapped up, and he looked at her with wide eyes. She wondered if he felt it too.

She quickly removed her hand and picked up her coffee, silently cursing the heat creeping up her cheeks. She was most definitely not interested in this man...or in the sparks he sent through her system.

He looked down at his coffee and took a moment before speaking again. "I knew she'd seen a doctor a few times, but she always said it was nothing major. No big deal. And then...she left to visit you."

Grace let out a loud breath and stirred her coffee, grateful to have something to keep her hands busy.

"Those doctor visits she told you about...well, she had a few ministrokes before she moved to Florida. Mama told me her movements had been affected, and she knew there was the potential for a much bigger stroke. She was afraid to drive and scared to be alone in case something else happened. It made sense for her to come back to Florida. I'm sorry she didn't tell you what was going on."

He asked questions, and she answered, telling him how quickly the dementia had come on, and how hard it had been to watch her decline.

"I had planned on trying to find you once we got things settled here to say thank you for being such a good friend to Mama, but I guess you've saved me the trouble," she said with a wry half smile.

"So what are you going to do now?" Carl asked. "I mean with this apartment? Are you moving here or do you plan on selling?"

It was tempting to tell him it was none of his business, but he didn't look like he was just being nosy. He was being a friend. She could see why her mother had enjoyed his company. He had kind green eyes and sexy dimples. She had to admit—at least to herself—she found his smile appealing.

But after Drake, she was definitely *not* looking for a guy. Good-looking or not.

Chapter 6

CARL

I'll never harden my heart, but I've tough-
ened the muscles around it.
Dolly Parton

SITTING AT THE TABLE he knew so well, Carl held the ice to his throbbing nose and studied Grace. He'd guessed she'd be tall, but she was even taller than he'd expected, only a few inches shorter than his own six-foot-one. And from what he'd seen earlier on the pole, a good percentage of her height was in the strong, shapely legs she kept trying to cover with her long sweatshirt.

Now that her face wasn't covered by hair, he could see her soft blue eyes, just like Marilyn's. But Grace's were warier than Marilyn's had ever been. He found himself wondering what—or who—had made her so skeptical. While her long, slender body was quite attractive and her face beautiful, he found himself distinctly drawn to her eyes. Some might think they were a little too close together and her nose a little too thin, but Carl knew he'd dream about those eyes tonight. *Only because she's Marilyn's daughter*, he told himself.

He hadn't meant to ask about the apartment; the question came out almost on its own. But he really did want to know. He had a lot of good memories in this apartment, and it made him sad to think it might be sold.

Carl realized he'd like to get to know Marilyn's daughter better. She seemed like she could use another friend right now...or maybe *he* could use another friend right now.

He didn't want to think about the electric spark he'd felt when she put her hand on his. *Static electricity*, he reassured himself. Certainly not *chemistry*. And while he was attracted to her, she wasn't his normal type.

He'd gotten the impression from Marilyn that her daughter was rather uptight and conservative. But looking at the beautiful, if slightly anxious, woman in front of him, he had a hard time seeing it.

His thoughts were interrupted by Grace's sigh.

"I'm not really sure what I'm going to do with this place, to be honest. I had no idea Mama had this. I was expecting a small condo, not a penthouse. I wish I'd made the time to visit Mama when she still lived here. I was always so busy building my business, and I thought we had plenty of time..."

The wistful comment seemed like something she hadn't realized until she said it out loud. Breena reached over and covered her friend's hand, giving it a little squeeze.

Carl felt like he was intruding on a private moment and was about to excuse himself when Grace continued.

"I have no idea where Mama got the money to pay for this. We weren't poor, but this is a huge step up from the middle-class lifestyle I grew up with. We didn't find any paperwork at the townhouse in Orlando, so hopefully, her files here will solve the mystery."

Breena jumped in again. "Mr. Pillingham might have some information, and it's apparent someone has been keeping up the place for the past three years. It was spotless when we got here yesterday, not covered in dust."

Grace's shoulders relaxed at Breena's observations.

"Well, whatever money was set aside for upkeep, I'm hoping it hasn't run out." Grace picked at the muffin in front of her, but none of it made it to her mouth.

"I'm pretty sure Marilyn paid cash for the apartment," Carl told her.

Grace's eyes widened. And while the worry lines on her face relaxed a bit, her confusion was still clear.

He had no idea where Marilyn had got her money, but he remembered a brief conversation when she mentioned paying cash for everything. It had never been his business, so the conversation didn't go any further. He'd known her to pay her bills in full and on time. She'd been an excellent customer.

Breena set her coffee down, then steered the conversation in a new direction. "Marilyn gave Grace a bit of a mission before she passed away."

The look Grace shot her told Carl this wasn't something she really wanted to talk about. He wouldn't be surprised if she was kicking Breena under the table, but his curiosity was piqued.

"Well, knowing Marilyn, that could be anything," he said with a chuckle. He plowed on despite knowing it wasn't any of his business; he really wanted to keep talking with Grace. "So what kind of mission did she leave you?"

He watched her play with the handle of her coffee cup before answering. "To be honest, I'm not really sure what Mama wanted me to do. She said to 'find Dolly,' but I don't know why. She said it had to do with my future, and it was very important for me to find Dolly."

"You mean like Dolly Parton?" Carl asked, confused. He knew Marilyn was a big Dolly Parton fan, but to ask her daughter to find her didn't make any sense. Even for Marilyn.

"I guess so? I mean, what other Dolly could it be?" Grace shrugged.

Carl thought about it for a minute. He knew Marilyn had based a lot of her life and style around

Dolly Parton. Just looking around the dining area, he saw three inspirational quotes on the wall, all Dolly quotes.

And he could only assume her colorful wardrobe was Dolly inspired. So he supposed it made sense, in a Marilyn kind of way. But why? *That*, he supposed, *is the big question.*

"I tell you what, Grace," Carl started before he could talk himself out of it. "How about if I offer my tour guide services for you and Breena? Having grown up here, I know Nashville. And I definitely know several 'Dolly' places. Maybe we can figure out this Finding Dolly Project together. This will be my way of thanking Marilyn for helping me through a hard time when we first met."

"Oh!"

Carl heard the surprise in Grace's voice. He was bewildered to discover he hoped she would accept his impulsive offer.

"That's, um...that's very kind of you." She looked at her friend, then back at Carl.

He had always wondered if women had a secret language that didn't involve words. It seemed they could communicate by only looking at each other. He'd noticed the same with his sister and mother. No wonder he never really understood women.

"Give us a couple of days to get ourselves organized...and hopefully, my luggage will show up by then." She looked sheepishly down at her sweatshirt and shorty-shorts. "It'd be challenging to go out in some of Mama's outfits." She grinned, but he could see she meant it.

He exchanged phone numbers with Grace, then stood up and headed to the elevator. "Oh, I almost forgot." He turned to look back at her. "One of the reasons I came over today. I have Marilyn's cat. I wasn't sure if I should bring her over...or what?"

"Mama had a cat?" Grace looked from Carl to Breena and back again. "Wow. I'm not even sure how long we're staying. Do you mind keeping it for a little longer, until I get things figured out?"

"Sure, no problem." With a grin on his face, he stepped into the elevator after the doors slid open, grateful he would keep Miss Kitty a little longer.

He was curious about Marilyn's daughter and glad he'd be able to get to know her.

A few hours later, Carl laughed as he stretched out on his brown leather couch with Miss Kitty curled up on his chest and an ice pack on his still sore nose. "We know how to party on a Saturday night, don't we, Miss Kitty?"

His plans to grab a beer with his buddy Gabe had fallen through. While he always had a good time with

Gabe, he was not disappointed to be sitting at home with a beer, a cat, and an ice pack.

Carl couldn't believe he'd offered to play tour guide for Grace. Sure, she was cute and looked a bit like a fragile flower, but she wasn't his business. The mission Marilyn had given her wasn't his business. So why was he inserting himself into her life?

He was already thinking about where he wanted to take her around town, but he had a busy week ahead of him with the new project. If he was going to play tour guide, he needed to make some space in his schedule. Ignoring the glare from Miss Kitty for interrupting her nap, Carl slipped out.

His office was a few hundred yards in front of his house, so the commute was pretty easy. Most mornings, when he wasn't at a jobsite, he'd walk across the yard with his coffee, Miss Kitty tagging along.

The log building consisted of five rooms—a reception area, a conference room, a bathroom, a break room, and his office. He'd built it expecting, at some point, he'd need to hire an assistant. He was probably there. It would be great to have someone handle the emails, phone calls, and billing for him. Someone to keep track of the jobs and schedules. Maybe his sister would know of someone looking for a part-time job.

He sat behind the big wooden desk he'd found at an estate sale Marilyn had dragged him to. She'd been looking for pieces for her penthouse, and he wound up leaving with a desk.

He stared out at the beauty of Whiskey Barrel Nature Preserve while his laptop powered up.

Nashville in October was stunning. The leaves were just turning, so his view was full of yellows, oranges, reds, and greens. He'd chosen this plot of land to be close to the city without being in the middle of it.

He planned to start a crew on demolition at the new Barn Reno project this week. He'd swing by early in the morning to check in with Jim, then let them do their thing. This demo was going to be slow since they were trying to salvage as much as possible to reuse.

It looked like he could entertain Grace and Breena for a few hours on Monday and Tuesday without causing issues in his schedule. Normally, demo day was a favorite, but it looked like he'd be missing some of this one. He hoped he'd be able to jump in later in the week and help.

He'd planned on ordering supplies Monday but went ahead and got started since, now, he'd be out. He did a quick check on materials in stock and what they would need for the new project and made a list of what needed to be ordered. Probably a good thing the Kline project stalled out a couple of months ago. At the time, he'd been pretty upset, but now he was able to repurpose some of those supplies for the new project. Worked out well.

As he was logging off to head back to his house to fix himself some dinner, he noticed the flashing red light on the answering machine. Marilyn had teased him for the antiquated tech, but he preferred customers calling and leaving a message at the office. He didn't like to answer his phone when he was at a jobsite.

He pushed play and listened. "Carl. This is Tony Kline. I just wanted to let you know we're ready to have you finish up our bedroom addition. Thanks."

Really? Carl couldn't believe it. *Now* Mr. Kline is ready to go ahead with the project? Now that he'd already filled the hole in his schedule? Well, Mr. Kline was going to have to wait a day or two while he played tour guide before he'd be able to even try to fit him in.

He turned off the lights and locked up his office, then breathed in the fresh, crisp air, stretching his arms over his head. The tension in his shoulders drained as he walked to his house. It was only a few hundred yards, but it was beautiful. Looking out over the nature preserve, he could almost forget he was pretty much in the middle of a city.

As he walked back to his house, he could understand, a little bit, his mom's argument about having someone to come home to. It would be really nice to have someone to share the load. Someone to vent to about Kline. Someone to enjoy a meal with each night.

His mind flashed briefly to Grace, and he immediately shut down the thought. Maybe he'd work on getting an assistant, then see if they could find him a housekeeper who could cook him some meals.

That would be easier. Or at least a lot less complicated.

Finding Dolly Project:
Here's what I know so far...

4. *I met Carl today. He is definitely not a sweet,*
lonely, old man! He's young, probably only a year or
two older than me, very good-looking, has gorgeous green
eyes, and a sexy dimple that peeks out when he smiles.
Nope. Definitely not an old man.

You could say I "fell" for him.

I'd decided to see what I could remember on the
pole. Apparently, I didn't hear the doorbell or the ele-
vator—the music was very loud—and when I saw him
standing there, watching me, it completely freaked me
out. If he hadn't moved quickly, I probably would have
broken my neck. As it was, I think I broke his nose. I feel
a little bad, but he scared the crap out of me. I'm not
quite sure why Mama thought he should be part of my
future, but I think it might be intriguing to figure it out.

5. *I hadn't really planned on spending any time*
on Mama's mission, but Breena and her big mouth
(LOL) mentioned it and now Carl has offered to show
us around Nashville on our quest to find Dolly. So I guess
the mission is a go, and he'll be part of my immediate
future in Nashville. I have no idea what Mama wants
me to find regarding Dolly. I can't help but think I won't
actually find her, but I think the search might be fun.

Too bad I'm not interested in dating right now,
because if I were, Carl Montgomery would be fun to get
to know. As it is, he'll take us around Nashville a bit,
we'll get the penthouse ready to sell, and that'll be that.

Chapter 7

GRACE

"I always count my blessings more than I count my money."

Dolly Parton

EARLY SUNDAY MORNING, WRAPPED in her mother's soft, bright purple robe, Grace wandered into the kitchen, yawning, and headed straight to the coffee maker. Her mind had been so busy thinking over everything that had happened during the last couple of days, it had made for a restless night.

First, showing up in Nashville to discover her mother lived in what she could only guess was a million-dollar penthouse had really thrown Grace off. Next, finding out that Carl, the friend her mother had mentioned so often, was young—and, if she were being honest, hot—left her intrigued. And finally, of course, there was that whole debacle with Drake, which didn't deserve any more time or brain cells thinking about it.

Though she *had* thought about Drake a little bit last night. It was hard not to. She was trying to figure out what happened. It took her back to her college days and the crushing end to her relationship with John. Why was she continually drawn to men who just wanted to use her? Men who weren't interested in a real relationship.

She wanted what her parents had had, a strong, loving relationship. She was beginning to think it just wasn't in the cards for her.

Then her thoughts had found their way to Carl, with his gorgeous green eyes and sexy dimples. But she quickly shut those thoughts down. Done with men, she'd reminded herself.

She was pulled out of her thoughts by the last sputtering of the coffee maker. She grabbed a mug from the cabinet and stood there frozen, staring at it.

When Breena walked in a minute later, she was still standing there, looking at the mug.

"Morning, Grace," Breena said through her yawn. She reached past Grace to grab a mug of her own and realized Grace still hadn't moved. "You okay there, honey?"

Grace, startled out of her reverie, walked over to the coffee pot and filled both of their cups. "I had no idea Mama still had this mug," she said in a soft voice. "I made it for her for Mother's Day when we were...oh, I don't know...maybe seven or eight? It was Miss Bennett's class, I think, when we made them."

Her mother had always loved bright colors and flowers, and she'd wanted to give her something special that year. The mug was covered with bright yellow, pink, purple, blue, and green flowers. Hand drawn then painted by a much younger Grace. The art teacher glazed the mug so it could be used and washed. It had taken Grace two weeks to finish the project at school.

"Oh, I remember those. It was right before my mama took off. I think she broke it within a week. She'd tried to act upset, but well..." Breena trailed off with a sad smile. "I remember it took you forever to paint yours. You wouldn't just scribble on it like the rest of us. You wanted yours to be perfect." She looked at the mug now. "It doesn't even look like the colors have faded. Wow."

"Yeah." Grace's voice was almost a whisper. "I didn't think Mama liked it because she never used it. And now...here it is. In her cabinet. In perfect condition, I don't know what to think."

Grace walked over to the wooden table they'd sat at with Carl just the day before. Each of the straight-backed chairs was painted a different color with a different colored cushion. A fun mix-and-match she knew her mother must have created.

"So what's the plan for today?" Breena asked as she sat down.

"Well, tomorrow, it sounds like we're going sightseeing with Carl. He offered to take us to the Country Music Hall of Fame to check out the Dolly display. Might be fun to see a bit of Nashville. So today, I was thinking about digging into Mama's filing cabinet."

"I think the tour offer was more for *you* than *us*," Breena said with a twinkle in her eyes.

"What?" Grace felt her face heat up. "No. His offer was definitely for both of us." Grace felt flustered. Carl certainly had no reason to think *anything* about her. "Why would you think that?"

"Oh, I don't know. Maybe the way he couldn't take his eyes off you yesterday?"

Grace blushed furiously and shook her head.

"Anyway, a nursing friend of mine lives in Chattanooga. We met on my last nursing assignment in Charleston, so it would be fun to reconnect. Since Chattanooga is only two and a half hours away, I was wondering if you'd mind if I use the rental car and go there for a few days? I can head out tomorrow when you leave with Carl."

"Oh." Grace was a little taken aback that her friend was leaving. "Sure, no problem. Go, have fun."

Of course she wanted Breena to visit her friend, but she wasn't sure she wanted to be here by herself. Among her mother's things. With nothing to do but think.

Especially after discovering the coffee mug. It scared her a little, not knowing what else she might find. And the thought that maybe she didn't know her mother like she thought she did was confusing.

She looked down at the bright purple robe wrapped around her body. For the moment, she was resigned to being surrounded by her mother's things. Especially the closet full of colorful clothes, since it didn't appear the airline was in a hurry to find hers. The thought of having to dress in her mother's clothing was unsettling. It brought back memories from her childhood; kids could be cruel. It looked like, for today anyway, she'd be dressing in something colorful. At least she wasn't going anywhere.

After breakfast, they headed into the small home office. The wall of colorful glass blocks made the room feel happy. The print over the desk that read Always count your blessings, not your money resonated with Grace. She wondered if it was one of Dolly's sayings.

Going through her mother's filing cabinet was today's top priority. Breena settled in front of the drawer and started pulling out folders. Grace, sitting on the floor as well, noticed the files were all neatly labeled and organized. That would certainly make their job easier.

There was a file for the job Carl did for her mother. Bills and details of what was done were included. It was fun to see what changes she'd made, and a little shocking how expensive those changes were.

Her mother's medical file was in the pile, so Grace went through it. She was happy to not find any surprises in the folder. Her mother had been up front about everything going on with her health.

The rest of the files were fairly mundane. Insurance for the house and a car, which made her wonder if her mother had a car. Where was it?

Grace looked over to see Breena engrossed in a huge file. "Hey, whatcha got there?"

"It's labeled 'Hope Files,'" Breena said. "It's filled with names of women who I think were abused. There are names, dates, pictures of injuries, an incident report on each woman, and a police report for some of them. It looks like it's about two, maybe two and a half, years' worth of incidents."

"Wow."

They looked at each other, confused.

"I wonder why Mama had these files. And who are all these women?"

They looked through the files some more but couldn't find any financial papers or anything about the penthouse.

"Hopefully, that information is with Mr. Pillingham," Grace said. "My meeting with him is a week from tomorrow. I hope he's got some answers because I have a lot of questions."

Monday morning, Grace's internal clock hadn't received the memo they were in the central time zone.
Even though the time difference was only an hour,
her normal six o'clock wake-up was at five.

She sipped her coffee on the screened balcony
twenty-five stories above the city. She'd never been
out on a balcony this high before. It was terrifying
but beautiful. She gripped the warm coffee mug
between her hands to stave off the early morning
chill. She'd had to wait an hour before watching the
sunrise, but she decided it was well worth the early
wake-up and chilly morning.

After finishing their coffee and bagels, Grace
and Breena went to their separate bedrooms to get
ready for the day. Dressed in the least colorful outfit
she could find—which, quite frankly, wasn't saying much—Grace checked herself out in the oval
mirror in one corner of her mother's bedroom. The
bright yellow sundress with large red daisy style
flowers on it looked good, much to her surprise.
She wasn't used to seeing herself in bright colors.
She'd stopped wearing fun, colorful clothes in middle school. But here she was, wearing a bright yellow
dress and working on being comfortable in it.

Grace headed from her mother's bedroom to the living room and looked around the space, imagining just how much her mother must have loved it here. While the apartment was huge, it felt homey. Her mother had a gift for making spaces comfortable and inviting.

Sitting on the couch, the infamous pole behind her, she loved looking at the city through the large windows on either side of the fireplace. It made for such a warm space. In the few days she'd been here, this had become one of her favorite spots in the penthouse.

The dining room probably had the better view; with windows all across the room, you could see downtown. At night, it was truly something to see, all those twinkling lights. And she got an amazing sunrise view while drinking her coffee that morning.

But the living room with the bookcases, fireplace, and cozy couch was where she found herself hanging out most.

She noticed that while the rooms all came across as bright and bold, it was all in the furniture, wall art, and accessories. The floors and walls were...well, normal. The floors were light, warm hardwood, except in the kitchen and bathrooms, which were tile. The walls were all a warm off-white and showcased her mother's colorful furniture and artwork. She wondered if Carl had influenced the wall and floor colors.

I'll have to thank him, she thought with a smile.

Just then, she heard a buzz from the lobby, informing her Carl was waiting downstairs. Breena came clattering out, dragging a huge suitcase behind her. Grace laughed, knowing her friend couldn't go anywhere with anything smaller. They loaded Breena's suitcase into the elevator and rode down together. After a quick hug goodbye to Breena, and with her purse and sweater draped over her arm, Grace headed out the front door, ready to tackle whatever the day brought her. She hoped so anyway.

It was a beautiful day, and Carl was waiting on the sidewalk when she got downstairs. She noticed how his worn blue jeans fit perfectly and his snug white T-shirt showed off his muscular chest.

Turning, he smiled. "Hey, Grace." He looked around. "Breena coming?"

"No, she's headed to Chattanooga today to visit a friend. I'm afraid it's just us." She tried not to act self-conscious but felt her cheeks get a little warm.

Carl didn't seem to notice her discomfort. "No problem. How do you feel about a little walk today?"

She looked down at the athletic shoes she wore with the sundress; they were the only shoes she had with her. She smiled up at him. At five-foot-ten, she'd always felt tall for a woman, and she liked looking up to meet Carl's eyes.

"A walk would be great, actually. I've been meaning to check out the area to see where would be a good place to run but haven't gotten around to it yet. And since I've got my sneakers on, a walk would be nice. Good thing I wore these on the plane because now I have to wear them with everything." She laughed.

"So no luggage yet?" Carl guessed, looking her up and down with an amused smile on his face.

"Nope," she said. "I hope it shows up later today or tomorrow. Believe it or not, this was the *least* colorful dress I could find in Mama's closet."

"Well, it looks great on you."

At Carl's smile, her stomach fluttered and her cheeks warmed again.

"You still up for the Country Music Hall of Fame today?"

Grace put on her sweater and pulled it tight around her body before nodding. She wasn't used to the chilly fall days here in Nashville. Or maybe she wasn't used to the way Carl looked at her.

"Sounds good. And I appreciate you shuffling your Monday around to make this happen."

"It's my pleasure," Carl said, his crooked smile making Grace shiver.

She really had to get her head on straight.

The walk took them along the Cumberland River for a few blocks. They stopped to take a quick picture with the Dolly mural on one of the buildings. When they turned onto Broadway, everything seemed to kick up a notch—the noise, the lights, the crowds. They walked past the red brick building housing Kid Rock's Honky Tonk bar, music streaming through its open doors and windows.

After crossing the street, they walked past a white brick building that used to house the American National Bank but was now, according to neon letters down the neck of a neon guitar, home to Luke's Honky Tonk. Again, all the doors and windows were open, lending to the festive atmosphere in the street. It was easy to see the source of all the colorful lights she noticed at night.

Carl entertained her with stories about the downtown area. There'd been a lot of changes in the last several years. So much so, it was now called NashVegas by the locals.

By the time they reached Fifth Avenue, she had taken the sweater off again. Even though she felt self-conscious, she was just too warm to wear it. Grace laughed as a bicycle bar rolled up with a group of women singing a Garth Brooks song. There were about eight women sitting on the two long sides of a bar. They pedaled to move the bicycle, drinking and singing.

She looked over at Carl. "It's a Monday, right?"

"Welcome to Nashville, Grace." He laughed.

They crossed the street with the crowd and headed on to the Country Music Hall of Fame.

"Is it just me, or does that building look like a piano keyboard?" The curved building in front of them was light concrete with thin dark windows at semiregular intervals.

"Huh. I've never noticed." He looked at her, then back at the building. "It's the Hall of Fame, so it makes sense."

As they walked into the building, Grace pulled the sweater back on. The entrance area was large and open.

Even though there were a lot of people in the space, it didn't feel crowded. She wasn't particularly a country music fan, but she was looking forward to wandering around with Carl.

She started for the ticket window, but Carl stopped her. "I already bought our tickets online. We can just head to the elevator." He steered her away from the crowd.

"Oh great. Just let me know how much I owe you." Grace chewed on her lower lip a little, thinking about her budget.

"Well, look at this." Carl evaded the comment. "Perfect timing." The elevator doors slid open, and they were on their way up.

She wasn't sure if she should bring it up again. She didn't want him to think he had to pay for her just because he was showing her around. This wasn't a date, after all.

The elevator took them to the top floor where they started a long, winding tour of the more than 350,000-square-foot museum. It was filled with everything country music, from the 1920s to the present. A feast for country music fans.

"So if you don't mind me asking, what's our Dolly plan?" Carl asked.

"Honestly, I'm not really sure. I can't imagine it was Mama's intention for me to *actually* find Dolly, but maybe I should focus on what lessons I can learn from her. That seems more plausible and attainable." She dipped her head a little, embarrassed to have shared her thoughts with him.

"That seems like a great place to start." Carl sounded thoughtful, and she looked up at him. "Let's see what we can learn from her here."

She nodded, her shoulders relaxing as they headed off on their quest. "So are you a country music fan?"

Carl laughed. "It's hard not to appreciate country music when you live here. You?"

"I grew up with Mama, so I know a lot of the '80s and '90s country stars. I don't know many of the newer ones though."

Keeping their eyes peeled for anything Dolly, they had fun taking pictures with Elvis's gold-plated Cadillac, Taylor Swift's tour bus, Laci Love's black leather outfit from one of her music videos, and some Paul Kaufman boots loaded up with Swarovski crystals that they agreed Grace's mother would have loved.

After nearly an hour of looking, they found the small Dolly Parton exhibit. Grace wasn't sure if she should be embarrassed or impressed by the fact that her dress matched Dolly's outfit in the exhibit—pants and a jacket in the exact same shade of yellow with remarkably similar red flowers. She knew her mother must have bought this dress because of Dolly.

Grace felt Carl come up beside her. "I wonder if they'd let you borrow her boots. They'd look awesome."

Grace tried to hide the redness in her cheeks. "Of all the dresses in my mother's closet, I chose this one today. Wow."

"You don't seem very comfortable wearing your mother's clothes. What do you normally wear?" Carl asked.

"Typically, I dress pretty boring, I suppose. A lot of black and white. Maybe a little khaki. But I'm not sure I have *anything* colorful in my closet back home anymore."

"Did you used to dress differently?"

"Not since I was young. Mama loved buying me very bright clothes—you know, like hers. Around middle school, I started getting comments about them, and I let it get to me." Grace shook her head at the memory. "Anyway, it's been a long time since I've worn anything this bold." Slightly embarrassed by the conversation, she read the placard and took a few pictures.

When Grace turned around, she saw a small crowd had gathered and were taking pictures of her with the Dolly exhibit. A woman who looked to be in her fifties sidled next to her to get a selfie with the three of them—Grace, the stranger, and Dolly.

She rubbed her temples, feeling a headache coming on. She didn't like crowds. Why did this group think it was okay to take pictures of her and invade her personal space? Her heartbeat was picking up as she looked around, trying to find Carl. Where had he gone?

Just as she started to panic, she felt a warm hand grab hers and pull her away from the display. Carl kept hold of her hand, which was tingling at his touch, and led her down the stairs and out the door. The warmth of Carl's hand soothed her and stopped the panic. Relief coursed through her body the further they got from the display.

"I hope you don't mind me pulling you away. You looked a little overwhelmed with the attention." Carl looked at her, still holding her hand even though they were finally outside on the sidewalk.

She gently slipped her hand from his before they started walking.

"Oh, no. I appreciate it," she said. "I wasn't prepared for that kind of attention. Especially over one of Mama's outfits. It was...well, overwhelming, to say the least. So thank you for getting me out of there."

"No problem," Carl said with a quick grin.

The walk back to her mother's apartment was quiet. Not uncomfortable, but not nearly as chatty as the walk to the Hall of Fame had been. Grace was thinking about the morning.

"So did you learn anything useful about Dolly today?" he asked, pulling her out of her thoughts.

Before Grace could answer, his cell phone rang. Looking at the number, he frowned a little and let the call go to voicemail.

Grace looked over. "Is everything okay?"

Carl sighed. "I have this client. It was a room addition. A bedroom. We started the project probably six months ago. We were halfway through, and they just stopped it, kicked us out. No explanation or anything. And now, he's apparently ready again and just expects me to drop everything else and come rushing back over to finish up the job. Rich people," he said with a snort. "Can't work with them, can't have a business without them. I'll deal with him when I get home."

She wondered at his comment about rich people. Granted, *she* didn't have money, but the more she was learning about her mother...had he felt the same disdain for her?

About twenty minutes after making their getaway from the Hall of Fame, they found themselves in front of The Athenian.

"Thanks for a fun morning. Well, other than my wardrobe malfunction," Grace said with a wry smile.

"My pleasure." Carl smiled back at her. "If you'd like, we could go to the Grand Ole Opry tomorrow, and then maybe find some of Nashville's finest hot chicken afterward?"

Grace looked at the leaf-strewn sidewalk and hugged her sweater around her body a little tighter. She looked up, her cheeks warm. "I'd enjoy that, thank you."

"How about I get you around ten tomorrow morning?"

She hated how easily she blushed around him.

"Sounds good." She dipped her head again, then looked up and smiled. "See you tomorrow."

Finding Dolly Project:
Here's what I know so far...

6. The Country Music Hall of Fame was impressive. The fact that my dress (well Mama's dress) was the exact same color and print as Dolly's outfit in her showcase was rather mortifying. Thankfully, Carl rescued me and got us out of there. When he grabbed my hand, I felt the same bolt of awareness travel up my arm I'd felt when I touched his hand on Saturday. I've not felt that before with anyone. I certainly didn't feel it with Drake. Not even with John. I'm not ready to make anything of it, but it's curious.

7. Carl has a way of making me blush, just by looking at me. I noticed a slew of butterflies hanging out in my stomach today as well. But I still had a fun time with him. He's easy to talk to. Too bad I'm not interested in dating right now.

8. Here's what I learned about Dolly today: Dolly is not afraid to wear bright colors, fun outfits. She's not afraid to stand out in a crowd. In fact, I think she dresses so she will *stand out in a crowd. I wonder where she got the confidence to be different and to embrace it. If Mama wanted me to learn lessons from Dolly, this seems like one she'd want me to embrace.*

Chapter 8

CARL

"Storms make trees take deeper roots."
Dolly Parton

ON THE WAY BACK to his office, Carl decided to swing by the new jobsite, the Barn Reno. He smiled just thinking about the project. The barn was around a hundred years old and in fairly good condition. The client wanted to keep the outside rustic but update and remodel the interior into a two-story home.

His clients had worked with an architect Carl respected, so this was a fun project all the way around. And while these clients obviously had money, they weren't throwing it around like some of his clients did. They were putting it into renovating an old barn on her family's property. They didn't want a lot of fancy fixtures or additions; they just wanted a place where they could raise a family and work on the farm.

Throughout the beautiful drive through the foothills, his mind kept wandering back to Grace and her lovely face. He enjoyed how easily she blushed around him; most of the women he dated were bold and brash. He could easily see himself falling for her...if he were interested in dating someone. She was smart, comfortable to be around, and helping her with the mission Marilyn left for her connected him to his old friend.

Pulling up next to Jim's old pickup, Carl hopped out and surveyed his crew. He was pleased to see the demo was moving along nicely. They wanted to salvage as much of the original wood as possible to keep the rustic look, which made the demo much slower. In the end, it would bring a rustic look to the updated interior that he thought was both smart and stylish.

After catching up with Jim about the three projects they had in progress, he headed back home to his office. He needed to touch base with Mr. Kline but wasn't sure where he could fit that project back into the schedule.

The next morning, Carl waited for Grace on the sidewalk in front of the building. He'd chosen a nicer pair of jeans and dressed them up a bit with a white button-down shirt, sleeves rolled to his elbows. It was weird not being at a jobsite, but this was definitely a nice way to spend a Tuesday morning.

He startled when she cleared her throat.

"Hi, Carl."

He turned and took in her colorful dress. "You look great. Still no luggage?" he asked with a knowing smile.

Grace laughed a little and looked down at her dress. "Yeah. I guess you can tell this is one of Mama's dresses, huh? I'm trying to embrace my inner-Dolly, to be confident and comfortable in color. The way it's going, I'm not sure I'll ever get my clothes back." She sighed. Today her dress was bright green with silver-and-pink cowboy boots, paired once again with her sneakers.

"That seems like a good Dolly lesson." Carl grinned and opened the passenger door of a black sedan in front of the building. "I thought you might find a car a little easier to get in and out of. And since you have a dress on today, I'm glad I didn't bring the pickup."

He caught the light scent of lemon as she moved past him to slide into the passenger's seat. He closed her door and walked around the front of the car to climb in beside her.

"So day two of your Nashville Finding Dolly quest, and we're off to the Grand Ole Opry. Seems like an appropriate place. I've booked a backstage tour, which should be fun. I've never been on it myself, and I'm looking forward to it."

"Sounds great," she said. "That was very thoughtful of you. How much do I owe you for the ticket?"

He noticed she chewed her lower lip whenever she mentioned money. He was glad he was able to help out during what he guessed must be a tough time, what with her mother passing away and the stress of dealing with two houses. He was confused about her finances though. It was apparent Marilyn had money, so why were things so tight for her daughter?

"I tell ya what." Carl slowed to a stop at the light and glanced over at Grace. "Since I already have the tickets, how about if you pick up lunch? I know a great place not too far from the Opry. Best meat-and-three joint around."

"Meat-and-three?"

Grace looked confused, and he chuckled.

"I forget that's not a common term everywhere, but it's pretty much what it sounds like. A choice of meat and three sides. We'll work up an appetite." He grinned at her.

"Interesting. Sounds delicious." Grace smiled, agreeing to the deal.

He wasn't sure whether he'd let her pay or not. He was used to paying when he took a woman out. Granted, this wasn't a date...but still.

The twenty-minute drive passed quickly and comfortably. Carl got a kick out of telling Grace about some of his favorite houses he'd worked on. She was a good listener and asked satisfying questions.

"I'm really enjoying the weather here." Grace was putting on her sweater, somewhat awkwardly while still in her seatbelt.

Remembering his bashed nose from a couple of days earlier, he leaned into his door to dodge a flying elbow.

"October in Florida is never this cool." Finally settled, she looked over at him.

"I've never been to Florida, but it does seem like it's usually hot and muggy. I'd miss the mountains if I didn't live here." He looked at the mountains surrounding the city he loved, before glancing down to the sneakers on Grace's feet. "You up for another walk today?"

"That'll be nice. It's so beautiful, it'd be a shame to not enjoy some of the day outside."

Carl parked the car and smiled at Grace. She returned a lopsided smile before hastily climbing out.

The walk from the plaza parking lot to the Opry was well-paved. Trees and flowers lined the walking path, making it enjoyable.

"How about a pic with one of the guitars?" Carl asked as they rounded the curve to the entrance.

There were two huge guitars in the walkway, and tourists were taking turns having their pictures taken with one or both of them.

"Oh, sure." She looked at her dress, then pulled her sweater tighter around herself as they hopped into the line to get a picture. Within a few minutes, it was their turn, so Grace walked up to the twenty-foot-tall wooden acoustic guitar.

"Hey, I'll take the picture if you'd like to join your girlfriend."

Carl looked behind him at the woman who'd made the offer. "Oh, um." He stumbled over his words. "Thanks, but we're just friends."

"Go on over. I'll get you two together," she insisted.

He handed over his phone and walked to Grace's side. They stood on opposite sides of the guitar and smiled at each other. The idea of claiming Grace as his girlfriend had been tempting...which completely confused him in a way he didn't want to explore.

Once finished, he reclaimed his phone. He didn't mention the girlfriend comment to Grace; he didn't want to make things awkward between them. "Want to wander a bit out here or head straight in?"

"If we have time, let's wander. It's lovely out."

They took their time exploring the beautiful walkways. It was like walking in a park, except for all the tourists.

After checking in, they only had to wait a couple of minutes before the tour started. There were eight people in the tour group, and their guide was an older man named Henry. Henry had been giving tours at the Grand Ole Opry for decades and felt certain he could answer any question they threw his way.

They walked through the beautiful building while Henry shared all kinds of details. Grace leaned over to Carl. "Have you seen a concert here?"

He shook his head.

"Seems like it would be pretty fun, wouldn't it?"

The idea of coming to the Opry with Grace and watching a show was suddenly something he wanted to make happen. He wasn't sure if it was possible, but the idea was now stuck in his mind.

His attention was drawn back to Henry. "A little trivia for you all. You know who Blake Shelton is, right?" Henry got lots of nods. "Did you know Blake Shelton is the only artist who was invited to be an Opry member via Twitter?"

After lots of laughs and exclamations, Henry continued, "When an artist is invited to become a member, they are inducted. It used to be they had to perform twelve times a year if they were a member, but these days, it's a little more relaxed because of everyone's busy schedules. Performers all get paid equally, whether they're Blake Shelton or a brand-new artist."

Henry continued with his spiel, but Carl lost focus on what he was saying. They peeked into dressing rooms, checked out where the in-house band practiced with the artists, saw the storage area for equipment, and so much more.

"Thanks for bringing me here." Grace's lemony scent surrounded him as she leaned toward him again. "This is such an amazing place. It almost feels sacred, know what I mean?"

"I was thinking the same. I'm surprised at how many of the names I know. It feels really special."

"Carl!"

Carl smiled at the tall man in black jeans and a black button-down shirt walking toward them with his hand out. "Gabe! Hey, what're you doing here?" He shook Gabe's hand.

"Laci's got a show here tonight. I was checking things over before she gets here."

"Laci? Laci Love?" Grace spoke up. Laci Love was one of the few newer artists she knew and listened to.

"Oh, sorry." Carl put his hand on Grace's back to bring her into the conversation. "Gabriel, this is Grace Parson. Grace, this is my friend Gabriel van Neugh. He's Laci Love's manager."

"Pleasure to meet you, Grace." Gabriel shook her hand. "Sorry, I've got to run. Shoot me a text, and we'll reschedule that beer." He walked away, around a corner.

"Wow. So do *you* know Laci Love?" Grace asked as they tried to catch up with the tour group.

"I wish." He laughed. "I've not met her yet. The one time Gabe gave me tickets to one of her shows, I wound up getting sick and not being able to go."

"We'll end the tour here, where it all happens." Henry stopped.

As they turned the corner, they realized they were standing backstage. Henry lined them all up, and they took turns stepping out onto the stage of the Grand Ole Opry. When it was their turn, Carl walked out with Grace. He let her go up to the microphone in the middle of the golden circle at center stage. Looking out at all the red pew-like rows was pretty amazing.

The photographer called over to him. "Hey, handsome, you two together?"

Carl looked around before nodding.

"Come on in, then. Let's get a picture of the two of you."

He looked over at Grace who gave a little shrug to say it was fine with her. As he walked to the golden circle, the photographer asked them to pretend they were singing together. Carl carefully held the mic stand an inch or two below Grace's hand, then leaned in. Their faces were so close, he could feel Grace's warm breath as they pretended to sing.

He looked at her, and their eyes locked for an intense moment.

His heart slammed against his ribcage in anticipation. He couldn't help reaching out his hand toward her face. Her skin looked so soft, so touchable.

Midway to her face, he realized he shouldn't be reaching for her. To cover his mistake, he tucked a stray hair behind her ear. But that just made him want to touch her soft hair again. He wanted to put his hand behind her neck, to close the narrow gap between their lips. His eyes lowered to her lips. He saw her tongue quickly snake out.

"Oh, you two make such a cute couple. This'll be a great picture." The photographer's words startled them and broke the moment.

Carl took a step back. He needed a little space to get his brain cells working again. He noticed Grace shaking her head a bit, like she was trying to get her bearings, then she moved alongside Henry so the next group could get their picture taken.

He could hear her talking to Henry but needed a minute or two to get his head back on straight. What had he been thinking? He'd almost kissed her. What would she have done?

No. He shook his head. *It doesn't matter.* He didn't need to be thinking about kissing anyone.

"You didn't mention Dolly Parton in your tour. What has been her connection to the Opry?"

Grace didn't seem to be overly bothered by their encounter. Maybe he didn't affect her the way she affected him.

Henry was armed and ready with all his Dolly facts. "Oh, we love Ms. Dolly around here. She became an Opry member way back in '69. She's sung here a lot over the years."

Carl let the conversation wash over him. He could hear them talking but didn't focus on the words. Instead, he stood back and watched Marilyn's daughter.

How on Earth had she worked her way into his system?

After the tour, they headed back outside for the walk to Carl's car. The sky had darkened while they'd been in the theater.

Carl looked up at the ominous clouds. "Lookin' like rain. You want me to go grab the car and pick you up?"

"Nah, I'm good. It's only a ten-minute walk or so."

They chatted about what they'd heard on the tour, neither mentioning the intense moment on stage. About three minutes into the walk, the first drops came down.

Carl put his hands out to make sure he'd really felt rain. "Uh-oh."

"Yikes. Maybe I should have taken you up on that offer." Grace laughed.

Within seconds, the floodgates opened. They ducked under the branches of a tree, but there was no way around getting drenched.

Grace looked at him, a grin on her face. "Feel like a run?"

And off they went. Carl liked that Grace didn't mind getting wet. He'd dated plenty of women who would have been miserable in this moment, but she seemed to be enjoying herself. He shook his head, trying to clear it again, as he ran behind her.

A few minutes later, they arrived at his car, soaking wet and out of breath. After unlocking the doors, Carl dug around in his trunk.

Closing the door behind him, he looked over at Grace and started laughing. She was soaked from head to toe.

Thankfully, she joined him in laughter. "I'm sure I look like a drowned rat."

"Right there with ya." He handed her a towel. "It won't do much, but maybe it'll get a little of it off." He cranked up the heater to stave off the chill he knew was coming.

"We're getting your car all wet."

"Ah, it'll dry out. No big deal." And it wasn't a big deal. Carl wasn't at all concerned about his car at the moment. "But I am thinking we might need a raincheck on our lunch date." He looked at his sopping-wet jeans and shirt.

"Probably for the best." Grace looked at her own soaked dress, clinging to her skin.

"Well, let me get you home so you can get changed." He smiled at her, then got the car moving.

Finding Dolly Project:
Here's what I know so far...

9. The Grand Ole Opry was pretty amazing. Standing center stage, I can understand why someone like Dolly would work so hard to get there. And from the sounds of it—at least from tour guide Henry's perspective—Dolly Parton is well-loved, not only at the Grand

Ole Opry but in Nashville. Heck, in Tennessee. Having a dream and working hard for it seems to be a good lesson to learn from Dolly.

While I love what I do, I'm not sure it's my passion. My dream. I'll have to think about that. If it's not my dream, what is? I hate that my brain went to Carl just now.

10. Being so close to Carl on the stage was a little unnerving. I'm surprised he didn't hear my heart thundering in my chest. He makes me feel things I didn't even feel for Drake. Makes me wonder about that relationship and why I was even in it. For a second there, I thought Carl was going to kiss me.

Would I have wanted him to? We only met a few days ago, but in that moment, I wanted him to kiss me. I feel this strong connection to him. When it was time for the next couple's picture, I had to put some space between us, so I went over to talk with Henry and was grateful Carl went to a different area. I have no idea what I asked Henry. I just needed to get my body and my brain to calm down.

11. The rainstorm came right as we were walking back to the car! We both got soaked to the skin. Yesterday, Carl looked really good in his jeans and white T-shirt. But today...wow! I had to look away. Carl with his white shirt plastered to his chest...took my breath away. I have to keep reminding myself I'm not interested in a relationship right now. Carl's making it hard for me to remember that.

Chapter 9

GRACE

*"I make a point to appreciate all the little
things in my life."*
Dolly Parton

THE EARLY MORNING LIGHT filtered through
Grace's closed eyelids, letting her know it was
time to get up. The storm lasted through most of yesterday afternoon and into the evening. She'd relished
putting on the leggings she'd worn on the flight with
one of her mother's long sweaters and settling in with
a good book.

Carl had texted the night before and invited Grace
to the coffee shop he and her mother had gone to every
Wednesday for two years. She loved that he wanted to
take her to the place where he'd spent so much time

with her mother. And on a Wednesday as well. For some reason, this felt big to Grace. Almost like this was something that would bring her a little closer to Mama. And maybe closer to Carl too.

She wasn't really sure how she felt about either of those thoughts.

She was uncomfortable with the new information she was learning about her mother. The fact that she could afford a million-dollar penthouse in downtown Nashville really confused Grace. It was like she didn't even know her mother, which brought up guilt that she should have made more time for her over the years.

And then there was Carl. He and her mother had been good friends, and it felt like he knew her mother better than she did. And why was he bringing up all these feelings in her? Feelings that had nothing to do with her mother. Feelings she thought had died with John's and Drake's betrayals.

She dressed with care this morning and wore a bright, lime green sundress printed with sunglasses, along with her trusty, well-used, still slightly damp athletic shoes. She chose a yellow cardigan to go with her dress and was quite pleased with the colorful ensemble.

Mama would be proud, she thought. *And maybe Dolly too.*

That thought made her smile. She'd come a long way in just a few short days. For so long, she'd avoided bright colors that brought attention to her. She was trying to be more confident and comfortable in her mother's clothes. Trying to embrace her inner-Dolly.

She remembered the cute colorful outfits her mother had bought her for school, outfits that made her look like a mini-Dolly Parton. For a while, she'd loved it, loved the bright, fun colors and the attention. But then the girls got meaner, and she became less confident in what she was wearing. She remembered when she told her mother she wanted black pants and plain, basic shirts for school. The disappointed look on her mother's face had stayed with her for years.

But now she wondered if her mother would be pleased with her wearing all these bright, colorful, fun outfits. Especially since they were Mama's clothes. She wasn't sure what she'd do when her luggage showed up and she didn't have to wear the bright clothes any-more. Would she *want* to wear them? She still wasn't completely comfortable, but she did enjoy how they looked on her.

Heading to the kitchen to grab a cup of coffee while she waited for Carl, she was excited to answer her cell when Breena called.

"Hey, Bree," she said. "How's Chattanooga?"

"Oh, Grace, it's so beautiful here. Right in the middle of the mountains. Such a cool little town," Breena gushed. "But I want to hear everything about you and Carl and your Finding Dolly Project. How's it all going?"

"Well, first, there is no *me and Carl*," Grace an-swered a little too quickly. Her cheeks heated a bit as she thought about the moment on stage at the Grand Ole Opry. Then, seeming to realize her misstep when Breena chuckled, she quickly went on, "I really don't know where we are on the Finding Dolly Project. I've learned a lot about Dolly. She's quite an amazing woman, you know, but I don't quite get what Mama wanted me to learn."

"Hmm, well tell me what you've discovered so far?"

Grace shared everything about their trip to the Country Music Hall of Fame on Monday and the Grand Ole Opry yesterday.

"Oh, Bree, the theater there, it was amazing. You and I need to see a show there one day." She laughed. "I don't even like country music, but what a fabulous place to see a performance."

She conveniently left out the heated look on stage that brought color to her cheeks. And Carl with his shirt plastered to his chest after getting caught in the rain.

Just then the buzzer rang.

"Oh shoot. I've got to go, Bree. I'm heading out with Carl to the coffee shop he and Mama used to go to." Grace walked to the entryway to grab her purse and sweater.

"Well, have fun with Carl and keep me updated on the Project. I'll be back soon. I miss you and want to see Nashville with you." Breena hung up.

The coffee shop, Music Row Joe, was a little funky, a little off the beaten path, but exactly what she imagined Mama enjoying. Inside, there were guitars, signed by famous musicians who had come through at one point or another, hanging all around the room. The color theme of yellow, bright pink, and lime green was bright, bold, and fun.

And today's outfit choice fit right in.

There was a coffee bar, painted black and white like the keys on a piano, where you could sit on a yellow stool and grab a cup of coffee, and tables seating two or four scattered around the room.

They chose a table on the patio, close to a large heater. The music was bluegrassy and suited the place.

Grace could easily see her mother thoroughly enjoying it here.

The two of them sat in comfortable silence for a bit before the waitress came to take their orders, each lost in their own thoughts about the person missing from the table.

Her mother.

"What can I getcha, hon?" the waitress asked in her very southern drawl. "Oh hey, Carl. Long time."

Grace put her menu down and asked for a half-caff vanilla latte, hot, with a little whipped cream and a blueberry scone. She looked up from the menu to see Carl staring at her.

"What?" she asked.

"That..." He took a deep breath. "That is *exactly* what Marilyn always ordered. Exactly."

Grace froze. She wasn't sure what to say. The waitress, not really sure what was going on, just stood there, looking between the two of them, waiting for Carl's order. After he gave it and the waitress moved on, they just looked at each other for another minute.

"You know," he began slowly, "from what Marilyn always said, I didn't get the impression you were very much alike. But the longer I'm around you, the less sure I am."

"I—" Grace started, then stopped. "I'm not even sure what to say. Honestly, I didn't think Mama and I had very much in common either. Growing up, it always felt like we were butting heads. I suppose that's not so unusual. And now, being here, I feel like I never really knew her at all."

"Do you mind telling me what the last couple of years with her were like?" he asked tentatively.

Grace took a deep breath. She appreciated Carl's interest. Most people didn't want to hear the sad stuff.

"When Mama came home, it was hard. I didn't know what she needed, and she was so used to being independent, she wouldn't ask for help. We had a few really difficult weeks before I finally reached out to Bree. She was able to be 'the caregiver' in Mama's eyes, which allowed me to just be her daughter. Even though I did a lot to help, it was easier if Mama saw Bree as the one in charge. She didn't mind telling Bree what she needed."

The coffee and pastries came with perfect timing. Grace took a slow sip, savoring the sweet, creamy, piping-hot coffee before going on.

"I'm not going to lie, it was hard, knowing Mama let Bree in but not me. I was really resentful for a while. Eventually, I was able to move past it, and the household ran much smoother. Mama's memory kept slowly creeping away. First, it was little things. Small memories she couldn't remember. Then, it was calling us by the wrong names. When she said her husband was Marco, I knew we were in a whole new phase. Daddy's name wasn't Marco. It was Martin. Martin Parson. And the relationship Mama was remembering wasn't the relationship she and Daddy had. It was all so sad and so confusing."

Grace took some bites of her scone and drank some more of the delicious coffee. It was nice to tell someone this story and not feel judged. She loved her mother, absolutely, but they hadn't always understood each other. As close as she and Breena were, she couldn't tell her all this. Breena's relationship with Marilyn was different from her own, and she didn't want to color Breena's opinion of her mother. Or of herself, for that matter.

"The last few weeks were hard. Mama called me Dolly a lot, instead of Grace. She would ask for Dolly, but when I came in, she would say I wasn't Dolly. It was...hard. Hard on everyone. I ran through most of my savings over the last three years, helping to care for Mama. Since I'm self-employed with my fundraising business, it was hard to commit to long-term projects. And now, not knowing the status of the penthouse, I have to admit, I'm nervous about the future."

Carl seemed to ponder what she'd said before he spoke again. "I can certainly understand how that would make you nervous. When you're ready to jump back into work, just let me know, and I'll intro-duce you to some of the movers and shakers around Nashville. Seems like a lot of my clients might be the same folks who could be your clients. Assuming you'll be in Nashville, I suppose."

She smiled at that. She wasn't sure if she was stay-ing in Nashville, but she was warmed at the idea that Carl might want her to. And she appreciated his desire to help her if she did. She looked around and knew she could see herself living in Nashville. It was a relaxed, friendly town. The outer neighborhoods were fun and comfortable, kind of like some of the smaller commu-nities around Orlando. She loved her mother's pent-house but couldn't really see herself living downtown. She missed having an outdoor space with trees.

They wound up ordering another round of coffees and pastries after finishing the first, both wanting the conversation to continue.

"So tell me about *your* relationship with my moth-er during the time she was here," Grace asked, ready to take the attention off herself. "You mentioned yesterday not really liking 'rich people.' Wasn't Mama 'rich people?' I mean, she must have had some money to buy her apartment and have it renovated."

"Well, as I mentioned earlier, we met when she wanted me to update her apartment." He smiled a little at the memory. "I remember she was wearing a bright pink pair of halfies...what are they called? The pants that come halfway down?"

"You mean capris?" Grace asked, an amused look on her face.

"Right. Yes, she was wearing these bright pink capris with bright yellow heels and a bright yellow hat. She was something to behold." He grinned. "When she told me where she lived, I was really interested in the job. I love that building and its history, and I was eager to leave my mark on it. But after she outlined some of the changes she wanted, I told her no. I was so disappointed because I really wanted the job, but who puts a pole in their *living room*?" He shook his head. "Well apparently, *I* do since I put it in there for her. She even offered to give me lessons." He laughed at the memory.

Grace smiled. "Even with not much money, I think I would pay to see that." She noticed Carl was comfortable laughing at himself. Not a lot of guys—at least the ones she knew—were.

"Ha. Never gonna happen. Anyway, that's when our coffee dates started, but I didn't realize it at the time." At this, he raised his black coffee as if to say *cheers* with it.

"She'd call and ask me to have coffee here with her to talk about the job. She'd changed some of what she wanted. I thought she was a typical eccentric rich client when I first met her. For two months, we met over coffee. She'd call, change something I wasn't willing to do, and we compromised our way to a deal. She figured out what I was willing to do, and in the end, we both agreed to it. My opinion of your mother changed through those coffee dates. We got to know each other, and I was really fond of her, of her zest for life. Her kindness and the way she genuinely cared for others. She definitely had a style of her own, no doubt about it."

"So how did the pole get into the living room then?" Grace asked, laughing but genuinely curious.

Carl chuckled. "We were about six months into the project, probably only a month left, and she sprung it on me. She knew exactly what she was doing." He smiled kind of sheepishly. "She asked if I would put up a bar for her to exercise on. I thought she wanted a ballet barre or something along that line. And I figured she'd want it hidden away in her office. But as you can see, I was wrong, and she got her pole right where she wanted it in the beginning."

Grace laughed at the story. "Yeah. That sounds like Mama. She was always good at figuring out how to get what she wanted."

"She definitely was," Carl said with kindness in his voice. "I never felt like she was using me or she thought less of me, like I feel with some clients. Some people feel like because they have a lot of money and are paying me, they can control my time and my projects."

Grace frowned. "Well, that certainly doesn't seem right. I'm glad to hear Mama was different. Though I'm not surprised."

"When Marilyn left," Carl said softly, "I really missed her. I kept coming here on Wednesdays for months, hoping she would be here to join me. And when you told me on Saturday she passed away...well, it broke my heart. I..."

Grace laid her hand over his, feeling the now familiar zing run up her arm. She wasn't sure if she should really be holding his hand, but it seemed like a good time to offer him support.

Carl looked down at their hands, took a steadying breath, and continued. "I'm really sorry for your loss, Grace. I'm not sure if I said that the other day. I was too consumed with *my* loss. Thank you for sharing this project with me."

"I appreciate your help. Especially with Breena out of town. It's definitely more fun to be shown around by a local." Grace squeezed his hand, then picked up her coffee cup.

They sat with their thoughts for a few minutes in comfortable silence, then Carl asked, "So where are you on the Finding Dolly Project?"

"Breena asked exactly the same thing right before you buzzed my apartment this morning." Grace smiled. "I'm not really sure, to be honest. I've definitely learned a lot more about Dolly than I knew before, but I'm not sure how *useful* any of it is?"

She gathered her thoughts before continuing. "So far, I've learned Dolly has never been afraid of wearing bright colors or crazy, sparkly outfits. She chose the look intentionally. I would love to have her confidence and to not care what others think about me. Another thing I've learned is, she's not afraid to dream. And to dream *big*. She didn't just *want* to be a superstar. She worked hard to make it happen. She's still working hard. I'm not sure how this is relevant to what Mama wanted me to figure out, but it's what I've found so far."

"Hmm," Carl thought for a moment before continuing. "One thing I remember about Marilyn is she always seemed to have a vision for the future. Like with her remodel project, she knew exactly what her end vision was and kept working toward it. I have no idea where all this will lead you, but it seems like Marilyn had an idea for you with this project. I think you should trust the journey your mother is sending you on."

Grace nodded. That was an interesting way to look at it. *The journey Mama is sending me on.* Grace wondered if her mother had known Carl would be part of this journey.

Probably.

She smiled at that thought.

Finding Dolly Project:

Here's what I know so far...

12. Mama and I apparently have the exact same taste in coffee and scones. I thoroughly enjoyed my coffee date with Carl. I'm not sure if calling it a date is appropriate, it felt like one. We sat and talked for a couple of hours. He wanted to hear how it was after Mama moved back to Florida. I don't think anyone has asked about that before. It was also interesting to hear about his relationship with her. I appreciate that he shared it with me.

13. Carl suggested Mama must have had a vision for what she wanted me to figure out with this Project. And I need to trust that the steps I'm taking will lead me closer to the answer. I guess as long as I know my next step, that's all I need right now. Tomorrow, I will do some computer research on Dolly. That's my next step.

14. The more time I spend with Carl, the more I like him. I can see why Mama enjoyed his company. He's an easy person to be around. He's a good listener and asks interesting questions. I'm a little jealous, maybe envious, of how well they got along. I wish I could have had that kind of friendship with Mama. While we never had big problems, we also never felt like friends. I hope I can call Carl a friend like Mama did. If I move back to Florida, I think I will miss him.

Chapter 10

CARL

"You need to really believe in what you've got to offer, what your talent is—and if you believe, that gives you strength."
Dolly Parton

C ARL HADN'T WANTED TO end his coffee date with Grace. Hearing and sharing stories about Marilyn helped heal the hole in his heart. He'd been back to the coffee shop several times over the last few years, but this time he'd felt Marilyn's presence.

He welcomed Grace's company. She was easy to talk to, and he couldn't deny he was attracted to her. He looked forward to the lemony scent he now associated with her. She brought up feelings in him he thought were long dead. He wasn't sure how he felt about that.

And he wasn't sure if it was wise to even consider trying to change their relationship.

As much as he adored being with Grace, he still had a business to run. Currently, he was bumping down the road to get the update on the Barn Reno project. He'd already popped into the other two work-sites for the updates on them. Things were progressing all around.

He'd listened to another message from Mr. Kline and knew he needed to call him when he got back to his office, but for now, his mind was on the historic barn he was happy to be putting his mark on. He loved bringing an old building back to life. He also loved the fact that this client had been open to some of his ideas to keep the historic feel.

Jim met him at his truck as soon as he pulled up. "Hey, boss. How's it goin' playin' tour guide?"

No such thing as a private life when you worked so closely with a group of guys. "It's fine." He chuckled. "No Dolly Parton sightings yet though."

"How's the daughter? Is she as crazy as her mama?" Jim had met Marilyn during the work on her penthouse and knew all too well just how colorful she was.

"Nah." Carl thought about Grace and how self-conscious she was in Marilyn's clothes. She looked great in them but didn't seem to want to hear it. "She's actually a lot of fun."

Jim looked at him through squinted eyes. "Yer fallin' for her, aren't ya?"

"What? No. Of course not." Carl frowned at Jim's declaration. "Well, I could potentially see myself falling for her...but no." He shook his head to emphasize the point.

"Didn't you learn nothin' from your mountain-cabin woman? I thought you didn't mess with rich women no more?" Jim rarely bothered learning clients' names. He just called them by the job.

"Well, Grace isn't rich—" Carl started before Jim interrupted.

"Of course she is." He looked at Carl, exasperated. "She's Marilyn's girl. Why wouldn't she be?"

Hmm. He'd have to think about that one. Marilyn was rich, so why was Grace having financial troubles? Maybe there was friction in their relationship neither had mentioned.

"Hey, I heard from Kline." He switched the subject. "He's wanting us back to finish the addition."

"What? Now? After months of nothin'? Now he wants us back?" Jim was not particularly forgiving. It was his guys who'd been out of work because of Kline. "What'd ya tell him?"

"Nothing yet. I'm going to call him when I get back to the office. But what're your thoughts? Do we have any wiggle room in the schedule?"

"Not really. We'd have to bring in a few extra guys to be able to handle that job along with the other three we've got runnin'. Most of the guys we usually hire are

already workin', not sure we'd be able to find anyone we'd want."

That wasn't what Carl wanted to hear. He was
going to have to put in more time than he'd hoped.
Time he'd rather spend with Grace. Maybe there
was an easy solution he just couldn't see yet.

An hour later, back in his office, Carl was pleased
when Kline's voicemail answered his call. That
might give him a little more wiggle room to figure
out the logistics.

"Mr. Kline, Carl Montgomery here. Sorry I've
missed you again." Carl wasn't sorry he had missed
him. "I've just put my guys on another project, but
I'll double-check the schedule to see if we can work
you in anywhere. I'll call as soon as I can make some
space on the calendar."

That task done, Carl's thoughts strayed back to
Grace. He was surprised at how open she'd been
during their coffee date. Sharing how hard the last
three years had been, taking care of her mother. He
thought of his own mother and was grateful she was
healthy and still around. He probably should take
her some flowers soon.

He'd also appreciated being able to share what his relationship with Marilyn had been. There weren't many people he could talk to about it, so he was happy she asked. Marilyn had been a friend, a genuine friend. And he felt some of the same feelings with Grace he'd felt with Marilyn. She was easy to be with, easy to talk to...and well, she just felt *comfortable*. He didn't really know how else to explain it.

He did, however, feel something for Grace. He was attracted to her. And not sure what to do about it. The sparks between them threw him off. Whenever they touched, the electricity was palpable. He hadn't had that type of chemistry in a relationship in a long time, if ever.

He was happy she'd let him help with the Finding Dolly Project, even though he was sure they hadn't really gotten anywhere with it. Other than checking out some Dolly murals around town, they'd done most of the Dolly sites in Nashville. But he wasn't ready to be done looking with her. He was having fun spending time with her.

She was the complete opposite of Krisi, the ex he didn't like to think about. Krisi was overly confident, pushy, and a fashion diva; Grace didn't seem to recognize her own beauty and strength. She was unsure of herself at times and really seemed to be thrown off by having to wear Marilyn's clothes. He was curious about her normal style.

As he thought more about Grace and her project, he decided that if she really wanted to learn more about Dolly Parton, she would need to visit Pigeon Forge.

That was Dolly country.

Between Dollywood, the Stampede, her childhood home, and all of the other Dolly activities up there, if Grace were going to learn anything more about Dolly, it would be there.

And he wanted to be the one to take her.

The idea of taking her there for a weekend was very appealing, but would she go with him? They hadn't known each other for very long. Less than a week. How could he convince her? And should he?

He'd have to ponder that one for a while. He'd had fun the last few days taking her around the city.

The ringing of his phone took him out of his thoughts, and he answered before checking the caller ID.

That was a mistake.

"Carl, I got your message. I appreciate you checking the schedule. Just wanted to see if you have anything yet?" Mr. Kline's voice boomed across the line.

"Well, Mr. Kline, I just walked in the door. Like I said, I just started the guys on a new project that's taking up a lot of our schedule, but I'll see what I can do."

"I need this done in the next two months, Carl. Make it happen." Mr. Kline ended the call.

Carl threw his phone down on his desk, startling Miss Kitty from her nap in the perch above him.

"Sorry, Miss Kitty." He reached up and gave her head a scratch. As soon as he sat at his desk, she hopped down to his desk, then to his lap. She walked in an awkward circle, before plopping down. His frustration was simmering, but Miss Kitty helped cool it down.

He didn't like the thought that he might have to give Miss Kitty up soon. He'd been waiting until Grace figured out her plans, but he hadn't wanted to ask or bring it up since that might mean losing the cat.

Carl scratched Miss Kitty's head as he thought about how to get Grace to go to Pigeon Forge with him. He hadn't been to Pigeon Forge or Dollywood for several years. It would be fun to go again. He wondered if she would find it fun to see the theme parks. She was from Orlando, after all. Was she a roller coaster girl? The idea made him smile.

Chapter 11

GRACE

"Well, I always just thought if you see somebody without a smile, give 'em yours."
Dolly Parton

GRACE'S PHONE STARTLED HER awake the next morning. She'd hoped to sleep in a bit. Looking at the clock, she was shocked to see it was already ten. She grabbed the phone as it trilled again.

"Hullo." She yawned.

"Hey, Gracey."

She smiled, as always when Breena called her by her middle school nickname. It took her back to the days when they were together day and night, when Breena was living in their house. And for Grace, it had felt like she had a sister. As sisters, they'd decided they

needed nicknames for each other—Gracey and Bree.
They hadn't been super clever in their nicknames, she
realized, but she still loved it when Breena used hers. It
was a reminder she wasn't alone in the world.

"Hey, Bree. I miss you, girl."

"I miss you too. What're you up to today? It
sounds like I woke you up."

"Yeah, late night with Dolly." Grace yawned again.
"I watched a couple of her movies and stayed up way
too late."

"Oh fun. Which movies did you watch?"

"*Best Little Whorehouse in Texas* and *Nine to Five*.
I hadn't seen either of them in a few years."

"Love those. So tell me what's going on with our
hunky contractor, and how was the coffee shop yesterday?"

"Sorry." Grace yawned again, evading the *hunky
contractor* comment. "I just woke up and need to get
some coffee going. I'll update you while it brews."

By the time the pot finished brewing, Grace had
told Breena all about the last few days. She sat down at
the kitchen table and took a long sip of coffee. "Ahh,"
she sighed. "Much better already."

"It sounds like you've been having fun with Carl
this week." Breena prodded a bit. "Breakfast yesterday
seems like it was pretty intense."

"Yeah. I really don't know him, but we've had
some pretty deep conversations. And I really appreciate he's willing to drag me all over town playing tour
guide."

"It doesn't sound like he's minded in the least. It sounds like he enjoys spending time with you. Is he sending you any signals he likes you?"

"I...um, hmm..."

Grace wasn't really sure what to say. Her mind flipped back to the moment on the Opry stage when they were only a breath apart. She remembered the intense look in his eyes before they had been shuffled off the stage. But there hadn't been any more moments like that.

She was pretty confused. She'd never been great with guys. And since Drake, her confidence—what little she'd had—was pretty much nonexistent.

"I have no idea," she said honestly. "I'm pretty sure I'm not ready for a relationship though."

Thinking back to Drake, she realized she was angrier and more embarrassed than heartbroken by what he'd done. John had broken her heart, but Drake...he'd just pissed her off. She wasn't sure she'd ever really let him into her heart.

She caught Breena up on the Finding Dolly Project, which was, basically, not a lot further along. She was going to spend the afternoon online, if she could get into her mother's computer, to see what else she could learn about Dolly and to look for any clues to the next steps.

"Good luck in your hunting today. I'll catch up with you tomorrow."

Breena signed off as Grace refilled her coffee and set up her mother's laptop on the kitchen table. She found the login information in the top drawer of the desk, which was helpful. Sitting there, in her mother's bright purple robe, drinking out of the mug she'd made for her so many years ago, Grace couldn't help but wonder what exactly her mama wanted her to figure out by chasing Dolly Parton.

Her respect for Dolly Parton had definitely grown over the past week. She appreciated how sure of herself Dolly was, and Grace wished she, too, could be more sure of herself. It was time to start standing up for herself and her business the way Dolly Parton did.

A few hours later, after watching multiple interviews and concerts and reading over a dozen articles, Grace knew what her next step needed to be. She wasn't exactly sure how to make it happen, especially on a budget, but she had to go to Pigeon Forge. Home to not only Dolly but Dollywood. She was certain whatever she was supposed to learn, she would find it there.

With her budget in mind, she made a list of the places she needed to visit. It wasn't outrageously expensive, and she felt like she could probably make the trip in a day. It would be a long day, but it could be done.

But how would she get there? That was the question. She could ask Breena to come back with the rental car. Or, she supposed, she could rent a second one. Her savings account wouldn't like it, but it was an option. Since she wasn't sure when she'd find work again, she was nervous to spend too much. She knew she could sell the two houses, but that took time, and she just wasn't sure what she was going to do in the long term.

Her cell phone vibrated as she pondered all this.

CARL: Hey Grace, how's the research going today?

She smiled, feeling the familiar flush of heat on her cheeks. She felt like she was back in high school.

GRACE: Hey there, knee deep in Dolly research

Then she typed some more, sending at the same time she received a response from him.

GRACE: I think I need to go to Pigeon Forge

CARL: You probably need to go to Pigeon Forge

GRACE: Great minds think alike, lol

CARL: LOL, I guess so.

CARL: I'd be happy to continue playing tour guide. I love Pigeon Forge & Dollywood

Grace looked down at her phone. Well, that would certainly be more fun than going alone.

GRACE: What'd you have in mind?

CARL: Maybe head over tomorrow night after work. Catch dinner. Then Dollywood on Saturday?

Oh boy. An overnight trip. It sounded amazing. She could picture the two of them walking hand in hand down around the quaint town, looking at all the trinkets. Maybe dinner at a romantic inn nestled in the mountains with twinkling lights in the trees. Waking up to a stunning mountain view with their coffee.

If he had romantic feelings for her, this could become complicated, quickly. She hadn't really dealt with her breakup with Drake, and she wasn't ready to jump into another relationship.

GRACE: Sounds like fun.

She'd have to set some boundaries.

Finding Dolly Project:
Here's what I know so far...

15. Dolly is a smart, savvy businesswoman who doesn't let anyone run her over. Heck, she once said no to Elvis Presley! He wanted to record "I Will Always Love You," but he wanted to own half the song's rights. Dolly said no, even though she loved Elvis and really wanted him to record it. She just couldn't give him half of that song. Can you imagine saying no to Elvis? To the Elvis Presley? But by saying no to him, she was saying yes to her future success and the future success of that song. Pretty cool. This is another instance of Dolly standing up for herself and her business.

16. It looks like Pigeon Forge is the next step in my mission to find Dolly. And I'm going with Carl. Apparently, he loves Pigeon Forge and Dollywood. Who knew? I wonder if he's a roller coaster fan. I can't wait to ride them. I also wonder how Dollywood compares to the Orlando theme parks.

I called on my inner-Dolly and set some boundaries with Carl for the trip. Two bedrooms. I think it'll be a lot of fun being there with him, but we haven't even been on a date. So I didn't want there to be any expectations on either side. This keeps it clear, and I feel much better after having told him. He seemed fine with that, so maybe friendship is all he wants after all.

Or maybe, he's okay with taking it slow and letting us get to know each other better. I'm hopeful.

Chapter 12

CARL

"You'll never do a whole lot unless you're brave enough to try."

Dolly Parton

IT WAS FRIDAY, AND Carl was grateful to be wrapping up his week. He'd been distracted all morning, thinking about his text conversation with Grace yesterday. He couldn't believe he'd offered to take Grace to Pigeon Forge; he was even more surprised she'd agreed to go. Not only did he offer to take her, he offered to make the hotel reservations—separate rooms of course—and dinner arrangements. Planning had never been his particular forte, so to straight-up offer these things was a little crazy.

He thought about Jim's comments that he was falling for her. Maybe he was.

If falling for her meant wanting to see her and looking forward to seeing her and counting the minutes until their weekend...then yes, he was falling for her.

He'd missed her today, which was ridiculous. But they'd spent so much time together since they met. It was hard to believe it had only been a week.

And now, he was trying to wrap up the week with his crew and to set up next week so he could take off a little early today to drive to Pigeon Forge with Grace. Hopefully, the Friday afternoon traffic wouldn't be too bad. Probably wishful thinking.

Having arranged the rooms at a resort near Dollywood and a reservation for two at the Dolly Parton Stampede, he felt he'd planned enough and moved on to next week's plans. The Kline project was still niggling at the back of his brain, but he had yet to figure out how to fit it into the schedule.

"Hey, big bro."

He startled out of his thoughts at the voice. He turned to see Jillian standing in the doorway.

"Well hey, Bean, what're you doing out here today?"

Jilly Bean. He couldn't remember when the nickname started, but it had stuck.

It was always a bit of a jolt to see his baby sister in her police uniform. She'd been hired by the NPD a couple of years ago, and he still couldn't figure out why she wanted to be a cop. But here she was in her uniform, long auburn hair in a ponytail, and two cups of coffee in her hands.

"I hear you took a lady to Joe's this week?" She offered him one of the insulated Music Row Joe cups. "I want to hear all the deets. Who's the new girl?" She made herself comfortable on the couch. Miss Kitty jumped down and wandered over to get scratches from the newcomer.

He laughed. Sometimes, living in Nashville was like living in a small town. You couldn't do anything or go anywhere without everyone knowing about it. Of course his sister found out he and Grace went to Joe's.

"Well, I appreciate you keeping up with my social life, such as it is, but there's not a lot to tell. I met Marilyn's daughter this week. Her mother passed away a month or so ago, and she's here figuring out what to do with the apartment."

Jillian looked at him, understanding in her eyes. "I'm so sorry to hear about Marilyn. She was a real nice lady. I was glad to have met her, and I know she was a good friend of yours."

Carl nodded his appreciation as she paused for a minute.

"So...how's her daughter?"

"Her name is Grace, and well, she's nice. Marilyn gave her a mission before passing away, and I offered to help."

"Ooh, a mission. Tell me." Jillian settled further into the couch.

"Well, you know how Marilyn was, well, obsessed with Dolly Parton?"

Jillian laughed. "Yep. What—did she set her daughter on a mission to find Dolly?"

Carl cocked his head. "Well, yeah."

"Really? I was just kidding."

"That's exactly the mission she gave Grace. To 'find Dolly.' So I've been playing tour guide, showing her some of the Dolly stuff around Nashville. I took her to the Country Music Hall of Fame and the Opry. Tonight, we're headed up to Pigeon Forge."

"Wait a minute." Jillian narrowed her eyes. "I know that look. Oh geesh, Carl. You think you're helping her, but...why do you always go for the society girls who take advantage of you?"

"No, no..." Carl started. He could feel his face getting warm. The problem with sisters was they know you too well. "She just seems a little down on her luck right now, so I'm happy to help. That's all."

"Well, from over here, it looks like you're falling for her, and she's taking advantage of you. Didn't Krisi teach you anything?"

Carl recoiled. "What? No, no. You've got it all wrong. Grace isn't a rich, society girl. She hardly has any money."

"Carl," Jillian said slowly, as if talking to a child. "She's Marilyn's daughter. Marilyn, who bought a penthouse apartment at The Athenian. Of course she has money."

What Jillian was saying made sense. It was the same thing Jim said. But it didn't really match up with the woman he'd been out with this week. Grace was concerned about how much she was spending, always asking how much things were and wanting to pay him back.

"I don't think she has a lot of money," he finally said. "And she's definitely not taking advantage of me. I offered to show her around a bit. That's all. It's kind of a farewell gift to Marilyn, I guess. And as for me falling for her, it's a little early. She doesn't seem interested in more than friendship."

He would take friendship, he realized, if it was all Grace would give.

They chatted for a few more minutes, then Jillian had to take off back to work. As he watched his sister drive away in her cruiser, he thought about what she'd said.

About Grace having money.

About him falling for her.

He definitely could...well okay, probably *was* falling for her, but he could handle it. He thought about the short trip in a few hours. He was excited to be with her again. To hang out with her. To learn more about her.

And he was pleased he could do this for her. She wasn't taking advantage of him, regardless of what his sister thought. He was happy to take her to Pigeon Forge.

Just, you know, as a friend.

Yeah right, he thought. He liked her and wanted her to like him. The least he could do was be honest with himself.

He paced around his office before stopping to scratch Miss Kitty behind her ears as she lounged in front of the window on her perch. Living her best life. Basking in the sunshine, as a cat should do. "Okay, big girl, time to head next door."

Going out the door with his hands full of files and Miss Kitty winding around his feet, he heard the office phone ring. He let it go to the answering machine; he needed to head to the house and get ready to pick up Grace.

Chapter 13

GRACE

"Never ignore your roots, your home, or your hair."

Dolly Parton

"I'LL BE SAFE, BREE, I promise."

Breena was not thrilled about Grace heading out of town—overnight—with a guy she barely knew. And now Grace was doubting herself, wondering if she'd made a really bad decision.

"Just remember Drake, Grace. He was very nice to you but ultimately seemed to be after your money. Money you don't have, but still. Don't get stuck with one of those guys again. Especially one who thinks you're rich because of your mother's apartment."

"But, Bree, I don't have any money. I told him that. I wish I did. I'd go shopping for a new wardrobe." She laughed. "My savings is doing pretty well since he's paid for so much, but I wish he wouldn't."

"Okay, okay." Breena dropped the subject. "So, since your wardrobe is limited, what are you going to wear on the trip?"

"Well, I've been going through Mama's closet. I decided to do some cleaning out and organizing, I guess. I made a pile of the clothes I know I will never wear to donate. But some aren't too bad. I even found a pair of cowboy boots that fit, which is weird since Mama's feet were smaller than mine." She laughed again. "So now I have the option of turquoise cowboy boots or tennis shoes to go with whatever I wear."

"Cowboy boots are fun." Breena laughed. "Turquoise, huh? Well, I guess the color shouldn't be a surprise. That was your mama's favorite, after all."

They talked for a few more minutes while Grace finished packing. She promised Breena several POL texts; they'd come up with the "proof of life" code in college, just keeping an eye on each other. It was one of those habits that stuck.

After saying goodbye, Grace checked the suitcase one last time before closing it. She looked at the colorful clothes and wondered at what point she'd stopped liking colors.

As a young girl, Grace loved wearing colors. She didn't like the attention garnered by some of the outfits Mama put her in, but she did like the colors. In her young mind, and maybe in her not-so-young mind, she associated color with negative attention.

Maybe it was time to rethink her wardrobe. Maybe it was time to add some color back into it.

She wouldn't go so far as rhinestones or anything, but she was enjoying looking bright and fun again. And some of the colors actually complemented her skin tone. She'd have to talk to Breena about it when she got back. Breena would be honest about what looked good and what washed her out.

Before she closed the overnight bag, she grabbed her Finding Dolly journal and tucked it inside. She was really hoping for some answers this weekend. If she couldn't figure out what it was she was supposed to find, she wasn't sure what she would do. She'd hate to fail in this last request from her mother.

Grace paced as she waited for Carl, chewing on her bottom lip, wondering if she'd made a mistake agreeing to go with him. Really, what did she know about this guy? Yes, he was good-looking, but Drake had been good-looking too. Carl certainly made her heart beat faster whenever she was around him. Drake had never gotten her heart going.

That thought startled her a bit. Why had she stayed with Drake for so long when he didn't even get her pulse jumping? Dolly would certainly never put up with that kind of crap.

Grace vowed to not stay in a relationship that didn't work for her ever again.

She wanted pulse jumping, heart beating faster, face flushing in her next relationship.

Her thoughts returned to Carl. He certainly did all of those things for her. She had to admit it, at least to herself.

Could she see herself in a relationship with him though? Hmm, maybe. She remembered Mama had been friends with him, and he was a great listener. Those seemed like good places to start if you were looking for a great relationship.

Was she?

Just then, Brian buzzed up, breaking off her thoughts. Suddenly, she was back to being nervous and wondering if going overnight alone with him was a big mistake.

The biggest risk for the weekend seemed to be her heart.

And Breena wouldn't be able to help with that.

"Okay, so who was your nightmare girlfriend?" Grace asked.

They'd been on the road for about an hour and had talked about everything. She was nervous to ask the question but really wanted to know. She wanted to understand more about this man who made her feel so much. Excited. Comfortable. Nervous. Beautiful.

"Well, that would have to be Krisi. She's the one I'd been dating shortly before meeting your mother. We broke up...well, I broke up with her about a month before I met Marilyn. I was still pretty raw."

"What was she like, Krisi?" Grace asked. She wasn't trying to be nosy. She was interested to see what type of woman Carl had been attracted to.

"She was beautiful, confident. She knew how to get what she wanted, but she got a bit too cocky with our relationship."

Grace squirmed in her seat, trying to smooth out nonexistent wrinkles. She forged forward with more questions. "What do you mean she got 'too cocky' with your relationship?"

"Do you really want to hear all this?"

His eyes looked wary, but she wanted to hear the story. "I'd really like to hear, if you don't mind telling."

"Okay. May as well tell the whole story then. Krisi and I met when she hired me to do some work on her mountain cabin. She called it a cabin, but it was basically a mansion in the mountains." He gave a bit of a snort.

Grace chuckled. "Kind of like Mama's apartment turned out to be a penthouse."

"Ha! Exactly. It's a beautiful place, the mountain cabin. I loved working there. I usually work on historic places or older homes, but I relished working with the wood, working with and around nature at that house.

Over the months, she was around a lot while I was working. She'd invite me to stay for a drink or something to eat, and we just kind of fell into a relationship. I stayed over a lot with her. I told myself it just made the job easier to get to. You know, saved me the drive back into town. But over time, she would ask me to do little projects for her, and make comments like, 'This is what a boyfriend does' so I knew she didn't expect to see it on her bill. This went on for months. After a while, I had basically redone the whole house. It turned out fantastic."

"Having seen some of your work, I'm sure it was beautiful."

He paused for a moment. "One weekend, I was going out of town to visit a buddy. I went back to my house to pack some clothes, and my buddy called to say his girlfriend was in an accident and he didn't want to leave her."

"Oh no."

"Thankfully, she wasn't hurt too bad. I decided to grab some wine and flowers and head back up to the cabin for what I hoped would be a romantic weekend. When I got there, there was another car in the driveway. One I didn't recognize. I figured she had one of her girlfriends up for the weekend since I was going to be out of town. But apparently, Krisi had the same idea of a romantic weekend. It just wasn't with me."

"Oh boy." Grace cringed, feeling bad she'd pushed him to tell this story. But he seemed to want to finish it.

"As I pulled into the driveway at her cabin, I noted a sleek, black Maserati in the driveway. I wondered which friend was visiting her and how quickly we could get her to leave. Just as I was about to get out of my car, Krisi skipped down the front steps toward the Maserati. She turned back to the house, said something to her companion, then laughed."

He hesitated for another moment, pulling around a tractor trailer on the highway before returning to the story.

"Then a man made his way down the steps, carrying Krisi's weekender bag. He dropped it by the trunk and put an arm around her to pull her close. I sat and watched as Krisi leaned in and gave the man a kiss. Not a chaste kiss. This was a kiss between lovers. Or soon-to-be lovers. The man pulled away, put her bag in the trunk, then walked around to open the door for her. I watched them drive away, blissfully unaware of my presence."

Grace put her hand on his arm. "I'm so sorry, Carl. What a horrible thing to happen to you." Her heart ached for what he must have felt.

"Somehow, I made it back down the mountain in one piece. The switchbacks seemed sharper and steeper than usual. I went home and drank that whole bottle of wine by myself. I paid for it the next morning, but I made myself get up and do something productive to keep my mind busy. I was working in the office, getting some billing done. Actually, I was billing Krisi for all the small *boyfriend* jobs. It might have been petty, but I was pretty pissed off.

"She showed up about eleven in the morning. She didn't even realize I knew until I handed her the bill. She was stunned and confused, trying to figure out how I knew she'd cheated. She quickly became angry and said she wouldn't pay because the work was shoddy anyway."

"Oh my gosh," Grace exclaimed. "Did she ever pay you?"

"Oh yes. I had a lawyer friend send her a letter that looked all nice and legal. It insinuated if she didn't pay, he would see her in court and she'd pay a lot more than the invoiced amount. Within a week, I had my money, and she had the key to her cabin back. I wrote off the clothes I'd left there as collateral damage."

"Wow." Grace didn't know what to say, but she knew the feeling. It had happened to her.

"So that," he said with a wry smile, "is my sad story. I met your mother shortly after all that happened. I was wary of getting into any kind of relationship with her while I worked on her place, even just a friendship. But Marilyn wouldn't take no for an answer. She was upfront about all our business dealings—paid quickly and made sure I included everything. She wouldn't let me do anything for free. Even when I wanted to."

"It's so weird to hear about your relationship with my mother," Grace said. "It feels like she had this whole other life I knew nothing about. I really enjoy hearing about it though, so thank you for sharing."

Grace appreciated Carl's openness. His story made her realize just how similar they were when it came to relationships.

Finding Dolly Project:
Here's what I know so far...

17. Headed to Pigeon Forge tonight and Dollywood tomorrow. With Carl. Something about this weekend feels magical. I hope I'll get some answers and figure out this silly quest Mama has sent me on.

Chapter 14

CARL

"If you don't like the road you're walking, start paving another one."
Dolly Parton

CARL HADN'T INTENDED TO share the whole Krisi story with her. He typically didn't share it with anyone. Usually, even thinking about Krisi was painful. But telling it this time, to Grace, he didn't feel the hurt in his heart. *Maybe enough time has passed*, he thought. Or maybe, it was the company he was keeping. Either way, it felt like a big step toward moving on.

He hadn't had a serious relationship since then. Usually, a date or two was enough. None of his dates had tempted him to want more. It surprised him to realize he'd spent more time with Grace than any woman since Krisi. Something to think about.

"Now it's your turn," he prodded. "Who was your last nightmare boyfriend?"

He saw her take a big breath before she spoke. "Well, my biggest nightmare was John in college. But my *latest* one is the man I was dating right before coming to Nashville."

Well heck, he thought. *No wonder she seems a little gun-shy.* Out loud, he asked, "So what happened? If you don't mind sharing?"

"Well, I guess I kind of have to share since you did." She laughed a little. "Companies hire me to organize fundraisers. I met Drake at the last company I was working for. He was one of the bachelors we auctioned off—"

"Wait, what? You auction off guys?" He glanced at her, appalled.

"Well...yes. We get several good-looking or popular guys from the company or the community, and I organize a bachelor auction. It's an effective way to raise a lot of money."

"But..." He paused, glancing quickly at her, very confused. "Is that even legal? I mean, are you like a modern-day *madam*?"

Grace burst out laughing. "No, no." She caught her breath. "No. I swear it's all above board. The auction is for a completely legit and *innocent* date with the bachelor. Usually, it's something like a balloon ride with a champagne breakfast or lunch at a horse ranch or something like that."

Carl was curious about the details but really wanted to hear the rest of her story, so he didn't ask the questions lurking in the back of his mind. Another time maybe.

"Anyway," Grace continued. "I met Drake while working on the auction. My sad story is remarkably like yours, except our relationship was...how shall I say? Much more platonic. I was in the midst of caring for Mama, so I didn't have a lot of time or energy, physically or emotionally. We went out semiregularly, he sent flowers, showed the proper amount of interest to keep things moving."

Carl raised an eyebrow but didn't interrupt.

"Bree never liked him, which I suppose should have been my first clue. Before Bree joined me in caring for Mama, I'd set up an alarm system with cameras and an easy call button in case Mama needed something while I was out. After she passed, I moved the alarm to the front door and completely forgot about the cameras. Until we were at the airport on our way here."

Now he was very curious. "So what happened when you were on your way here? And...just out of curiosity and not that it matters, but does Breena like me?" He gave her a cheeky grin.

"Ha. Yes, actually. Bree does like you. She appreciates that you've been my tour guide, so she can visit a friend without guilt."

He tried not to smile too big, but it made him happy to have passed the Breena test.

"So back to Drake. While Bree and I were at the airport, the alarm for my townhouse went off. When I logged into the app to see what was going on, it showed the cameras were still on. That's when I saw two people walking around my townhouse." Grace paused to take a deep breath.

"Drake obviously didn't know about the alarm, and he definitely didn't know about the cameras. But for whatever reason, he was using my townhouse for an 'assignation' with a woman he works with," she said, including air quotes.

"Oh my," Carl's right eyebrow ticked up. "So then what?"

"Well, Bree called the cops and said the alarm went off, but we were heading out of town. They arrested Drake and Deanna." Grace had a wicked gleam in her eyes.

Carl waited, knowing there was more.

"While we were in the air, he left quite a few messages for me. I checked them when we arrived in Nashville. At first, he tried to make it sound like he was just keeping an eye on my house while I was out of town, and it was all a big mistake. Then he was mad about being at the police station, and I wasn't around to say he was allowed in my house. And then he got ugly. After we landed and we listened to his messages, Breena just texted back a screenshot of him and Deanna in my bedroom. I called a locksmith and got the locks changed so it wasn't an option for him to try again."

"Oh geesh." Carl exhaled. Then a little hesitantly, he asked, "So did you hear from him again?"

"Nope. That was it. Good riddance as far as I'm concerned. Deanna can have him. And that, Carl Montgomery, is my sad tale."

"You don't seem super heartbroken, if you don't mind me saying," Carl ventured. He figured it was a good time to get a lay of the land, so to speak. Was she heartbroken and not at all interested in a relationship? He wanted to know.

"More embarrassed and angry than heartbroken, I've discovered." Grace sighed. "He used me, thinking I had money because of our address in Orlando. And I guess since Mama was sick, he probably figured—correctly as it turns out—I was vulnerable. He had even been talking marriage right before I left for the airport."

"Oh wow. *Marriage*? Is that something you were considering?"

"Not really." Grace looked thoughtful. "I was comfortable with Drake, but I didn't feel any sparks or passion for him. I suppose I didn't really have the capacity for more at that point in my life. I hope marriage will be part of my path one day, but I'm certainly not in a rush for it. I feel like I'm just figuring out who *I* am. I'm not sure I want to think about being part of a couple yet."

"Seems like you're thinking pretty clearly, Grace," Carl said with a smile. "Hopefully, this weekend will help bring some answers to you and for your Finding Dolly Project."

Chapter 15

GRACE

"The magic is inside you. There ain't no crystal ball."

Dolly Parton

GRACE HADN'T ENJOYED RELIVING her whole sad tale, but since Carl shared his, and he was a good listener, she'd found herself telling him everything. It was curious they had both been cheated on. Maybe one day, she'd have the courage to share about John.

As the miles rolled by, the conversations continued to roll as well.

"Your mother was so proud of you, you know," Carl said, quickly glancing her way. "She never said anything bad about you."

Grace sat for a moment with this information, playing with her watch, twisting it around her wrist. It confused her when she heard comments like that about her mother. "I feel like I never really knew my mother. Or maybe I'm just getting to know her now. And the sad thing is, I feel like the Mama I'm getting to know, I would have had a lot of fun with her, but it's too late."

She looked out the window so Carl couldn't see her watery eyes. She appreciated that he let her have silence when she needed it. He didn't fill every moment with chatter.

Thinking about her mother, Grace wished she could have used the last couple of years with her differently. But even if she'd tried, her mother had been in no condition to have those kinds of conversations. The last year in particular was really rough. The day Mama said her husband was Marco...well, Grace was just glad her dad wasn't around for that heartbreak.

It was interesting though; even at the end, Mama always responded to music. Especially Dolly's music. Grace could put on one of the twenty or so CDs they had, and her mother would hum along, right in tune. There were some songs she remembered better than others. Some she'd clap her hands along with it. Just the thought brought a smile to Grace's face.

It wasn't all bad, the last three years. Yes, it was hard, but she wouldn't have *not* done it. There were some very tender moments during her caregiving years, and she would always hold on to them. The spontaneous dance parties to one of Dolly's songs, or sitting together, watching *Steel Magnolias* with her mother reciting certain parts because she'd seen it so many times.

Looking out the car window at the mountain view, she could certainly see why her mother chose to live in this area. Grace felt Carl's eyes on her, but he didn't intrude on her thoughts. She appreciated the kindness.

The sun was getting lower in the sky, even though sunset was still a few hours away. The shadows were stretching longer across the mountains. They had stopped in Knoxville about a half hour ago and were rolling through Sevierville now.

Grace looked at him for a minute. "It's beautiful here. I've never driven through the mountains like this."

"This is Dolly country. She was born and raised in this area. We'll be there in about ten or fifteen minutes. I was thinking we could walk around for a while, see Pigeon Forge a bit, then head to dinner. We're going to Dolly's Stampede tonight."

Grace smiled. "That sounds great." She turned a bright shade of pink when her stomach rumbled loudly. "I guess it's good we're headed to dinner soon."

Carl laughed a little. "Yeah, I'm hungry too. The menu looks like we'll be eating pretty well tonight. So probably good we're going in hungry."

They rolled into Pigeon Forge a few minutes later, and Grace laughed. "I'm not sure I was expecting it to be so touristy. It reminds me of I-Drive back home. This will be fun."

She looked at her old-school Mickey Mouse watch. "Looks like we made good time. It's 6:10."

They hopped out of Carl's car and headed down the main drag. Grace savored strolling down Old Mill Street with Carl. It reminded her of some of the touristy areas in Orlando, but the atmosphere was completely different. Here, the buildings were all wood, with names that included *hickory* or *smoky*. Some even had front porches with rocking chairs.

They wandered through a couple of the tourist shops, looking at the fun, sometimes tacky, souvenirs. She paused to examine a few necklaces, then moved on. She was drawn to one with a silver chain with a blue butterfly on it. It reminded her of Dolly Parton, but it also reminded her of her own missing necklace. Her hand touched her empty neck, like it always did when she thought of the necklace. Maybe when she came back here with Breena, she could get one to replace it.

As they headed back out to the street, Grace stopped to take a selfie with him and the Pigeon Forge strip in the background to send to Breena. As she pulled out her phone, she looked confused.

"Everything okay?"

"My phone says it's 7:17." She looked up at him with a furrowed brow.

Carl looked alarmed and pulled his phone out of his pocket. Sure enough, 7:17, and ticking.

"Oh crap." He looked at her, his eyes wide. "Our dinner reservation is at 7:30."

Chapter 16

CARL

"I never have considered myself a per-
fectionist, but I do think of myself as a
'professionalist'...I always strive simply
to be my very best."
Dolly Parton

THEY JUMPED INTO THE car, and Grace found the directions on her phone while Carl pulled out of the lot, speeding onto Island Drive toward the Parkway.

"I am so sorry. I forgot about the time change."

"There's a time change between Nashville and Pigeon Forge?" Grace asked.

"There is. Nashville's central and Pigeon Forge is eastern. I don't come this way often enough to remember." He shook his head.

While it was only two and a half miles to Dolly Parton's Stampede, it felt like forever. Cars kept pulling out in front of them, going slow, enjoying the view.

Finally, he pulled into the parking lot next to the large red barn-like building, and they raced up to the front doors. The doors were already closed, but he noticed an employee standing off to the side. He ran over to the older woman.

"Can we still get in for the 7:30 show?" Carl panted, trying to catch his breath.

She looked at him, a little startled. "I'm sorry, we've already closed the doors."

"Please," he begged. He looked at Grace, standing a little bit away, then back at the woman. "We drove here from Nashville, and I screwed up the time change. Is there any way you can let us in? Please."

She looked like she was about to say no again, and Carl was getting desperate. "Listen..." He glanced at her nametag as he fumbled with his phone to pull up the reservation. "Mindy. I don't want you to break any rules or anything, but this is our first time away together, and I hate I've already gotten it off to a rocky start. I really like her and would love to turn this evening around. If there's any way you could help me out, I'd be grateful. I do have a reservation."

Mindy looked around conspiratorially, then said, "Okay, honey. Grab your young lady and come with me. I'm always happy to help with a new romance."

Carl ran over to Grace and grabbed her hand. He was starting to get used to the zing running up his arm when they touched. If the reaction to just holding her hand was this strong, he wondered what kissing her would feel like.

Grace looked down at their entwined fingers but didn't pull her hand away.

They followed Mindy to a side door. "Follow me and I'll get you to the right place. Let me see your tickets."

She glanced at Carl's phone, then led them down a couple of hallways and through a door into the arena seating area.

"Okay, kids, stick close."

Carl kept a tight hold on Grace's hand, even though he probably didn't need to. It warmed him to hold her hand and feel that link.

And she hadn't pulled her hand away yet.

They followed Mindy downstairs, closer and closer to the arena floor. They passed a sign that said Preferred Seating and kept moving. Carl was confused. He hadn't paid for preferred seating, but Mindy seemed to be on a mission. And their mission was to keep up.

There were two seats, front and center, where she finally stopped. She waved her hand to indicate they should sit down.

"But I didn't pay for preferred seating, Mindy," Carl said softly.

"For late arrivals, I'm pretty sure these are the only seats available, honey." She gave him a wink and was on her way.

He saw her stop and talk to one of the servers on her way out, and within a minute, the server was asking for their drink orders.

Grace was wide-eyed, looking around the arena.

They were in the front row. The very front row.

"I'm not sure why she sat us here." Carl interrupted her thoughts. "I paid for seats much higher up, but I think this is going to be amazing."

"How curious she sat us down here. And that there are only two seats in this whole row. So odd. But I agree, this is going to be a lot of fun."

Grace shot a couple of selfies, then leaned in close, indicating she wanted a picture of the two of them. There was something about her scent that always got his blood humming. He leaned close, enjoying the frisson of energy between them. She took the picture, then turned her head toward him, only to find herself within a breath of his lips.

"Oh!" she exclaimed.

But she didn't move. Her gaze moved down to his mouth, then back up to his eyes. Her tongue darted across her lips. She cleared her throat and leaned back, creating some space between them.

The disappointment he felt in her absence was palpable. He'd wanted, desperately, to taste her lips.

And if he was reading her correctly, it seemed she had been thinking about a kiss too.

"I have to send 'proof of life' pics to Breena this weekend." Her laugh was a little shaky as she sent the text.

"I thought Breena liked me? She doesn't trust me?" Carl leaned back as well, trying to get his thoughts off kissing her.

"She doesn't know you, so I'll be sending a few pics this weekend." But Grace said it with a smile.

Carl smiled back at her as the server brought their drinks and appetizers. It seemed the front row got premium service. The evening was turning out better than expected.

Chapter 17

GRACE

*"I'm not going to limit myself just because
people won't accept the fact that I can do
something else."*

Dolly Parton

G RACE LOOKED AT HER empty plate, a little
embarrassed. "Guess I was hungry." Dinner, as
expected, was delicious. It was Dolly's down-home
cookin' and definitely hit the spot.

"It was good food." Carl looked down at his own
empty plate. "Besides, I like a woman with a healthy
appetite." He waggled his eyebrows, which made her
laugh.

After their dishes had been cleared, they sat back
to enjoy the show and dessert. Grace got a kick out

of the show. She had always liked horses, even though she'd never been around them much. Sitting in the front row, she could see just how massive and majestic these animals were. It was exciting to feel the ground rumble, to hear the jangling of the horse's saddle and whatever went around its head, to smell the earthy, musky scent as the horses galloped past.

As they were finishing up the show, the lights went low, and several spotlights flashed around the crowd. Music was playing, appropriately one of Dolly Parton's songs. Grace couldn't quite figure out which one though.

Up on the big screen, she watched as the cameras panned the crowd. And then, a heart-shaped frame outlined the camera shots; outside of the frame, it said Sweetheart Spotlight. She smiled at it. She'd seen the kiss cam at different sporting events but was a little surprised they had something like that here.

The panning of the crowd had gone on for a good minute or so before it started zooming in on couples. Grace had fun seeing the couples it paused on. There was a young couple, sitting with kids. She laughed at the way the kids tried to hog the camera shot before it moved on. She thought the older couple the camera stopped on next was sweet. They looked so comfortable with each other and still very much in love. The man put his arm around her, and they smiled at each other.

Grace looked forward to having moments like that in her life.

And then, inexplicably, embarrassingly, when the music climaxed—Grace now recognized the song as "I Will Always Love You"—the camera focused on her and Carl.

This time, though, the camera didn't move on.

"Ladies and gentlemen, I think we've found our sweethearts," the announcer began in his perfect ring-master voice. "Let's see who our cute couple is. Tell us your names and how long you've been together."

As if by magic, someone was next to Grace with a microphone. She and Carl had the same stunned look on their faces when they turned to each other. The microphone was pushed a little closer to her face.

"Go ahead and say your name," the guy whispered.

"Um, hi. I'm Grace and this is Carl."

"Carl, my man, she's already doing the talking for you."

The crowd laughed.

Carl and Grace looked at each other; her cheeks grew hotter and redder, but he just smiled.

"So, Carl, how long have you two been sweethearts?"

Carl looked at Grace, and she looked back at him, a little panicked.

"Well, Jed." They'd learned the announcer's name earlier in the evening. "To be honest, Grace and I haven't been sweethearts all that long. We had one of those moments where we fell hard for each other as soon as we met."

Grace looked at Carl incredulously. "What?" she whispered.

"Well...we did fall hard for each other, didn't we? Right on the floor," he whispered back with a chuckle.

"Awww," Jed drew the word out. "We have new sweethearts, folks. How sweet is that?"

The crowd, of course, enjoyed Jed's antics and Grace and Carl's awkwardness.

Well, Grace's awkwardness. Carl seemed to be enjoying the situation just fine.

"How about we help our young couple along? What d'ya say, folks?"

Of course, the whole audience thought that was a good idea.

Again, Carl and Grace looked at each other. She with a look of panic, he with amusement.

"Carl, this isn't a good idea." She leaned over to whisper to him.

Carl, recognizing her panic, put his arm around her. "I'm sorry, Grace," he whispered back. "I wasn't trying to embarrass you. I just thought if I said we weren't a couple, it might be even worse."

He rubbed her back a bit, trying to alleviate her anxiety.

She nodded. "You're probably right. And he can't go on too much longer, right?"

"How about if our sweet young couple kisses each other while Dolly sings to them? After all, they *are* on the Sweetheart Spotlight." Jed was definitely enjoying his role as cupid. "How about it, Carl? You got a kiss for Grace tonight?"

Grace noticed Carl's ears getting pink as he turned to her. If it weren't them in the spotlight, she would have laughed.

Carl tightened his arm around her shoulders, pulling her close to him. He looked straight into her eyes, very seriously. "Well, this certainly isn't how I pictured our first kiss."

Her eyes widened, and butterflies fluttered in her stomach. "You've thought about our first kiss?"

He nodded and murmured, "I definitely have."

She didn't hear the crowd chanting "Kiss, kiss, kiss" around them.

For this moment, they were in their own world.

He leaned closer, his lips a whisper from hers. "Well, you only get one shot at your first. Right?"

And then his lips were on hers.

She wasn't sure if it lasted a second or an hour, but the old cliché of time standing still seemed to be true. His soft mouth pressed onto hers. She felt the heat of his lips sear her body. Her heart was pounding hard as his hand moved from her shoulder into her hair to cradle the back of her head.

And then, all too soon, it was over. The crowd came back into focus, and they could hear the cheers.

The rest of the show went on, but Grace had a hard time focusing on it. She was still trying to get her brain back into gear.

Finding Dolly Project:
Here's what I know so far...

18. Carl shared his past with me. I know he's very wary of women, especially rich women. Guess it's a good thing I'm not rich. But even if I were, I'd like to believe it wouldn't be a problem between us.

19. The trip to Pigeon Forge was fun. The car ride was easy. Carl and I talked the whole way. We even talked about our big bad breakups. His was with Krisi. Seems like she used him for free labor before breaking his heart. I told him all about Drake—the good, the bad, the ugly. It felt nice to get that out in the open.

20. We went to the Stampede for dinner tonight. After a little bit of a timing mix-up, we got in and were seated way down at the front of the arena. The show was really interesting. Full of everything Dolly. We learned a bit more about her commitment to the community she grew up in and loves.

21. And then there was the kiss. I probably shouldn't make such a big deal about it. Jed, the ringmaster at the Stampede was just having a little fun with us. We were in the "Sweetheart Spotlight," and he had us kiss in front of the whole arena. We were on the big screen—kissing! Okay, it wasn't much more than a peck, but still...it felt like a lightning bolt started at our lips and coursed through my body. I'm not really sure how it felt for him, but I've never had that reaction to a kiss in my life. I don't know what it means. Well, I do. But I'm not sure I'm ready to go there yet. Not even in my own head.

22. I'm really looking forward to going to Dolly-wood tomorrow. It just feels like something important is going to happen.

Chapter 18

CARL

"As long as we're together we'll never walk alone."

Dolly Parton

WHILE THE EVENING MIGHT have started off rocky, it had certainly ended much better. Carl drove to the hotel with a smile on his face. He couldn't read how Grace felt about the evening's events. Hopefully, she didn't think he'd set up the whole Sweetheart Spotlight.

"Thank you for being such a good sport during the Sweetheart Spotlight." He looked over at her quickly.

She glanced at him, a blush creeping up her cheeks. "It was rather embarrassing, wasn't it?"

Hmm, embarrassing. That wasn't how he would have described it. Sure, he'd pictured their first kiss differently, but he could still feel where her soft lips had briefly touched his. He felt branded. The electricity he'd felt when their lips touched still pulsed through his body.

"I want you to know, I didn't plan that." He glanced over again to make sure she heard him. "I wouldn't ever put you in that position on purpose."

"Yeah, I know. I think your new friend Mindy might have been playing matchmaker sitting us up front like that. And then Jed..." She shook her head and leaned back on the seat.

The well-lit resort had the feel of luxury right in the middle of nature. Carl pulled up under the awning reserved for check-in, still pondering her reaction. While he hadn't planned the kiss, he certainly didn't regret it. Hopefully, she didn't either.

"Well, let's check into our rooms so we can get a good night's sleep and rest up for a fun day at Dollywood tomorrow." He looked at her small overnight bag as he grabbed his own backpack. "I appreciate a woman who can pack light for an overnight trip. My sister would never have just a small bag."

"Well, it's not like I have a ton of choices." She laughed. "Since I pretty much have no clothes, it was easy packing."

They walked into the lobby together and took in the cozy, rustic atmosphere. It was everything you'd want in a mountain lodge—dark greens, tans, and cozy. The couches looked like you could just sink right into them. The chandelier was made of antlers but wasn't tacky, and the wall sconces had little bears on them. He looked around, pleased with his choice.

Grace wandered around the lobby while Carl stepped up to the desk. He set his backpack at his feet.

"Carl Montgomery, checking in please."

"Welcome, Mr. Montgomery. I hope you and the missus have had a wonderful day in Pigeon Forge."

Carl took a quick step back and almost fell over his backpack, righting himself just before he landed on his backside. "Oh no, we're just friends. That's why I reserved two rooms for tonight." He chuckled awkwardly.

The clerk looked at his computer again and frowned.

Oh boy, what now, Carl thought.

"I'm sorry Mr. Montgomery, the reservation was for one room with two people." The portly desk clerk shook his head as he started typing again.

"No, the reservation was for two rooms. Two people, two rooms." Carl let out an exasperated breath.

Grace quietly approached the desk and looked at Carl. She had a worried look in her eyes. "Is there a problem?"

"Well, it seems our reservation was somehow messed up." Carl was completely frustrated. Would she think he'd done this on purpose too?

"Listen. I'm not sure where the problem occurred, but if you could just get us two rooms, then no harm done."

The clerk continued to look at his computer, still frowning. "Excuse me for a moment." He walked to the back to talk to another employee.

Carl ran his fingers through his hair and paced in front of the desk. He would pay whatever price needed to be paid to make this situation right. While the idea of sleeping in the same room as Grace was appealing, he didn't want to make her uncomfortable. She was already looking at him when he glanced over at her.

"I'm not sure what happened, but it seems our reservation was messed up. I asked for two rooms, but it seems he's only got one on my reservation. I'm pretty sure he's going to get us two rooms."

He wasn't sure.

Not at all.

He was hopeful.

"I think I'm going to go to the restaurant to grab a glass of water while they work on this." Grace headed down the hallway toward the dining room.

The desk clerk came back with another man, and together, they looked rather seriously at the computer.

"I will take any two rooms you have, Roger," he tried again. "I don't care about the price. I just need two rooms."

The desk clerk looked up at him with one eyebrow cocked. "Well then, I might just have a solution for you. The only other room available tonight is the two-bedroom suite. It's quite a bit more expensive than your other room, but it does have two bedrooms in it. Would you be interested in that, sir?"

Without blinking an eye, Carl put his credit card on the counter. "Sold."

With a sigh of relief, Carl finished the check-in process, thanked the clerk for his help, and headed to the dining room to find Grace.

When Carl unlocked the door to their suite, they both stood there, stunned. The door opened into a large, beautiful living room with a small kitchenette behind the door. The living room had a comfortable couch in a tan color and a wood-and-glass coffee table.

But it was the windows along the far wall with the view they'd see in the morning that was the real star in this room.

They had just closed the door when there was a knock.

They looked at each other, confused, as Carl turned to answer it. A woman from room service was standing there, pushing a cart with a bottle of champagne in a bucket of ice, two champagne flutes, and a tray full of fruit.

"Um, I think you have the wrong room." Carl smiled at the woman. "We didn't order anything."

He glanced at Grace to confirm she hadn't ordered it while in the dining room. She shook her head, looking curious.

"Oh no, sir. This is from the hotel. Roger, the desk clerk, said he was sorry for the confusion with your reservation." She wheeled the cart in and unloaded the bucket with the bottle, setting it on the table in front of the couch, along with two glasses and a fruit tray before heading back to the door with her cart.

"Enjoy your evening," she said with a smile, and she was off.

Carl and Grace looked at each other, then burst out laughing.

"I didn't think this evening could get any weirder," he said. "Guess I was wrong." He walked over to the table, grabbed a strawberry off the tray, and bit into it. "Well, Ms. Parson, can I interest you in a glass of champagne?" He held up the bottle and grinned at her.

"I suppose it would be rude to not have at least one glass, right?" She walked over to the couch and curled up in one corner and smiled at him. "Probably a good thing they didn't serve alcohol at the Stampede."

Carl got busy opening the bottle. After several seconds of twisting and turning the cork, it finally popped out, landing across the room. Grace giggled at his theatrical bow, and he poured two glasses. After handing one to Grace, he settled himself at the other end of the couch.

"Well, cheers." He held his glass toward her, and they clinked glasses. "Here's to more fun in Dolly country."

He watched, fascinated, as Grace took a sip, closed her eyes, and got a look of pure contentment on her face.

"Mmm, this is delicious. I can't even remember the last time I had champagne." Grace opened her eyes and looked at him. Her cheeks turned a little pink under the intensity of his stare. "I know this had to cost you a fortune, Carl, but thank you for getting this suite so we could have two bedrooms. I really appreciate it. I'm happy to help with the expense."

"Nah. Thanks, though. I truly have no idea what happened with the reservation, but I'm happy to pay for this. It's a great room, isn't it?" Carl refilled their glasses. "It has been a day of mistakes and awkwardness. Thanks for being so understanding and flexible. You're amazing, you know that?"

Grace's face flushed with heat as she smiled at him. "It's been a great day. Everything seemed to work out in the end, so no problem."

Carl stretched his long legs out in front of him and settled more comfortably into the couch. "So what'd you think of the Stampede? Did you enjoy it?"

"It was a lot of fun. And the food was tasty—I thought the soup was fantastic. And I was really glad to see they had silverware." She giggled a little. "We have a few dinner show places in Orlando. They don't all give you silverware. They're always fun, but I'm not a fan of greasy fingers."

He could see Grace was relaxing, probably because of the champagne. Carl was feeling pretty relaxed himself.

"Are they caveman-themed? Why don't you get silverware?" He wouldn't have even thought to make sure they used silverware at the Stampede, but he was grateful they did.

She giggled again. "I can't even remember what the theme was, to be honest. Oh my gosh!" She looked out the windows. "I can't wait to see the view in the morning. I bet it's going to be amazing."

Carl followed her gaze. "Yeah, just think, coffee and a view of the mountains. Too bad we're only here for one night."

Realizing what he'd just said, Carl quickly took a gulp of his champagne and looked out the black window even though he couldn't see anything.

After the kiss, he'd been thinking too many thoughts about sharing space with her, and when they left the Stampede, he was ready to get to his room to get away from her for the night. But now he was really enjoying her company. It felt good to be stretched out on the couch together, legs within a breath of each other. *I could get used to this.*

"You could get used to what?"

Carl startled a bit. He hadn't realized he'd said it out loud. Now, he was wondering what else he might have said. He looked at her, down at her lips, then back up to her eyes.

"Um, staying in a suite instead of a regular hotel room. I'm enjoying all this extra space." While it was true, it was certainly *not* what he'd been thinking about.

"This is rather cozy, isn't it?" Grace looked flushed. He wasn't sure if it was because of the champagne or because she'd been thinking about him. "So tell me, Carl, what'd you think about our kiss?"

Oh boy, she was going there. He hadn't been sure if they were going to pretend it didn't happen, even though his lips still tingled a little when he thought about it. He looked at her mouth again. She bit her lower lip, like she was nervous.

"Well, it certainly wasn't how I pictured our first kiss."

Crap! He needed to stop drinking. His tongue was too loose right now. He felt his neck get warm.

"So how exactly *did* you picture our first kiss?"

Her face turned a darker shade of pink. She wore it well, but he did not need to be thinking about how good she looked right now. He decided it was best to ignore the question.

"I, um..." He cleared his throat. "I liked the kiss. It probably would have been less awkward without hundreds of people watching."

Realizing what he'd said and where the conversation could lead, he decided he needed to get out of there. He couldn't trust himself to keep his mouth shut. He knew Grace wasn't a one-night stand kind of girl, and he wasn't a long-term relationship kind of guy.

"Listen," he said softly. "It's late and it's been a long day. I think I'm going to hit the hay."

He stood up and hurried to his bedroom door. He was already away from her before she could even unwind her legs.

She looked at him over her shoulder, confusion clear on her face. "Oh. Well. Good night then. Thank you for a fun, if different, day, Carl."

He stopped before going into his room, turning to look at her. He saw the hurt in her eyes. He felt bad about it but couldn't trust himself at the moment. All he wanted to do was go back to the couch and wrap Grace in his arms. Instead, he just nodded and walked into his room.

Chapter 19

GRACE

*"We cannot direct the wind, but we can
adjust the sails."*
Dolly Parton

WELL, THAT WAS WEIRD. And a little abrupt.

He said he could get used to this. She was pretty sure he hadn't intended to say it out loud. And she was also sure he hadn't meant staying in the suite.

But she had to admit, it *was* nice having the extra space.

And then he said he *liked* the kiss but bolted for his room without even a good night.

Grace didn't think she'd ever understand men.

She carried the champagne glasses to the kitchenette and set them on the counter, pouring the rest of the bottle down the drain. They wouldn't be drinking anymore. After filling a large glass with water, she turned the lights off and headed to her own room.

Because of the whole mix-up at check-in, Carl had given her the room with the king-size bed. It hadn't really mattered which room was hers; she was just grateful for separate bedrooms. He'd been very tempting tonight while they were sitting on the couch.

Ending her day with him in this hotel suite had been lovely. It had crossed her mind that she, too, could get used to it when he'd spoken those words. Hmm.

Maybe it was for the best he'd made it an early night.

She went into the bathroom to wash her face and get ready for bed. Rubbing moisturizer on her face, she traced a finger over her lips. They still tingled where his lips had touched them.

Truth be told, that kiss had rocked her world. It felt like lightning struck when his lips met hers.

Which was silly since it was such a short kiss.

It should have been a throw-away kiss.

A fake kiss.

Except it wasn't.

And he said he liked it.

She lay in her bed, her Kindle next to her, unable to focus on the words on the screen. Her mind kept trying to figure out the puzzle that was Carl Montgomery. Her brain kept telling her to forget about any feelings she might have regarding Carl.

But her heart was getting into the conversation now. And it was getting tougher to stop her heart from feeling what it wanted to feel.

She hadn't thought she wanted a relationship. After Drake, she was sure she was done with men for a long while. She thought about Drake and her feelings for him. What was it about him that led her to say yes to drinks that first time? It was probably ego. After all, he was a good-looking guy, and him asking her out had felt good.

While she hadn't felt any flutters or passion in Drake's kisses, it was nice to have someone show interest in her. That certainly wasn't an inspiring reason for a relationship, but she was glad she hadn't slept with him.

She'd been in such a hard place taking care of her mother. Most of her social life had come to a screeching halt because she just didn't have the time, the energy, or the mental capacity for it. She was so grateful for Breena and her willingness to walk through the journey with her—not just as her mother's caregiver, but as Grace's friend. It was so nice to have someone to talk to, who understood what was going on and how hard it was.

The first time Drake had kissed her, she remembered thinking it was nice. But it certainly hadn't set off fireworks like that short kiss with Carl. And now, instead of getting a good night's sleep, she was thinking about Carl sleeping a few yards away in his room. She wondered if he was having the same trouble sleeping as she was.

She thought about him and how he came into her life. He'd thought he was coming to see her mother. It wasn't about *Grace* at all. He was honoring his friendship with her mother.

She frowned a bit. So maybe he wasn't interested. He was just trying to be a friend because of his relationship with her mother.

But her mother had thought maybe she and Carl had some sort of future together. Maybe just as friends.

Her heart reminded her, *he liked the kiss too.*

That must mean something, right?

Ugh, she felt like a teenager crushing on the cute guy at school. She glanced at the bedside clock. One o'clock. Tomorrow was going to be long. She decided to refill her water glass before trying to sleep again.

She quietly opened her bedroom door and walked through the dark living room to the little kitchenette.

"Can't sleep either?" Carl's voice had a sleepy, husky tone that incited a shiver down her spine.

The glass fell from her hand and shattered on the floor, but she stood rooted to the spot. She felt a piercing pain on the top of her foot where a piece of glass must have nicked it.

"Oh crap, I'm sorry," he apologized. "Hang on a sec. Don't move." Carl ran to his bedroom and quickly reappeared with shoes on.

"Here, let me help you so you don't cut up your feet."

He easily lifted her into his arms. Her own arm automatically went around his neck. Her other hand went to his chest. She could feel the beat of his heart.

Or maybe it was hers. She wasn't sure.

Hers was definitely beating loudly. Wildly. She wouldn't be surprised if he could hear it.

She'd never had a man sweep her off her feet and was entirely unprepared for the feelings rushing through her now. She felt completely protected as he held her like precious cargo. She felt very feminine and a little swoony at the way he carried her, as though she didn't weigh much.

He gently set her down in front of the couch. "Here you go. I'll sweep this up since it was my fault."

His deep green eyes locked on hers. They were standing very close. His hands were on her shoulders, helping her balance.

She felt the heat from his body.

His eyes wandered down to her partially open lips and stayed there for a second. His eyes darkened as he looked back into her eyes.

He took a step back and cleared his throat.

"Um, I'll see if I can find a broom."

She stood there for a few seconds longer then sat on the couch; her knees were a bit shaky. She needed to catch her breath. Her heart was still pounding. She closed her eyes and put her head in her hands on her knees as she tried to slow her breathing and get herself together.

The shock of Carl picking her up and holding her close to his warm body was *not* going to help her sleep tonight.

"Hey, you okay?" Carl's concerned voice was close.

She looked up and gave him a wobbly smile. He'd finished cleaning up the glass and was standing by the couch.

"Yeah, just getting my breath back. You startled me, and then when the glass broke, it just..." Her voice faded out.

"I...um, yeah. I'm sorry about that. I didn't want you to turn around and see me sitting there and scare you. Guess that plan didn't work so well." He chuckled softly. His gaze lowered down her body. "Oh no, you've got blood on your foot."

She had forgotten the pain in her foot when Carl swept her up in his strong arms, but now she noticed the dripping blood. She'd never been great with blood, especially her own. She leaned back and closed her eyes for a second to stave off the woozy feeling in her head.

"Oh, I'm sure it's fine," she mumbled, trying and failing to sound like it was no big deal.

"Hang on a sec, and I'll get a washcloth. We'll get you cleaned up." Carl hurried to his bathroom and returned with a wet washcloth and a dry hand towel.

"Oh, I hate to get blood on their white washcloth," Grace groaned and quickly averted her eyes.

She leaned her head back against the couch as Carl propped her foot up on the coffee table and wiped off the blood.

She could feel his fingers touching her leg as he cleaned up the cut and covered it with a Band-Aid.

This was not helping her body calm down.

"You looked like you were going for water." He went to the kitchenette, filled a glass, and brought it back to her.

"Thanks. I was having a hard time sleeping. Must have been the champagne. I figured a glass of water would help." She felt like she was rambling, but there was no way she was telling him that *he* was the reason she couldn't sleep.

Why was she nervous? She'd been with Carl all day. They were comfortable around each other.

She noticed her heart ramping up again. It often happened around him.

He looked down at her body, then back to her face.

"Marilyn's?" he asked.

Confused, she looked down. Then, she felt her face burn.

"Oh my gosh. I completely forgot I had this on."

She looked down again at white cotton from head to toe. There was a ruffle around the neckline, which was truly at her neck, nothing showing there. The sleeves were long with their own ruffles. And the whole ensemble buttoned up the front, probably twenty or thirty buttons.

Her mother might have been bright and fun and loud with her clothing, but her nightwear was a completely different story. Grace had discovered it her first night in her mother's penthouse.

She looked up, her face still hot. "Like everything else, Mama seems to have her own style for sleepwear. Her daytime clothes are fun, colorful, and a little crazy, but her nighttime choices are positively Victorian."

Very chaste.

She certainly hadn't planned on running into Carl at this hour.

Carl laughed. "I'm trying to reconcile this"—he waved his hand up and down in front of Grace—"nightgown? With what I knew of Marilyn. Are you sure this is hers?"

"Yup. There must be twenty of these in her drawers. She was a woman of paradoxes."

Grace suddenly stood up, wavering a bit as she got her balance. Carl's hand shot out to steady her, her pulse ramping up again at his touch.

"And on that note, I'll say goodnight. Again."

Finding Dolly Project:
Here's what I know so far...

23. I got up in the middle of the night to get a glass of water, and Carl was up too. He startled me, I dropped the glass I was holding. He literally swept me off my feet and carried me to the couch. I have never been swept off my feet before. It felt so good being in his arms. And then...we had a moment when he set me down. I thought he might kiss me again. He has gotten all kinds of fluttering going inside of me. I'm really starting to like him and would like to see if our relationship could work.

I don't even know if he's interested in a relationship. I suppose time will tell.

Chapter 20

CARL

"You need to really believe in what you've got to offer, what your talent is—and if you believe, that gives you strength."
Dolly Parton

E ARLY THE NEXT MORNING, Carl sat in the living room with a cup of coffee, watching the sun start to peek over the mountains. The view, as they had suspected, was spectacular.

Sleep had not come easy. He hadn't been sleeping well anyway, but after the middle-of-the-night encounter with Grace, it had been impossible.

That ultraconservative nightgown shouldn't have been sexy.

And the way her body had felt next to his when he carried her away from the broken glass...it shouldn't have felt so right.

He'd tossed and turned, thinking about kissing her. About standing there looking down at her, his hands on her shoulders. Her lips looking soft and inviting. *That* was more of what he'd envisioned for their first kiss.

Minus the blood, of course.

He'd been tempted though. Too tempted.

He remembered how her lips had felt during their brief kiss at the Stampede. He couldn't believe he told her he liked it. Well, *like* was putting it mildly. Even though the kiss had only lasted maybe a second, he'd felt hot shock fill his body, starting at his lips. He'd never had that kind of reaction to a kiss before. And he'd kissed and been kissed quite a few times in his life, thank you very much.

He'd lain awake for hours, wondering what it all meant. Why had Grace's kiss had that effect on him?

Last night, he'd gone to the kitchen for his own glass of water and had just finished it when Grace came out.

The sound of her bedroom door opening startled him out of his thoughts.

"Good morning."

She was fully dressed, but her big yawn led him to believe her sleep had probably been as good as his. Her eyes looked a little bloodshot with some purple underneath. Today, she wore black leggings, a long, collared, white button-down shirt, and turquoise cowboy boots.

He smiled at her outfit.

"Morning. Coffee is hot and fresh if you want some."

After filling a cup, she sat in the chair next to his to watch the last remnants of sunrise. They sat in comfortable silence, drinking their coffee, admiring the mountain view.

"I knew this was going to be amazing," she said. "I wasn't wrong, was I?"

"You definitely weren't." Carl looked at Grace with a grin. "I don't recall your mother ever wearing black leggings or a plain white shirt. The boots though, they look like they could have been hers."

Grace laughed. "True, true. This is the one out-fit of mine in the state of Tennessee. Well, minus the boots. But I thought the boots were appropriate for Dollywood."

"Well, it looks great. Fun to see you in your own clothes for a change," Carl said with a smile. "So what would you like to see today?"

"Well, when I was doing my research on Dolly, it seemed like the Chasing Rainbows Museum would be an important stop. And maybe pop into her Tennessee Mountain Home. Then, I was thinking roller coasters."

"I wondered if you were a roller coaster girl," Carl said with a grin. "Sounds like a great plan."

Grace stood up and looked at Carl's coffee cup. "Need a refill? I'm headed that way."

He passed his cup over and waited until she returned to continue. "The hotel has a breakfast buffet included with our room, so I figured we could eat here before heading out. After our coffee, of course." He held up his mug, as if to toast.

After finishing their coffee, they packed their backpacks, did a last sweep of the suite, and headed downstairs to the hotel restaurant. Carl swung by the front desk to check out, while Grace went to the dining room to find a table.

From the looks of the crowd in the lobby, they weren't the only ones headed to Dollywood today. Most of the guests were dressed in some sort of Dolly wear—a T-shirt, a hat, even sunglasses. It was fun to see.

Carl appreciated her consideration when he saw the cup of coffee waiting for him as he sat down. *I really could get used to being around her more.*

The park was hopping when they arrived. Grace, seemingly unfazed by the crowds, waited in the line without complaint. She used the time to look up information about Dolly and the park.

After grabbing a map of the park, they headed in the direction of the museum.

"So what's on our Dolly agenda today?" he asked. Carl was curious. He wondered about her progress on the Finding Dolly Project but hadn't wanted to bring it up last night, or even this morning. It had been so nice just sitting and watching the sunrise together.

"I'm not really sure," Grace admitted. "I feel like something will be made clear today. It sounds kind of silly, but I feel like something...I don't know...something kinda magical is going to happen."

Carl looked at her and smiled. "Well, this certainly seems like the right place for magic."

"Okay, looks like we need to head to the left here."

He was thrilled when Grace reached over and grabbed his hand as they headed into the crowd. He wondered if she felt the connection too. She looked at him with a cheeky grin and squeezed his hand. Then she took off into the madness with Carl in tow.

First stop, the Chasing Rainbows Museum was just inside the entrance of the park. Once inside, they started upstairs in Dolly's Attic. Carl grinned at the chaos around him. Stacks of furniture, pictures, toys, and so much more.

"What's got you smiling?"

"I was just thinking how much this looks like my Granny's attic. She has stuff everywhere too. I don't think she's ever thrown anything out."

Grace smiled. "How sweet."

"Well, I don't think my mom finds it very sweet." He laughed. "She's the one who's going to have to clean it out after Granny's gone."

"Hmm, yeah. I can see where that could be an issue," Grace said diplomatically, trying not to laugh. "My dad was the one who kept things organized and clean. There are a few things remaining from my childhood, but nothing like this."

After wandering through the attic, they found the stairs that took them down into the museum proper. This part of the museum was organized by different parts of Dolly's life—her beginnings, recording career, film career, causes important to her, and of course, her clothes throughout it all.

"Oh my gosh." Grace stood, looking a little flummoxed.

"You okay?" Carl asked, concerned.

"Dolly was in her high school marching band too." Grace looked at the white wool marching band uniform with purple embellishments. "And we were both in drumline. It's so weird to think that The Dolly Parton was in marching band. It's just such a normal thing to do."

"Well, I'm pretty sure she was a 'normal' person for at least part of her life," Carl said, using air quotes.

"You know what I mean." Grace laughed. "I never thought I'd be able to say Dolly and I did the same thing. Senior year, we played a medley of Dolly tunes in our halftime show. Mama loved it, of course. It was my favorite show we did. It was so much fun."

"I was never in band." Carl wanted to keep the conversation going. "I had some friends who raved about it. What did you like most about your experience?"

"For one thing, as a freshman, it was nice to have band camp over the summer because when school started, I knew more than a hundred people. And the school didn't feel quite so new since I'd already been there for a couple of weeks. I wonder if Dolly appreciated that about marching band?" Grace looked at the display again, thinking about her own high school days for a moment before they continued wandering around, checking out the records on the walls.

"It was like being part of a huge family. Well, Dolly already was part of a huge family, but for me...I was an only child until Breena moved in, so it felt really good to have this big band family. The band parents were amazing too. It didn't matter whose kid you were, they treated us all like their own." She had a faraway smile on her face.

"Sounds like a great thing to be part of." Carl smiled at her. "Hey look at this."

He'd wandered over to the section with Dolly's wedding dress and was reading the information plaque.

"Dolly and Carl." He looked at Grace, surprised.

"Uh, no. *Grace* and Carl." Grace pointed back and forth between them.

"No, no." Carl laughed. "Dolly Parton's husband's name is Carl. Carl Dean. Did you not know that?"

"Wow, no. Carl, huh?" Grace asked with a surprised look on her face before becoming quiet and thoughtful.

After finishing up with the museum and looking through Dolly's Tennessee Mountain Home, they found themselves heading deeper into the park. The scent of sugar and cinnamon brought them both to a stop in the middle of the walking path.

Grace's stomach rumbled a little at the smell, and her face turned a light shade of pink in response.

"Oh my gosh, what smells so good? We have to find whatever it is," she said rather emphatically.

They looked around and noticed several people walking around with cinnamon bread. After asking for directions, they headed to the Grist Mill. Walking in was an assault on the senses in the best possible way. Carl watched Grace as she just stood and breathed in for a minute or so, a smile on her face, her eyes half closed. It was hard not to appreciate her enjoyment of the moment.

After ordering a loaf of cinnamon bread and two coffees, they headed out to find a place to sit. They found a covered seating area with a stage at one end and grabbed a picnic table to enjoy their treats.

"I'm sorry. Do you mind if I take this?" he asked Grace as his phone rang.

"No problem. I'm going to make some notes in my journal."

"This is Carl." Carl wandered away from the tables but stayed close enough to see Grace. She had her head bent over her journal and stopped writing every few minutes to pull off a hunk of bread and eat it slowly.

"Carl, Tony Kline here. I've been trying to reach you to get you back out here to finish up the job you started."

"Right, Mr. Kline. I'm sorry I haven't been able to get back to you. I'm out of town right now. I left you a message stating I scheduled a new project a few days ago, so I'm not sure I'll be able to get you on the schedule for another few months. I'm not at my desk, but I can call you with a date as soon as I get back to my office, if you'd like."

"A few months? No, that will definitely *not* work," Mr. Kline said rather loudly. "We need this project finished within the next two months."

"Two months? I'm afraid that's impossible, Mr. Kline. I—" But Carl was cut off.

"Listen, Carl. You started this project six months ago, then stopped. You haven't worked on it for three months. We need this finished now!"

Carl tried to keep his voice calm. "Mr. Kline, the project would have been finished by now, but *you* stopped it. Not me. You told me and my crew to leave and—"

Kline interrupted again. "Well, now I need it finished. You can't just push us off for months. We were your client first. Push the other client's project back and make this happen."

"Listen, Mr. Kline, as I said, I'm away for the weekend, so I can't help you with anything right now. I'll call you when I get back to my office. I don't—"

"Carl, you need to call me back with the date you'll be here. And it needs to be next week."

"I'll be back in my office on Monday, Mr. Kline. I'll talk to you then." Carl hung up before he could be interrupted again.

He took a couple of deep breaths, trying to calm himself. Some clients felt entitled to his schedule. This was why rich clients always frustrated him. With some clients, it was a pleasure when the job was done and he could move on, never hearing from them again.

Except Marilyn. She'd been the exception to that rule.

To most of his rules.

Mr. Kline was confusing him though. His first experience with him had been great. He'd been easy to work with, but then one day, everything fell apart. Carl had no idea why. And now Kline was back. Carl just wasn't sure what to think of it. He'd have to deal with it eventually, and he would as soon as he got back to his office.

Carl walked back to Grace, still sitting at the picnic table, still buried in her journal. She was sitting next to a petite woman with dark hair.

"Grace, I'm really sorry, but do you mind if I make a few more calls? I have a client who's being unreasonable, and I'd like to get some wheels moving before we get back into town."

Grace looked up at him and gave him a kind smile. "No problem. I'm fine here."

Carl wandered away again to try and get a hold of Jim to see what possibilities were even available for Mr. Kline. He did not want to move his new client around, that was for sure.

Chapter 21

GRACE

*"I'm not offended by all the dumb blonde
jokes because I know I'm not dumb...and
I also know that I'm not blonde either."*
Dolly Parton

G RACE SAT AT THE picnic table with her delicious cinnamon bread, coffee, and journal.
The lack of sleep was starting to catch up to her,
so maybe a little sugar and caffeine would keep her
going.

She was so excited about the visit to Dollywood.
Even though she had no logical reason to think anything would be revealed today, she couldn't shake the
feeling that *today was the day*. The day she'd learn what
her mama's mission was all about. She felt so strongly

about it, she was almost a little sad the Project would be over.

But here she sat, no closer to answers than when she started. She pulled out her journal and decided to do the only thing she could think of—write a letter to Dolly.

Dear Dolly,

Well, I'm not really sure how to start this, but suffice it to say, I'm trying to keep a promise to my mother. I think. You see, Mama passed away a couple of months ago.

Well, I guess I need to go back further.

Mama was, for as long as I can remember, a huge Dolly Parton fan. So much so, that when she saw she had a blonde baby, she named me Dolly.

Dolly Grace Parson.

I go by Grace, because...well, being Dolly Parson was just too hard, I guess. There were all kinds of expectations. It got to be too much. So I became Grace. With Grace, there were no expectations. Writing that sounds pretty lame, but it felt like the right decision when I made it.

For the past three years, I've been a caregiver for Mama. She lost her battle with dementia recently, but growing up, and especially during the last three years, we listened to all your records, watched your movies, and well, other than my job, everything else in life just kinda faded away.

So now you're caught up with me and Mama.

The hospice nurse was with Mama in her room the night before she passed. Mama knew her time was short. I suppose we all did. But before she went, Mama had the nurse write a note for me. She told me she wanted me to be happy in life.

And then she told me to "find Dolly." I honestly have no idea why she would ask such a thing of me.

I have no idea how to find you. I mean, it's not like I can just look you up and find your address on the internet. But I'm in Nashville right now. Well, Dollywood. Pigeon Forge. So who knows? Maybe one day we'll bump into each other.

Yeah, right. LOL.

I've spent the last week learning all about you at the Country Music Hall of Fame, the Grand Ole Opry, and digging around online. It's been a pleasure getting to know you better.

Well, I just wanted to say thank you for being someone Mama truly enjoyed for so many years. She had great respect for you...and I guess I just wanted to let you know.

Respectfully,
Grace

A tear started a slow trek down her cheek, and she looked around for a napkin. She noticed a petite, dark-haired woman sitting on the bench near her with a couple of extras, so she leaned over a bit. "Excuse me, ma'am. May I use one of your napkins please?" Grace kept her head down, trying to hide the fact that she was crying at Dollywood.

The woman gave her a kind smile and handed her the extra napkins.

"Thank you." Grace gave her a sheepish smile as she wiped her eyes and cheeks. "I really thought today was going to be magical. I guess my expectations were too high." She laughed.

The woman, comfortably dressed in a baggy pink hoodie, skinny jeans, and athletic shoes, cocked her head a bit and had a curious look on her face. Like she was waiting for Grace to go on.

So Grace found herself pouring her heart out to a complete stranger at Dollywood.

She told this woman all about how much her mother had loved Dolly Parton, and how she'd named Grace after her. She told her about her Finding Dolly Project, and how, thus far, she didn't feel like she was any closer to finding Dolly than when she started.

And while the woman hadn't said a word through the whole conversation, she had put her hand over Grace's and was looking at her with kind eyes.

For some reason, Grace felt it was safe to tell her all about her frustrations, her inadequacies, her hopes that finding Dolly would give her some clarity on where she should go with her life. Just as she was finishing up her monologue, Carl came back.

"Hey, you okay?" he asked softly, a questioning look on his face.

The woman sitting next to Grace scooched over a bit, giving them space to talk.

Grace looked up at him, her eyes still watery. "Yeah, just thinking about all the things I don't know yet."

"Do you mind if we talk for a minute?" He gestured away from the table, to where he'd been on the phone.

"Oh sure, hang on a sec." Grace looked at her journal, water bottle, and tote bag, then leaned toward her new, nameless friend. "Would you mind keeping an eye on my stuff?"

The woman smiled and nodded, so Grace grabbed her phone and moved away from the table with Carl.

"You sure you're okay?" he asked again, a concerned look on his face. "That woman wasn't bothering you, was she?"

"Oh no, she's fine. Great, actually. I was just sharing my frustration at not getting anywhere with the Project. She's a kind listener," Grace finished with an embarrassed smile.

"Oh." Carl seemed a little stumped by that one. "Well, okay. That's nice, I guess."

Grace cocked her head. "I feel like I should ask you the same question you asked me. Are *you* okay?"

Carl rubbed his hands over his face. "Yeah, just really frustrated. I told you about the Kline project the other day, the one that stopped partway through?"

"Right, I remember it."

"Well, Mr. Kline just called asking for the impossible. He's being really pushy, which is out of character for him. When we worked with him before, he was always a very considerate and likable guy. Now he's being unreasonable and rude. He wants us back on his project next week, but we just committed to another job. He wants us to abandon the new job to finish his. I don't know what to think of all this."

"Huh. How odd. He didn't offer any explanations?"

"No, that's the thing. He's just giving orders, no explanations. I talked to Jim, my foreman, to see if we even have the option of moving things around. He's going to talk with the crew, and tomorrow, I'll talk to our new customer, but I'm not sure how this is going to play out. Even if my new customer is willing to move things, I'm not sure I want my guys working on the Kline job." He shook his head, perplexed.

"Do you need to head back early?" Grace asked.

"No. I don't want to let him ruin our time here. Let's go have fun on some roller coasters."

Grace smiled up at him. "Okay, hang on a sec while I grab my stuff."

She sat down again next to the woman and smiled at her. "Thank you for being a kind listener. I know I babbled on and on, and I really appreciate you letting me. I feel so much better, just having gotten all of that out."

The woman scooched over and put her arm around Grace's shoulders, leaning in close. "Honey," she said in a husky whisper. "You just figure out who *you* are and be the best damn version of *you* that you can. *That* is all your mama wants for you. Go, be happy, Grace." She gave Grace a wink and turned, swung her legs over the bench, and Grace watched her walk away.

Grace hugged her journal to her chest for a moment, smiling at the kind stranger in the sweet butterfly hoodie. Then, realizing Carl was waiting, she packed up her bag and headed over to where he was pacing.

"You sure you don't want to go back early?"

"I don't want to ruin our day together." Carl stopped in front of her.

"I get that, but if your mind is going to be elsewhere, then we may as well get back and deal with it. We can do this another time."

Carl took her hands in his. "Thank you. I really don't want to go, but that's where my mind is. I'm sorry for letting my job spoil our day."

Grace laced their fingers and headed for the exit. "It's all good, Carl."

The long walk back to the car was quiet, each of them lost in their thoughts. As soon as they settled into the car, Grace opened her journal and wrote the words the woman had told her. They felt important, and she didn't want to forget them or how the woman had made her feel. Safe, understood, heard.

Maybe Dollywood had been magical after all.

Maybe she already had the answers she'd spent the last two weeks looking for.

Finding Dolly Project:

Here's what I know so far...

24. The Chasing Rainbows Museum was amazing. Dolly Parton was a band kid. How cool is that? Not only were we both band nerds, but we were both drumline. It was a fun connection to make.

And then Carl noticed that Dolly's husband's name is Carl. Dolly and Carl. Hmm. Makes me wonder if Mama had some matchmaking thoughts about Carl and me after all. Dolly and Carl. That would be just like Mama, getting the last laugh in from heaven.

25. While sitting at a picnic table, devouring the most delicious cinnamon bread and listening to some great bluegrass music, I met the kindest woman. Well, "met" might be a stretch. But it felt like we had a connection. Anyway, I wound up telling her all about the mission Mama gave me. When I was ready to leave, the woman said the most interesting thing:

Figure out who you are and be the best damn version of you that you can. That is all your mama wants for you. Go be happy, Grace.

Just writing this makes me tear up a bit. Maybe this—well she—was the magic I was hoping for today.

Chapter 22

CARL

"When I got somethin' to say, I'll say it."
Dolly Parton

ABOUT HALF AN HOUR outside Nashville, Carl's phone rang again. He saw it was his sister since his phone was attached to the car stereo system and hit a button on his steering wheel to answer.

"Hey, Bean, what's up?"

"Hey, Carl. Just finished feeding Miss Kitty and wondered how your weekend with your mystery woman is going."

"Just so you know, you're on speaker phone in the car, and said mystery woman is next to me." Carl chuckled and looked over at Grace, whose eyes were a little wide and questioning. "Jilly, I'd like you to meet

Grace, a.k.a. the mystery woman. And, Grace, I'd like you to meet Jilly, my big-mouthed little sister."

Jillian laughed. "Geez, Carl, you could have given me a little heads-up. Anyway, Grace, it's nice to meet you. Sorry for the mystery woman comment."

Grace looked a little unsure. "Hi, Jilly. I've never been a mystery woman in my life, but I think I kinda like it." She laughed.

"Carl, you should invite Grace and me out for dinner. We need to meet each other."

Stalling a bit, Carl responded, "Geesh, Jilly, don't you have any manners? You can't just go inviting yourself to dinner. Listen, we're just getting into the city. How about if I call you when I get home?"

Jillian laughed. "I look forward to meeting you, Grace. Talk later." She hung up.

"My sister heard we were at Joe's together and has been dying to meet you." Carl took a quick glance at her.

"Joe's?"

"Oh, sorry. Music Row Joe's. The coffeehouse we went to the other day. We just call it Joe's."

"Oh. Right." Grace paused for a minute. "She's been dying to meet me? Why?"

"Well..." Carl avoided looking at her, keeping his eyes on his road. "I, uh...I suppose because I haven't dated anyone in a while. Not that we're dating."

"Oh."

He could feel Grace's eyes on him, but he couldn't quite look her in the eye yet.

Carl pulled up in front of The Athenian, put the car in park, then ran his fingers through his hair. He reached over and put his hand on her arm before she could open the door.

"Listen, Grace," he started. He was flustered. His sister had completely thrown off his game. "Okay. I was planning on asking you out for a real date when we got back today." He took a breath and looked at her, somewhat expectantly.

"And now you don't want to?" she asked slowly, confused.

"What? No, no. I—" Carl rubbed his hands over his face. This was not going well. "I suppose I should have started with this. I had a really great time this weekend with you. Even though everything went wrong, I'm glad I was able to spend time with you. And I'd love to take you out on a date. A real date."

Grace grinned but took her time answering him. It was torture.

"Carl, I'd love to go out on a date with you. But..." She paused, stopping his heart for a beat. "I'd also love to meet your sister."

He grinned. "So just to make sure I have this correct, that was a yes. Right?"

Grace laughed. "Yes. It was definitely a yes."

His whole body relaxed with her answer. "How about we do a cookout at my house tomorrow afternoon? You can meet my sister and your mother's cat. Then, we can have a date night after your lawyer meeting Monday. That sound okay?"

"Sounds perfect." Grace laughed a little. "Kind of funny having our first date after spending almost two weeks together and just getting back from an overnight trip."

Carl laughed with her. "Well, that'll certainly make our first date a lot less terrifying, won't it?"

He grinned as he watched her walk into the building. Now, he just had to figure out where to take her on that first date.

Driving back to his house, Carl felt lighter and happier than he'd been in a long time. They'd gotten so close over the past two weeks. Going into a first date knowing he wanted more was something he hadn't experienced in years. He hadn't wanted a serious relationship since Krisi, but he could see one with Grace. It should have scared him.

She was worth the risk.

He wasn't sure if her future plans included staying in Nashville, but he hoped he could persuade her to do just that. As he pulled into his driveway, he pictured Grace here. In his space. In his home. In his life.

He let himself daydream for a bit, even knowing he had work to get to.

While grabbing his backpack out of the back of the car, he noticed Grace's journal on the floor. He picked it up and put both the journal and the backpack in his bedroom to deal with later. He leaned down to pet Miss Kitty, who was weaving her way in and out of his legs.

"Come on, big girl. Let's head next door. Tomorrow, you get to meet your new owner." Miss Kitty looked up at him and cocked her head. He could swear sometimes she understood what he was saying.

They went across the yard to the office where Carl got down to work, trying to figure out where they'd left off on the Kline job. He knew he'd have to head over there this week to check out how the room looked and what supplies they'd need. Some they still had, but others he'd have to reorder.

Miss Kitty immediately jumped on her climbing structure and made her way across the top of the room to the window. She walked to the spot right above his desk and got comfortable, settling in so she could keep an eye on the squirrels and birds outside and be near Carl at the same time. It always made him smile to have her there.

His heart clenched at the thought of handing her over to Grace. Even though he was sure Grace would be a great cat mom, it was hard to think about.

He grabbed his phone and relayed the cookout info to Jilly, knowing if he didn't, she'd call at an inconvenient time.

Then he opened the Kline file to dig in.

Chapter 23

GRACE

*"Dreams are of no value if they're not
equipped with wings!"*
Dolly Parton

As the elevator doors opened, Grace was
met with delicious scents coming from the
kitchen. That could only mean one thing—Breena
was back in the penthouse. She dropped her bag in the
living room and headed to the kitchen, excited to see
her best friend.

"Yay, yay, yay! You're home." Grace gave Breena a
big hug.

Breena laughed. "I'm surprised you even noticed I
was gone. Seems like a certain Mr. Hotty's been keeping you awfully busy."

Grace blushed but laughed. "I still missed you."

"Well good, because I missed you too. Now tell me all about the wonderful things you've been busy doing with Mr. Hotty while our spaghetti sauce simmers."

"Would you stop calling him that?" She laughed, her cheeks pink. "I'm so glad you're back. And not just because I had no idea what to eat for dinner tonight." Grace didn't enjoy cooking and mostly ate sandwiches when she was alone.

Breena covered the large pot and turned the burner to low, then took Grace's hand and led her back to the living room where they both fell onto the couch. Grace pulled her legs up underneath herself, and Breena stretched hers out.

"Ooh, hang on a sec." Breena jumped up and ran back to the kitchen. Grace could hear cabinet doors and drawers opening and closing, and then Breena was back with two wineglasses filled with red wine.

"A souvenir from Chattanooga." She offered a glass with a smile.

"Oh lovely. Perfect." Grace took a sip, savoring the taste of a good red wine and having her best friend back. "This is delicious."

Grace pulled her phone out of her back pocket before sitting and noticed a message. "Hang on a sec," she said, putting a finger up while listening to the message.

"Mr. Dreamboat calling already?" Breena teased.

"No." Grace blushed furiously. "It was Mr. Pillingham. He requested that you join me Monday at his office."

Breena cocked her head. "I wonder why."

"I guess we'll find out on Monday at ten."

"I'm happy to go with you. But for now, why don't you tell me how your *overnight* trip went." She waggled her eyebrows as she emphasized the word, making Grace laugh.

"Well, it was a weekend of one mix-up after another." Grace proceeded to tell Breena about the time change confusion at the beginning of their trip, getting to the Stampede late, and then being seated way down front. "And then they did this Sweetheart Spotlight at the end."

Breena raised a brow as if to say *continue*.

Grace huffed out a breath and failed to keep the blush from her cheeks. "They chose Carl and me as the highlighted 'sweethearts,'" she said, adding the air quotes.

"Oh my." Breena laughed. "So how'd that go? What happened?"

"Well, we had to kiss in front of the whole crowd." She tried to sound indignant about it, but her blushing cheeks gave away her true feelings.

"So let me get this straight." Breena was still laughing. "You had your first kiss with Mr. Hotty in front of hundreds of people?"

"Bree, his name is Carl." Grace figured it was easier to focus on that than the kiss.

Suddenly serious, Breena asked, "So how was it?"

Grace instinctively touched her lips, then quickly put her hand down. "For a kiss that lasted all of maybe a second, it was…" She paused, searching for the right word. "Amazing. Bree, it felt like a bolt of lightning coursed through my body. It left me breathless."

Breena touched her heart with her empty hand. "Oh my."

Grace was a little dreamy. "And then, back in the hotel room, I thought he might kiss me again."

"Whoa, whoa, whoa. You two *shared* a hotel room?" Breena was suddenly serious and protective again.

"Well, that was the next mix-up of our weekend." Grace told her about the two-bedroom suite. And about the broken glass, about Carl carrying her to the couch, the near-miss kiss, and the granny pajamas she had worn.

"Wait. I'm all over the place here, not knowing what to think. So Carl, Mister-I-Don't-Like-Rich-People, shells out what had to be a huge chunk of money for a two-bedroom suite instead of just going to a different hotel?"

"Um, yeah. I guess so. And from the sound of it, he didn't bat an eye at the cost."

"Hmm. Okaaay." Breena dragged the word out. "So then, he goes all romantic hero on you and sweeps you off your feet to carry you across the room to the couch? Then stares longingly into your eyes. Was there glass all the way across the room?"

"Well, um, no. Just in the kitchen." Drat, why hadn't she thought of that earlier? She probably would have left it out of her recap. "And I didn't say any-thing about him *staring longingly* into my eyes."

"Poetic license." Breena laughed. "That's pretty romantic, Grace. I've never had a guy carry me any-where. And I've certainly never had a kiss that left me tingly and breathless. It all seems pretty special, if you ask me."

"I guess we'll see. I hope you're right."

"We need more wine." Breena jumped up and ran to the kitchen to grab the bottle.

"Oh, I need to tell you what happened at Dolly-wood. I met the most amazing woman there." Grace was talking with her hands and carefully set her glass down before she spilled it all over.

Breena looked confused. "Weren't you with Carl?"

"Of course I was with Carl. But I sat down at a picnic table to write in my journal while he took a phone call. That's when I met this woman. Hang on, let me grab my journal."

Grace raced to her overnight bag and rummaged through it looking for the journal. After not finding it, Grace walked back into the living room. "Well, that's weird, I can't find it."

"Oh no, I hope you didn't lose it."

"I think I'll shoot Carl a text to see if it fell out in his car. Hopefully..."

GRACE: Hey there, I can't find my journal. Did I happen to leave it in your car?

CARL: Yep, I found it when I got home. I'll give it to you tomorrow if that's ok.

GRACE: Sounds good, thanks! Oh hey, Bree's home. Is it ok if I bring her tomorrow?

CARL: np, the more the merrier :)

GRACE: Thanks! What can we bring?

CARL: I've got it covered. See you tomorrow

"Oh, thank goodness, Carl has it." Suddenly, a worrying thought occurred to her. "You don't think he'll look through it, do you?"

With a raised eyebrow, Breena half grinned at her friend. "You got some juicy stuff about Mister—uh, Carl in there?"

Grace blushed a bit again. "Well, there are a few things I would be embarrassed if he read."

"Ha, excellent!" Breena laughed. "I doubt he'll read it. He's got a sister, so he probably got in trouble for that crime when he was younger."

Grace relaxed, knowing her secrets were—probably—safe for now.

Chapter 24

CARL

"He's always loved who I was, and I loved who he was, and we never tried to change each other."

Dolly Parton

CARL KICKED HIS BACK door closed behind him and finished setting all the food on the table, pleased with his efforts. Burgers from the grill, mac and cheese, sweet potato fries, baked beans, and coleslaw.

Grace and Breena had brought a bottle of wine, so he topped off the women's glasses and grabbed another beer for himself. After he sat down, they all filled their plates. It always felt good to feed people.

"So then Kline calls me while we're at Dolly-wood. Can you believe it?" Carl was sharing stories about some of his clients. Most of them were pretty great, the jobs were interesting and challenging, but for some reason, Kline had become a nightmare lately. "We even wound up leaving the park early. I still feel bad about that," he said to Grace.

"It was too bad we didn't get to do any of the roller coasters," she said.

"Sounds like reason enough to go back—roller coasters and cinnamon bread," he suggested.

"Mmm." Grace got a faraway look on her face. "Oh my gosh, it was so good." Looking over at Breena, she continued, "If I'd known you were home, I would have grabbed a loaf for you."

"Would it have made it home?" Jillian laughed. "Like Carl said, it's a good reason to go back. I'm in for roller coasters and cinnamon bread. That would be a fun girls' day."

"Ooh, I'm in," Breena agreed.

"That'd be a lot of fun!" Grace said.

"Hey." Carl felt a little left out. "I like Dolly-wood too."

Jillian laughed. "Well, we might let you come with us."

Carl's phone dinged with a text. "Oh shoot. Looks like Gabe can't make it today."

"That's too bad. Gabe's always good for some fun stories." Jillian looked a little disappointed.

"The same Gabe I met at the Opry? The one who works with Laci Love?"

"*The* Laci Love?" Breena asked.

"One and same," he responded.

"I would have enjoyed hearing some of his stories." Breena grinned.

"Maybe next time." Carl smiled at the thought of there being a next time.

"This is delicious, Carl. Did you actually make all of this yourself?" Grace asked between bites.

"I did. I had to call my mom for the mac and cheese recipe."

"Man, I'm envious. I'm pretty hopeless in the kitchen. Thankfully, Breena enjoys cooking, so we don't starve."

Carl caught his sister's eye and laughed, remembering their mother's comments about Carl finding someone who could cook for him. "Well, Jilly, good idea to have dinner together. Glad you all were able to come today." And he was glad. He wasn't sure how it was going to go with the three women, but they seemed to be getting along.

"So, ladies, how do you like Nashville so far?" Jillian asked.

"To be honest, I haven't spent much time here yet, but I'm looking forward to checking it out. I spent the last few days in Chattanooga," Breena said.

Jillian added another scoop of mac and cheese to her plate before turning to Breena. "I've not spent much time there. How'd you like it?"

"It's beautiful. You're right in the middle of the mountains. The people were friendly, and there were some great places to hike. All in all, a good time, but I'm happy to be back here with Grace."

Carl enjoyed listening to the women talk. It had been a while since his sister had good girlfriends to hang out with, so Carl was happy to see they were all enjoying each other's company.

"What about you, Grace? What're your thoughts on Nashville?"

Grace put her fork down and looked at Jillian. "So far, it's been great. It's been very Dolly Parton–focused, so it'd be fun to see some other things around here."

They continued to eat while Jillian and Carl talked about different places they'd been to around Nashville and Tennessee that were fun to visit. Lots of hiking trails, caves to explore, and interesting museums.

Sitting next to Grace, Carl found all his senses on high alert. Their legs kept touching, and he tried to ignore the sensations running through his body. There hadn't been anyone to get his heart rate up in a long time.

It felt good to feel all of the feelings again.

After dinner, Carl offered a tour of the property to anyone interested. Happily, Grace was the only one to take him up on it. Jillian and Breena opted to stay on the deck to enjoy another glass of wine while their meal digested.

"Let's walk around outside while it's still light out." He grabbed her hand as they went down the steps to his backyard. He could feel his sister's eyes on him, but he was fine with that. They walked the brick path he'd built that wound around his yard. "I waited a few years to find the perfect property, and when this came up, I knew it was the one."

They stopped at two Adirondack chairs looking out from his yard. "This is where I like to watch the sunset."

While standing there, they watched a mother deer and her two babies walk along the edge of the property, darting in and out of the trees. Seeing wildlife never failed to impress him, even after living here for a few years.

He looked over at Grace to see a look of wonder on her face.

She must have felt his gaze because she turned her face up to his. "That's amazing," she whispered.

"It really is, isn't it?" He reached out and rubbed his knuckles down her cheek. He put his arm around her shoulder and pulled her close as they watched the little deer family.

Grace leaned her head on his shoulder, and suddenly, everything in his world clicked into place.

As soon as the deer were out of sight, they turned to gaze deep into each other's eyes. The moment felt magical, watching the deer, and he was grateful to have shared it with her. He dipped his head a little lower.

"I've been wanting to do this all night," he said quietly. Then he touched his lips to hers.

Her lips were soft and warm and inviting. He wanted more, so much more, but he needed to go at her pace. He pulled back to look at her.

She had a smile on her face and looked as content as he felt. She lifted her arms and put them around his neck. "Well then, here's what I've been waiting to do all evening."

And she pulled his head down but stopped when their lips were only a millimeter apart. He could feel her breath. His heart was already pounding.

She gave him a little smile, then her lips were plastered to his.

All his brain cells seemed to fuse together, and his cognitive function went out the window. His arms immediately went around her. His right hand cupped the back of her head while his left grabbed her shirt in the small of her back and held on.

This wasn't a sweet kiss.

This was a blow-your-mind kiss.

He angled his head slightly, but their lips stayed fused. She tasted of sweet wine and...well, Grace. He could steep in this taste for the rest of his life.

The thought startled him, he pulled back slightly.

Breathless, they separated.

"Well," he said once he caught his breath and got his thoughts back on track. "I have to say, I like the way you think." He gave her a suggestive eyebrow waggle and grinned.

She grinned back at him and blushed. "Well, this tour is certainly more exciting than I expected. I really do want to see your property though."

Holding hands, they continued their walk around his yard. He pointed out where he wanted to put a garden in the spring, the trees he wanted to put a swing or maybe a hammock under, and then they headed inside.

Jillian and Breena were on the couch, so Carl and Grace sat on the loveseat across from them. As soon as they sat down, Miss Kitty came out to sniff everyone's shoes. She jumped up on Carl's lap, then walked over to Grace's.

"Oh, well, hello there."

Grace scratched the cat behind her ears and waited while she turned in a circle before settling down. "Miss Kitty, I presume?"

Carl was surprised Miss Kitty had settled on Grace's lap. He looked up and noticed Jillian watching them. She lifted an eyebrow, then looked pointedly at the cat. Miss Kitty never went to any of the women who visited his house.

An hour later, the cat finally jumped down. "I guess it's safe for me to get up now." Grace laughed. Both she and Breena stood up. "This has been a lot of fun. Thank you for having us over."

Jillian and Carl stood up, and the women all exchanged hugs. Carl walked Breena and Grace to their car. He opened the car door for Grace, then hugged her.

"I'm very much looking forward to our date to-morrow night." She looked up at him with a gleam in her eye.

Leaning his head down, he whispered in her ear, "Me too."

He watched them drive away with great anticipation for their date, then turned and hopped back up the steps, knowing the next day was going to be pivotal for them.

Chapter 25

GRACE

*"Everybody has their own journey, they
have their own way of doing things. And
who am I to judge?"*

Dolly Parton

"HULLO?" WOKEN BY HER ringing phone,
Grace yawned, hoping it was Carl saying
good morning.

"Grace? Hey, babe. Guess who's in Nashville and
excited to see you?"

"Drake?" Grace's mind snapped alert. What the
heck was Drake doing calling her? She'd never expected to hear from him again. "Why are you calling me?"

Why would he *ever* think she'd welcome his call
after catching him with Deanna? In *her* house?

Sounding contrite, Drake sighed dramatically. "I just want to tell you, I know I let you down." Another big sigh. "I mean, I even let myself down. But...well, you know...I wanted to apologize and see if we could have dinner tonight?"

"Dinner? I don't think so, Drake."

"Well, how about a drink then? I have things I'd like to say, and I'd rather not do it on the phone."

Grace sat up on her bed, dumbfounded that he had the gall to call her, to expect her to forgive and forget. She didn't say anything though. She just sat there, quietly waiting.

"Um, Grace? Are you still there, babe?"

"I'm here. I just wanted to make sure you were done talking," Grace said drily.

"Um, yes? I'm done talking." Drake sounded confused.

"Why would I want to meet you for anything, Drake? You cheated on me. There's nothing you need to say, and nothing I need to hear from you."

"Well, I also wanted to let you know, I found your butterfly necklace in my car. Did you know those are real diamonds on your necklace?"

"You-you have my necklace?" The gift from her father. Drake had it? How was it possible he had her most treasured gift? "Listen, Drake, there's no way we're going out for dinner. I'll meet you for coffee tomorrow morning. Make sure you bring my necklace. And my house key." She gave him the name of Music

Row Joe's since it was the only coffee shop she knew, and they arranged a time.

She hung up and wondered what the heck he was up to. He's what her mother would have called a *bad penny*. If he didn't have her necklace, there was no way she'd even bother with meeting him.

She switched gears and started getting ready for her meeting with Mama's lawyer, grateful she'd have Breena by her side. She was more than a little nervous to hear what Mr. Pillingham had to say.

Or, maybe more accurately, what *Mama* had to say.

The law offices of Pillingham, Grand & Blanck were located downtown, so it only took about fifteen minutes to maneuver through traffic and find parking. The reception area was classy and classic, tastefully decorated without being ostentatious.

"Grace, Breena, I'm pleased to see you again." Mr. Pillingham walked around the corner into the reception area to greet them. He was dressed as sharply as he had been at Mama's funeral. His gray suit looked to be tailor-made. Grace didn't know men's suit labels but guessed this one cost a pretty penny.

He shook hands with both women. "Please come back to my office."

Grace and Breena followed him down the hallway to his corner office.

The decor was similar to the reception area but felt more comfortable. Maybe it was just Mr. Pillingham. He seemed like a nice man, and Grace was glad her mother had found a good lawyer to work with in her later years.

"I'm waiting on one more...Ah, there you are, Mr. Montgomery. Please come in, have a seat. Ms. Parson, this is Carl Montgomery. Your mother requested him to be here today as well. I hope you don't mind."

"Carl!" Grace jumped up and gave him a quick hug, then turned back to Mr. Pillingham, her cheeks a little warm. "Yes, Carl and I have already met. He's been playing tour guide for me for the past week. We've gotten to know each other pretty well, haven't we?" She laughed, a little embarrassed at her outburst, then found her seat again.

"Well, that certainly makes this easier." Mr. Pillingham smiled. "Shall we get started?"

She nervously rubbed her hands on her slacks and nodded. Breena, sitting next to her, patted Grace's leg, offering comfort and support. "Yes, let's do this."

Opening his file, Mr. Pillingham took several colorful envelopes out of the folder and set them aside. He put on his readers and started. "Well, first off, Ms. Parson, with a few exceptions, your mother left you everything."

Grace nodded her head, understanding. It made sense since she was Mama's only family.

"Before we go too much further, Ms. Parson, I'd like to talk with Mr. Montgomery and Ms. O'Malley, if that's okay."

Grace nodded. She was curious what her mother left each of the other two in here with her.

"Mr. Montgomery. Mrs. Parson left a letter and a box for you. The box will be delivered to your house this afternoon, and the letter is here." He held up a lime green envelope. "She also requested I read this note aloud in the presence of Grace and Breena before I give it to you."

Carl chuckled, but nervously rubbed his hands on his thighs. Grace wondered if he was feeling some of the same emotions she and Breena were.

"That sounds like Marilyn. She was accustomed to having things done her way." He looked at Grace and gave her a wink and a smile.

"'Carl,'" Mr. Pillingham read from the note. "'You have been an absolute gem to have in my life. Thank you for all you've done for me over the past few years. I am going to miss you more than you know when I move to Florida.

"'Now, I don't know how long it's been since I left Nashville, but the last thing I told you is "Don't get so busy making a living that you forget to make a life." You know it's one of my favorite Dolly Parton quotes, and I hope you've taken it to heart.

"'Somehow, I doubt you have, so I've left you something to help you remember to take time to smell the roses.

"'Please don't read the letter until you get home and open your package. I'll say my final goodbye in that letter. Marilyn.'"

Mr. Pillingham handed Carl the note and a lime green envelope with his name written in black cursive. Grace noticed Carl's eyes were a little damp and smiled at him.

"Now, Ms. O'Malley," Mr. Pillingham continued. "I have an envelope and a smaller box for you from Mrs. Parson. Again, with a note to be read aloud."

Breena reached over to hold Grace's hand, then nodded for him to continue.

"'Breena,'" the note started. "'Thank you so much for being such an amazing friend to Grace for so many years. It was always a pleasure to have you in our home and in our family.

"'I'm guessing after I moved to Florida, Grace would have reached out to you for help. And I know you would have given it. So thank you! Thank you for being there for Grace and for me.

"'I think you, like me, are a bit of a free spirit. So I've left you something for when you want to let your hair down, so to speak. After you've read your letter and opened your box, check with Brian, the doorman at The Athenian (hopefully he's still there). He can help you from there.

"'You are a caregiver at heart, Breena, which is no doubt why you excel as a nurse. But make sure you take care of yourself too and have some fun in life.

"'With much love, Marilyn.'"

Tears leaked down Breena's cheeks; Grace plucked a couple of tissues out of the box on the table next to her and handed them to Breena. Then she got a tissue for herself. This was already emotional, and it wasn't even about her yet.

Mr. Pillingham handed Breena the note, a bright yellow envelope with her name written in black ink, and a small rectangular box wrapped in gold paper with a purple ribbon. The box was about three inches long and an inch or so wide. Breena took the items from him and set them gently on her lap. Grace was curious about what her mother had left each of them.

Mr. Pillingham sat back down in his seat and opened the folder on his desk. He looked at Grace. "I'm not sure how much your mother told you about her assets, but I have everything listed out for you."

Grace looked a little confused. "Other than the two properties, what assets did Mama have?"

Mr. Pillingham gave a little sigh. "I see Marilyn did not have that conversation with you. Ms. Parson, you are now a very wealthy woman."

"W-what?" Grace stuttered, a little louder than she intended. She looked at Mr. Pillingham, trying to understand what was happening. For a moment, her brain seemed to shut completely off.

Her initial thought was relief that she didn't have to worry about her dwindling savings account. And she'd be able to go shopping for some clothes for herself.

But then the word *wealthy* registered.

"I'm rich?" Grace rubbed her hands on her pants again, her heart beating quicker.

"Oh yes, Ms. Parson. You are *very* rich," Mr. Pillingham said with a smile.

Grace looked at Breena, then at Carl, with a big smile on her face. "Oh my gosh." She laughed, feeling slightly hysterical. "I'm rich!"

Relief flooded her. She wouldn't have to worry about money or a job for the near future.

Carl flinched at Grace's enthusiasm. He looked at her, an unreadable mask on his face. "Excuse me." He stood up and left the room without looking back.

Grace looked at Breena, then at Mr. Pillingham, confused by Carl's reaction.

Mr. Pillingham, clearly also confused but a professional who had seen a lot over his years, cleared his throat. "Well, shall we continue?"

Grace looked at the door, then back at Mr. Pillingham and nodded.

Back at the penthouse that afternoon with Breena, Grace's head was still swimming with all the information Mr. Pillingham had gone over with her. Her mother had left her millions of dollars.

Not just millions, but *hundreds* of millions.

It was mind-boggling, to say the least. She wouldn't have to worry about finding a job for the rest of her life, not just for the near future.

Where had this money come from? Why had her mother never spoken about being wealthy?

She and Breena decided to read their letters together. Sitting on opposite ends of the couch with glasses of wine on the coffee table, they each had their letter ready.

While Grace opened her bright pink envelope with silver lettering on the front *Grace— Read First*, Breena had her bright yellow envelope ready to open as well.

Grace pulled out pale turquoise pages from inside the envelope. The pages smelled like Mama. She held them close and took a deep breath, then settled back to read.

My Darling Grace,

There's so much I need to tell you, and I'm afraid that when I get to Florida, I may not have enough time or mental capacity to share it all. The doctors tell me my memory may go quickly. Hopefully, we had the opportunity to talk about all this in person, but if we didn't, I'm so very sorry for not saying all of this sooner.

I guess when my mortality was challenged, I realized how much I hadn't told you over the years. I'd always thought we would have plenty of time, but I realize now I should have talked with you much earlier. I've left a second letter with a story about my past I think you need to know. It will hopefully answer all the questions you must have right about now.

First off, I want to say what a privilege it has been to be your mother. I know we've butted heads on a lot of things over the years, but I've never regretted that I had the honor to love and raise you. You are, and have always been, the most precious part of my life.

Second, I want to apologize for "saddling" you with a name that caused you so much grief. That was, of course, never my intention.

But in my defense, I still think the name suits you. I know you're rolling your eyes but hear me out.

The name Dolly means "gift of God," and you truly were a gift from God for me. The second letter will explain more of this, but for now, I want you to know that from the beginning to the end, I have always seen you that way, as a gift from God.

Another reason I think the name Dolly suits you (even though I didn't know these things when I gave you the name)—I think you share a lot of the same qualities I admire in Dolly Parton.

Dolly Parton has been not only a stand-up woman, but she was always one to stand up for women. Even before it was popular, she lived in a man's world and spoke her truth. I recognized this quality in you at a young age. You always stood by your friends and weren't afraid to stand up to other kids, even when they were bigger.

Dolly is a smart businesswoman and a hard worker, and so are you. The fundraisers you organize and put together are amazing. I know you probably think I haven't noticed, but I have. And the amount of money you are able to raise for the charities you work with is staggering. And you do all this by working hard, doing it on your own terms, and with style. How Dolly is that?

Dolly may have come from the hills of Tennessee and reinvented herself, but even as a superstar, she didn't forget her people. She's made hundreds of millions of dollars over her career, and she gives back to the land and the people she loves. In you, I see the same sense of loyalty to those you trust and love.

There are so many other qualities I think you share with Dolly, but I'll just add fun and kind. Don't let anyone, even me, steal your sense of fun or the kindness that has always been in you.

Somewhere along the way, you started doubting yourself. If I had a hand in that, I am truly sorry. Please know you have everything you need inside of you. You can trust yourself and your decisions.

As Dolly says, "Figure out who you are, and do it on purpose."

I love you so very much and am sorry I'm not here to say all this in person.

Mama

When Grace finished her letter, she looked up to see Breena was finished as well, and she also had tears running down her cheeks. Grace grabbed a couple of tissues and handed one to Breena before wiping away her own tears.

Grace picked up her wineglass and took a healthy sip before inhaling deeply. "Shall we swap?" She held her letter out to Breena. They shared everything, and she wanted to share this letter with Breena too.

Breena handed Grace her letter and took Grace's from her. They each settled back in for another emotional reading.

Dearest Breena,

I want to thank you again for being part of our lives and part of our family. I couldn't love you more if you were my own flesh and blood.

We met you as an eight-year-old needing a friend and a lot of love. At the time, I had no idea how unsettled your home was. And then, when you went into the foster system, I realized just how bad it must have been for you. Martin and I immediately started the process to become foster parents so we could bring you into our family.

As you know, it took months before we were able to officially bring you home. The years you were part of our family were a gift to all of us. Martin and I always felt like you were our own.

But once we had secured you in our home, I have to confess, I wanted more. I wanted you to officially be ours. I never told you, but I tried to figure out how we could adopt you and truly make you part of our family. We ran into trouble finding your biological parents so we could get them to release their rights.

This process took years. Tracking them down was quite a project. Especially since we weren't sure who your biological father was. I am sorry we were unable to complete the process before you turned eighteen and became a legal adult. The wheels of justice turn slowly.

But I wanted to tell you, we did find both of your biological parents. If you have any desire to see that information, Mr. Pillingham has it in his office and will share it with you.

Now, because you are family, even if it wasn't official, along with the gift in the small box, I've left the townhouse in Orlando to you along with a trust you have access to at any time. You are welcome to do whatever you want with the townhouse, of course. I always felt like it was as much yours as Grace's. Again, Mr. Pillingham has the paperwork already sorted for you. I also put the money we received from the foster system in an account for you, and it is immediately available to you as well.

Live well and love well, my darling girl,
Marilyn
PS Don't forget to open your gift and talk to Brian.

Again, Grace and Breena looked at each other with tears on their cheeks. "I had no idea Mama tried to adopt you. Oh, I wish that could have happened. But even though it never became official, you're still my sister, Bree."

"I know. She never mentioned it." Breena was quiet for a minute. "Grace, I don't need the house, you know. I feel like I'm taking something that's rightfully yours."

"No, no, no." Grace scooched over on the couch next to Breena and took her hands. "I love that Mama left you the townhouse. I've always felt like you were my sister, even if we didn't have the paperwork to prove it. If you don't want the house, I have no problem with you selling it."

"Are you sure you wouldn't mind me selling the townhouse? I really like it here in Nashville and wouldn't mind staying."

Grace smiled at her. "I really like it here too and was thinking of staying."

"If you don't mind me asking, what's going on with Carl?"

"I have no idea. Yesterday, I thought we were getting close, and I could actually see us trying to make a future. I'm not sure what happened in Mr. Pillingham's office. But my decision to stay in Nashville doesn't rely on Carl one way or the other."

"Grace, I feel like everything your mother said in her letter to you is basically the mission she gave you. I wonder if she didn't remember she wrote it?"

"I wondered the same. But I'm really glad she gave me the mission. Even though it was frustrating and confusing, I learned a lot about myself. And reading Mama's words just helps me believe it all."

Breena picked up the wineglasses off the table and handed one to Grace. "To Mama Marilyn," Bree said with a smile as she clinked her glass to Grace's.

"To Mama." They each took a sip, then Breena jumped up and ran to her room. She came back holding the small golden box Mama had given her via Mr. Pillingham.

"I almost forgot about this. I'm so curious to see what she left that could fit inside this little box."

"Ooh yes. I can't wait to see." Grace set her wine down on the coffee table.

Carefully, Breena undid the purple ribbon, then peeled the tape open, slowly unwrapping the little box. Once all the ribbon and paper were off, she sat staring it. "I don't know if I can do this," she whispered. "Will you open it for me?"

"You sure?"

At Breena's nod, Grace took the box and opened it. She looked inside, and a big smile bloomed across her face. "You're going to love this, Bree!"

She held the open box out so Breena could see the set of car keys sitting inside it.

Breena reached over and picked up the keys. "A Mercedes?"

"Let's go down to find Brian and see what he has to say about this. I'm guessing he knows which car those belong to."

They headed down in the elevator, curious to see which vehicle Breena now owned.

"Oh my gracious." Brian's southern accent still made them smile. "I have been waitin' and waitin' for someone to come to me with that key. Follow me, ladies."

They headed out the side door to the garage—it was a short walk when you didn't have luggage weighing you down. They stopped next to their rental car, confused.

Brian smiled, and with flair, he said, "Well, here she is!"

And he pointed to the sassy red Mercedes next to their rental car.

Breena's eyes went wide. "Oh my gosh. That's *my* car?" She looked from Brian to Grace. She clicked the button on the keys to be sure. A little *beep beep* confirmed the little red convertible they'd parked next to when they first arrived was Breena's car.

Ten minutes later, after a quick run back upstairs to get their purses and jackets, Breena and Grace were tooling along in the convertible.

"Are you sure we need the top down right now?" Grace asked, teeth shivering along with the rest of her body.

"It needs to be down for this first drive, Grace. At least for a few minutes, then we can put it back up." Breena laughed. "Hey, why don't we go down to Orlando on Wednesday and clean out the house? I'll visit Mr. Pillingham tomorrow, get the paperwork signed, and we can put it on the market while we're down there. We can drive my zippy new car."

"Oh my gosh. So much has happened today, I completely forgot to tell you Drake called this morning."

"What? Did you hang up on him?" Breena's Irish was up now.

"Actually, I'm going to have coffee with him in the morning."

Breena pulled over to the side of the road, stunned into silence for a minute. "Are you crazy?" She pushed the button to get the top back in place. "Why would you want to do that? You're not thinking of getting back together with him, are you?"

"No, no. I can assure you, that will *never* happen." Grace over-enunciated the words to make it clear. "He has the butterfly necklace I've been trying to find. He said he found it in his car. He also said he wanted to apologize in person, so I guess I should let him. I'm curious what he really has to say. But mostly, I just want my necklace."

Chapter 26

CARL

"A peacock that rests on his feathers is just another turkey."

Dolly Parton

AFTER WALKING OUT OF the lawyer's office, Carl headed to the Barn Reno to work off some of his frustration and anger. He couldn't believe how excited Grace had been about becoming rich. It felt like a slap in the face.

He'd been helping with the demolition, but after an hour in his company, Jim told him to take his sour mood elsewhere. They had the job covered and didn't need his help or his attitude.

Carl knew Jim was right. It wasn't fair to share his crappy mood with his guys at the worksite.

Currently, he was sitting on his back deck, beer in hand, Miss Kitty on his lap. He was wallowing and feeling sorry for himself, angry at feeling betrayed by Grace.

He couldn't believe he'd fallen for another Krisi. Or worse, someone like his mom. Someone more interested in money than a relationship. It took him straight back to standing on the front steps of the house he'd grown up in. His mom—well his bio mom—driving off with a man who wasn't his father or her husband. He remembered clearly her laughing when he asked why she didn't love them anymore, him, Dad, and Jilly.

"Honey," she'd said in her twangy southern accent, reeking of the new perfume her boyfriend had bought her. "You'll learn when you get older, there's thangs more important than love. *Money* is more important than love. Love might be all you need in a song or a movie, but in real life, money's what's important. Remember that and you'll go far, kiddo."

He could remember everything about that day. The beautiful spring morning seemed to mock him in his misery. He still couldn't stand the smell of Dior Poison. And he had an unfair hate for the white Cadillac she'd rolled out in. Her new boyfriend had been old. Even at five, when everyone's old, the man looked more like his grandpa than his dad.

Shaking off the memories, he wondered how he had missed the signs this time.

Every once in a while, he felt a niggle that maybe he'd screwed up by walking out of the lawyer's office. But he quickly squelched those feelings.

He wanted to feel the hurt, the betrayal, the anger.

He couldn't believe Grace had been so blatantly enthusiastic about money. Had she just been playing him about being on a budget? She had to have known Marilyn was wealthy. How could a daughter *not* know? But she'd seemed genuinely surprised.

Just then, he heard tires crunching down his driveway. He really didn't feel like dealing with anyone.

He wondered if it was Grace.

Hoped it was Grace.

Hoped it wasn't Grace.

He wasn't in a place to talk to her right then. She would definitely get the brunt of his anger. And while he felt justified in that anger, he really didn't want to say anything to her at the moment.

He walked around to the front of the house and found a delivery truck waiting for him. The delivery man was manhandling a large box off the truck.

"Hey, want a hand?" Carl offered.

"Oh hey. Thanks. If you could just grab that end. It's not heavy, just bulky."

Between the two of them, they maneuvered the box up the front porch steps, through the door, and into the dining room. Carl signed the paperwork and went back to his chair on the back porch.

He wasn't in the mood for Marilyn's gift at the moment.

Just as he was getting resettled, he heard another car pull into the driveway. *Geesh, Grand Central Station today*, he thought.

This time, though, he stayed in his chair. Nausea roiled in his stomach while he waited, wondering who was visiting this time.

Within a few minutes, he heard the crunch of footsteps on the gravel path leading to the back. Looking up, he saw Jim walking toward him. He knew he'd behaved poorly at the jobsite earlier, so it wasn't surprising Jim was here.

Jim gave him a nod and walked past him into the kitchen, grabbed a beer from the refrigerator, and came back out to sit in the chair opposite Carl.

They drank their beers in silence for a few minutes before Jim said, "So you wanna talk about it?"

"Talk about what?" Carl was feeling contrary, unwilling to make the conversation too easy. He also knew Jim would wait him out.

Which he did.

"Went to Marilyn's lawyer's office today for the reading of her will."

Still, Jim just sat, quietly drinking his beer, and waited.

Carl sighed heavily. "Apparently, Marilyn was quite wealthy. Her daughter inherited it all and was excited at the thought of being so rich."

Jim took another drink of his beer. Waiting.

"I walked out. The thought of her being just like Krisi burned my butt."

This time, Jim chose to respond. "So 'cause she's excited about inheritin' lots of money, that makes her like Krisi? How exactly did you draw that conclusion?"

"Well, the whole time we've been hanging out together, I had the impression she didn't have much money."

The waiting game again.

"I paid for everything every time we went out," Carl grumbled. "We went to the Opry, the Country Music Hall of Fame, and Dollywood."

Even to his own ears, he was whining.

"So she expected you to pay for everything? She never offered to pay?"

"Well...no," Carl mumbled.

"'Scuse me. What's that?"

"No, she didn't expect me to pay. She offered to pay every time."

"Why didn't you let 'er?"

"I enjoyed being able to help her out," Carl admitted.

"And so what? Now she don' need your help, you're mad at her?"

Carl hated Jim's patient logic. Why couldn't Jim just understand *he* was the one who was wronged? *She* betrayed *him*, not the other way around.

He took another drink to avoid answering Jim's question.

"Carl, you like bein' the hero. You like swoopin' in and helpin' people out. You're very generous with your time and money, but now she's an equal, *more* than an equal financially, and that scares you."

Carl spit his beer out in his shock. "What? What the heck are you talking about, Jim? I'm not scared. I'm mad. I'm mad she betrayed me. Mad she used me."

"You just said she offered to pay her own way, but *you* declined. And now she's got money, she's somehow evil? I don' buy it, man. Seemed like you were really into her. Is this inheritance just an excuse to drop the relationship? Like you done with every woman you gone out with since Krisi? Who cares if she's rich now?"

Carl didn't like the direction this conversation was going. Jim worked for him. Sure, they were friends, but shouldn't Jim be on his side?

He sat there, fuming. Jim's comments were hitting a little too close to home. They were making him squirm, and he didn't appreciate that.

"Listen, man," Jim continued. "You know I love workin' for you. You're a great boss and one of my best friends, but if you're still in a lousy mood tomorrow, don' bother comin' to the site. My guys don' deserve that."

Carl looked at Jim and nodded. He was right. The guys didn't deserve his wrath. He wasn't mad at them.

"You're right. Sorry about that. I shouldn't have come by this morning. I just wanted to work my mad out. Instead, I took it out on the guys. I shouldn't have."

Jim set his beer down and stood up. Having said what he needed to say, he'd be on his way again. "You know I respect you a lot, but I think you're wrong here." And with that, he hopped off the porch and headed back to his truck out front.

JILLY: Joe's?

The text from Jilly the next morning was a welcome distraction. He hadn't slept well and coffee at Joe's sounded particularly good right now. At some point during the night, he'd decided there was the possibility he'd been off base yesterday with Grace. Maybe he hadn't read the situation accurately, and a conversation was needed.

Heading through the dining room to the front door, he bumped into the box from Marilyn. How had he forgotten it? He decided he'd open it as soon as he got back from coffee. Then he would get some flowers from Mrs. Snowden and apologize to Grace.

He pulled into the parking lot at Joe's but didn't see Jilly's car in the lot. He scanned the porch to see who was there this morning. Since Nashville was basically a small town, it was unusual to not see anyone he knew when he came here.

His eyes came to a dead stop when they landed on Grace.

He realized he wasn't quite prepared to apologize to her. He wanted to talk it through with Jilly first.

Then he noticed Grace's companion, a slick city guy. Fancy suit. Dark hair, styled. A fancy smile. She smiled at the sparkly necklace he had just put in her hand. Carl's stomach clenched, and his heart hammered as he watched the man take hold of Grace's hand.

Carl texted his sister that something came up, put the car in reverse, and headed home. He'd seen all he needed to see.

Chapter 27

GRACE

"I'm very real where it counts, and that's inside!"

Dolly Parton

GRACE STARED AT THE diamond butterfly necklace her father had given her for her sixteenth birthday. She smiled as it sparkled in the morning sunlight.

"Thank you for this, Drake."

Grace had dressed carefully that morning. The new coral cardigan matched her new jeans with a coral butterfly on them. She and Drake found a table on the patio near one of the heaters, and they'd just ordered their coffee. Now he was trying to pretend like nothing was wrong between them. She put her hands in her lap, rubbing the necklace like a talisman, hoping to stave off the headache she could feel coming.

"Drake, you said you needed to talk to me. What exactly do you want to say?" She was trying to be patient, but he was testing her. "And why the heck are you in Nashville?"

"Well, Nashville is where you are, so it's where I need to be, babe. I feel like we need to clear the air between us."

"First off, don't call me *babe*. My name is Grace. And second, you are welcome to share your side of the story if you feel the need. Although, the cameras told a pretty convincing story of their own."

"Well, that's not fair, ba—Grace." Drake was getting whiny; it wasn't attractive.

"Drake, cut the crap. Why were you in my house? And how the heck did you get a key? I certainly didn't give you one." Grace wondered if he'd taken her keys and made a copy when her purse had been missing a few months earlier.

"As I tried to explain to the cops, I was just keeping an eye on your house while you were gone."

"And you thought it was best to keep an eye on it naked? With Deanna?"

Just then, the drinks came. They stopped talking and let the server put their orders down.

"Grace, hey."

Grace turned to see Jillian heading her way. *Oh boy.*

"Hey, Jillian, how are you?" Grace gave her new friend a genuine smile. Despite what was going on between her and Carl, Grace was happy to count Jillian as a friend.

"Aren't you going to introduce us?" Drake took one of Jillian's hands. "I'm Drake. Grace's boyfriend. I'm sure she's mentioned me."

Jillian extracted her hand and looked at Grace, confused.

"Jillian, this is Drake. My *ex*-boyfriend. *Very* ex."

Jillian looked between the two of them and shrugged. "You and Breena got plans tonight?"

"Not that I know of." Her curiosity was piqued.

Drake cleared his throat and ran a hand through his perfectly coiffed hair, trying to regain the attention of the women at the table.

"I'll swing by at seven and grab you two. Dress for dancing," Jillian said. And with a wave of her hand, she was off.

Grace's smile quickly turned to a frown when her gaze landed back on Drake.

"May I assume I'm invited?" Drake asked.

"What?" Incredulous, Grace stared at him. "No. You're not invited. Listen, Drake, I'm not sure what you hoped to accomplish by meeting today. I'm not interested in being used by you anymore. I know you're not interested in me, so why are you here?"

Drake stood, looking ruffled. "Listen, Grace, I can see this just isn't going to work between us anymore. I'm feeling very attacked by you. I had hoped we could clear the air, but that doesn't seem possible if you're not going to move forward here. I think I should go."

Grace felt like she was in an alternate universe. It had obviously been a mistake meeting Drake. He was making no sense, offering no explanations or apologies. But she was happy to have her necklace back.

"Yes, Drake. I absolutely agree with you. Go."

Drake stared at her for a second. "You've changed, Grace."

For the first time since sitting down, a genuine smile stretched across her lips. "Thank you, Drake."

He walked away, shaking his head and looking confused.

Grace took a deep breath and put the necklace around her neck. It felt good to wear it again. It was worth the ten miserable minutes with Drake to have it back. She drank her coffee in peace and pondered the last few days.

So much had changed in her life. She couldn't fathom the changes her mother's inheritance would bring. But for the moment, she was just happy to not have to worry about her dwindling savings account.

She was glad to be done with Drake. It was clear he was using her for her money, which was ironic since she hadn't actually had any when they were dating.

Last night, she'd decided she would swing by Carl's to figure out what happened yesterday. She didn't want to leave a misunderstanding between them.

After finishing her coffee, she left enough to cover both drinks plus a nice tip. It was a quick trip to Carl's, and soon her tires were crunching on his gravel driveway. As she was getting out of her car, his front door opened, and he stood on the top step.

Waiting.

Something about his stiff stance made her uneasy. The coffee she'd just finished all of a sudden wasn't sitting well in her stomach.

She put on a smile and headed toward the house. "Hey there," she said. "I just wanted to pop over and see how you're doing."

He stared at her with cold eyes. Something was definitely off.

"Peachy," he said. "I'm just peachy, Grace."

"Um, okaaay." She drew out the word. "You left Mr. Pillingham's office in a hurry yesterday?"

"I'm fine, Grace. I just don't enjoy it when people play me." His voice was cold.

Grace looked at him, confused and hurt. Her brain was working overtime trying to figure out what was going on. "I'm sorry, Carl. I have no idea what you're talking about."

"I told you all about how Krisi used me and hurt me, and now you do the same thing? You expect me to be happy?"

"Carl, I haven't done anything to use or hurt you." Her heart beat faster, and her palms started to sweat. This was not the conversation she'd been expecting.

"Well let's see." Carl's tone was dripping with sarcasm. "First, you use me to pay for your sightseeing around Nashville. Then you hook up with your rich *boyfriend* after you get your inheritance. Nice necklace," he added sarcastically. "And me? Are you planning on keeping me around for fun?"

Grace's hand went to her necklace. Everything was starting to click into place. Finally. She'd heard enough. Hands on her hips, she glared at him. "Okay, first off, I offered to pay my way. Every. Single. Time. If this is about money, I'll gladly pay you."

Carl took an involuntary step backward. "Yeah, that's what you rich people do, isn't it? Throw money at your problems."

"What? What the heck are you talking about Carl? If you're angry you paid for me, I'm happy to pay you back. That's not throwing money at my problems. And *that's rich*, coming from you." She glared at him across the driveway.

"What is that supposed to mean?" Carl glared back at her.

"I've seen *you* throw money at problems to fix them. Don't be such a hypocrite, Carl."

"*I* don't throw money at problems."

"So that hotel 'problem' in Pigeon Forge you paid to fix, that wasn't throwing money at a problem? Please." Before he could answer, she continued. "And secondly, I don't have a boyfriend. I thought *you* might be my boyfriend, but based on this..." She waved her hand up and down, encompassing his whole body. "Yeah, I don't think I'm interested anymore."

"So you're going to tell me you weren't just having coffee with your boyfriend?" Carl asked, triumphant. "I saw him give you that necklace you're so proudly wearing."

Grace's hand automatically touched the necklace. "Drake *returned* my necklace to me. My father gave it to me for my sixteenth birthday. It's one of the few things I have left from him." The anger left, and in its place came sadness. "Again, I don't have a boyfriend. I was having coffee with my *ex-boyfriend*. You must have seen us right after we sat down. You should have waited because it certainly didn't last much longer than that. But you were more comfortable jumping to conclusions and running instead of sticking around and asking questions. I can't be with someone who doesn't trust me to have coffee with another guy, Carl. Actually, I *won't* be with someone who doesn't trust me. First John, then Drake, and now you. I've got a crappy track record with men. And the fact that I was fine before I inherited money from Mama, and now you think differently about me? That's messed up, Carl. But that's your problem, not mine."

She spun on her heel, got in her car, and pulled out of the drive without looking back at him. She had to get away before she broke down. There was no way she was going to let Carl see how much he'd hurt her.

She pulled into the parking area for the Whiskey Creek Nature Preserve, about a quarter mile from

Carl's house. The tears were flowing before she turned off the engine. Blindly, she reached into the glove box for a couple of napkins. Hastily wiping her tears, she was surprised at how much he'd been able to hurt her.

Her thoughts went back to John. He was the first man to break her heart and completely shatter her trust. It was graduation day, and she was so excited to have her mother and Breena there to celebrate.

She'd met John midway through her freshman year of college. They started as study partners, then became friends, by junior year, they were dating, and senior year, they lived off campus together. She had been so in love. They talked about the future and what it might look like. Graduation was the first step toward that future.

Mama had offered to take Breena and Grace, along with John and his family, out for a fancy dinner to celebrate both of them. After the graduation ceremony, even before finding Breena and her mother, she looked for John. She found him with his family and was excited to finally meet them. She saw a tall man who looked like an older version of John. His blond hair short, his belly trim, his suit perfect. The woman next to him wore a stylish outfit and fit the description John had given her of a tennis enthusiast. The younger woman with them had long blonde hair and was stunning. She hadn't known John had a younger sister.

John rushed over and greeted her with a hug and a kiss on the cheek, then introduced her to his father.

He shook her hand. "I'm not sure John would have graduated without you." He winked at her.

After his mom was introduced, she gave Grace a warm hug and told her it was nice to finally meet her.

Then John introduced her to Rachel. His *fiancée*.

Her world fell apart.

The loud rumbling of a noisy muffler startled Grace out of her memory. After getting herself under control, she drove back to the penthouse. Her heart felt battered and bruised. She realized she wasn't angry so much as disappointed and hurt. She'd thought Carl was different.

Or maybe, she'd hoped.

Hoped he was one she could actually have a good relationship with. A real relationship.

But he didn't even trust her to have coffee with someone else. Well, that certainly wasn't a stable foundation for any kind of relationship.

And why did he think she'd changed in the span of a few minutes, just because she'd inherited money?

She angrily wiped the tears from her eyes again. She wasn't going to waste any more time crying over stupid men. And today had already been filled with two too many of them.

She headed back to the bedroom and saw the second letter from her mother sitting on the nightstand. She hadn't had the energy to read it last night. She wasn't sure she was any more ready now, but she really needed her mother. Plus, she had so many questions, and hopefully, this letter would answer them.

She propped herself in the comfy window seat and took a deep breath before opening the letter.

My Darling Grace,

I know you must have a million questions, and I hope I can answer them for you.

We must go back many years to when I was much younger. Younger than you are now. As you may have guessed, I was a bit of a free spirit in my youth.

Grace smiled at that. Her mother had always been a free spirit. Even when she was older.

In the late 1980s, I was on a road trip across the United States. I won't go into all the details, but in February 1989, I found myself in Las Vegas. Las Vegas then certainly wasn't what it is today. But it was still the place to go to have a good time.

And that's what I was after.

I wound up in the casino at the Stardust Resort. I didn't have a lot of money, but it was fun watching the big-time players. There was one man who caught my eye. He was very handsome. Looked Italian with dark hair, dark eyes, and olive skin. He was winning a lot, so I propped myself up by him and watched the show.

It was Valentine's Day, and we wound up having a fun night hitting all the casinos on the strip. One thing led to another, and by the end of the evening, he'd won quite a bit of money and we'd had quite a bit to drink. When I woke up the next morning, I wasn't surprised by the hangover, but I was shocked by the marriage certificate.

I take marriage very seriously. Even though I didn't remember the ceremony and I had just met the man, I wanted to try and make it work. He, on the other hand, had other ideas. He was fine with me taking our vows seriously...in fact, he insisted on it. But he didn't like that I expected him to take them seriously too.

A few days into our marriage, my husband told me he'd taken out a life insurance policy on me for several million dollars. I told him that was fine as long as he had purchased one on himself as well. The next day, he presented me with a life insurance policy for him with me as the beneficiary. I kept it in my purse since I didn't have anywhere to file it.

It wound up being fortuitous that I kept it with me, but I'm getting ahead of myself.

The first week or so of the marriage was good and fun. We lived in the Stardust Resort—he had a suite there. But after three or four weeks, he started getting pretty tired of me. He didn't like me asking things like when was he going to be home, and he expected me to ask him for permission anytime I wanted to go out and explore. His impatience came out as abuse. Initially, it was verbal, but it quickly escalated to physical.

One night, about two months or so into our marriage, he banged me up so badly, I needed to go to the hospital. The doctor, Dr. Denise Stanton, knew what had happened. She'd seen it enough in her time as a doctor to know what she was looking at. When my husband came that night, he tried to get me checked out of the hospital immediately, but the doctor wouldn't let him and insisted I stay at least one night.

She talked to me for a long time about abusive relationships and what kind of help there was for me to get away from it. The thing that really made up my mind for me was that she told me I was pregnant.

Yes, my darling girl. I was pregnant with you. I know that's a bit of a bombshell, but don't let it change who you know you are and who you know your father is. None of that has changed.

A *bit* of a bombshell? Really, Mama? Grace reached up and touched her necklace, wondering where her dad fit into all of this. She wasn't sure she would like where this went, but she needed to know the truth.

After talking to the doctor, I agreed to go to an abuse shelter, but the shelter was in Nashville.

A gentleman she knew gave me a ride from Las Vegas to Nashville. It was a long, grueling trip. I was still pretty banged up, and it took us three days of hard driving to get here. That man and I became friends during our long journey. He was kind, understanding, and just wanted to help me...and you.

On the drive across the country, I told him everything about what had happened to me. I even told him who my husband was, Marco Martinelli. Once he got me settled at the shelter in Nashville, he came to visit me every few days. He wanted to make sure my wounds were healing, which they were.

*And he wanted to make sure you were growing,
which you definitely were.*

*About a month after I arrived at the shelter, this
gentleman brought me a newspaper and asked me to
read an article. The article said Marco Martinelli, Las
Vegas mobster, had been found shot and killed on the
strip. The article went on to say more about him and
his mob connections, which I had known nothing about.
I was flabbergasted after reading it. First, he was a
mobster. And second, he was dead.*

*I told my friend about the insurance policy I had in
my purse and wondered if it was real. He said he had
a friend who was a lawyer who could help me. Since
Marco was dead, I really didn't need to stay in the
shelter, but I didn't have anywhere else to go. And no
money.*

*We went to see his lawyer friend the next day, a Mr.
Edward Pillingham.*

*You will have met Mr. Pillingham by now. Eddie
wound up getting the money from the insurance company for me, all $50 million of it! He then recommended
a financial adviser who helped me make some really
good investment choices over the years. That, my dear,
is where the money came from. I'm sure you've been
wondering.*

*The gentleman who drove me to Nashville and
helped me so much, who had become such a good friend,
was named Martin Parson. You, of course, know him
as your father. We wound up getting married shortly
before you were born. It was his name I put on your birth*

certificate. We moved to Florida with enough money to buy a house, but after discussing it with Martin, we left the rest of it with the financial adviser for you.

So that, my dear Grace, is my story. I hope you can forgive me for not sharing it with you sooner.

Love, Mama

Grace walked out to the kitchen to get a drink of water, still holding the letter in her hand, hardly believing it. It was such a fantastic story. Like something out of a novel. But this had been her mother's real life.

She heard the elevator doors open, and Breena walked in. "Wow. I'm guessing the coffee didn't go well?"

Grace shook her head. "Girl, it has been a day. Grab something to drink and let's talk." Sitting on the couch with the fireplace offering a cozy warmth, Grace proceeded to enlighten Breena about her coffee with Drake, her argument with Carl, and then gave her the letter to read.

"Holy moly, Grace!" Breena looked up from the pages after reading Marilyn's story.

"Crazy, right?" Grace shook her head. "But what the heck am I going to do with all that money, Bree?"

Chapter 28

CARL

*"We're all just a bunch of sinners, but we
do the best we can."*
Dolly Parton

AFTER GRACE DROVE OFF, Carl sank down to the step and sat there for quite some time with his head in his hands. How had everything become such a mess?

He should be feeling relieved he'd dodged a relationship with another conniving woman. So why didn't he feel good? Why didn't he feel relieved?

He'd been so sure he knew Grace's motives. What he'd seen with his own eyes and what he'd heard her say.

Had he twisted them to fit into an old story?

The sun was much lower when he looked up at the sound of another car coming down his driveway. *Great*, he thought as he watched Mr. Kline get out of his SUV and walk toward the house.

"Mr. Kline." Carl didn't stand but nodded in greeting.

Kline nodded in return and sat next to Carl on the step. He sat with elbows on his thighs, leaning forward a bit, looking out toward the road.

Not looking at Carl, he finally spoke. "I wanted to apologize to you."

Carl's right eyebrow raised, but he didn't say anything.

Kline focused on the road and continued. "Six or so months ago, when we hired you for the addition, my wife and I were in the middle of an adoption. It was our first child, and we were over-the-moon excited. The birth mother had signed the paperwork, we paid all her medical bills, it was all going smoothly until..." He took a deep breath, and when he continued his voice trembled. "Until our young mother was in a car accident. She survived, but our baby didn't."

Carl looked at Kline. He could see the pain in his eyes, could hear it in his voice. "I'm really sorry. I can't imagine how hard that must have been."

"In one moment, our whole world came crashing down." Kline paused. "That's when we stopped the work on the room. We couldn't even bear to look at it. It hurt too much."

They sat in silence for a few minutes while Carl absorbed what he'd heard and Kline composed himself.

"And then, about two months ago, we learned my wife was pregnant. She wasn't supposed to be able to have a baby. That's why we were adopting." He paused again. "When we first found out, we were nervous and scared of everything that could go wrong. But things are going well. The baby is growing like crazy, and Jenny is healthy. But it's been scary as hell. We have been so afraid to get our hopes up and just be excited. What if something goes wrong and our world crashes down again?"

Carl looked at him with new understanding. "So that's why you need the room finished."

"Yes." Kline looked down at his feet. "I...um. The way I've conducted myself with you recently is not the man I am. I'm sorry. I'm not going to make excuses for being rude, impatient, all that. Yes, there are circumstances, but that's just an excuse. I won't do that to you or to me. It's not who I want to be, and it's not right for me to act that way."

Carl sat for a minute with Kline's words. "Already twice today, I've had the *opportunity*," he began rather ruefully, "to realize I've made some poor assumptions about people." He looked at Kline. "Thank you for sharing that with me. It couldn't have been easy."

"Well," Kline said with a small smile, "Jenny made me. She said if we wanted the room finished, and we wanted you to do it, I needed to apologize since I'd been such a cow—her words—to you. I don't know if you have a wife or someone who you're willing to do anything for to make their world right, but if you do, you probably understand."

"I think I may have just screwed up my chance at having that kind of relationship in my life." Carl heaved a sigh and stood up. "Mr. Kline, can I get you a drink? Let's go to the office and figure this out."

"I think, under the circumstances, you should call me Tony. And thank you."

Carl led Tony around to his office to figure out how they could get his room finished.

Later that night, Carl sat in his living room, a muted football game on the television. The Titans were losing rather badly to the Colts, but he wasn't paying attention to it anyway. While football always entertained him, he just couldn't concentrate tonight. He kept it on in the background to keep an eye on the score. Although that was making him feel pretty miserable too.

His wandering mind kept mulling over the events of the last few days. He realized how wrong his assumptions about Tony Kline had been. He wasn't just a rich-jerk client trying to control Carl's time and schedule by flashing dollars.

No. Tony was hurting and scared and just trying to protect his family. Yes, he'd been a rude jerk, but he came clean and apologized for his behavior.

After their conversation, Carl and Tony sat in his office for a couple of hours and mapped out the timeline to complete the addition. If all the pieces came together as planned, they would finish the room before the baby was due.

After Tony left, Carl got on the phone with Jim, then with his Barn Reno client, and then with suppliers. It felt good to help Tony and Jenny. He was hopeful for them and their growing family.

But that brought his thoughts back to Grace. How had things become so messed up between them? Why hadn't he trusted her?

Seeing her sitting there at the coffee shop, receiving jewelry from that man had immediately brought him back to the day he had walked out on Krisi. And just like with Krisi, he hadn't stuck around to ask questions or listen to explanations.

Grace had said he was her ex-boyfriend. He remembered the story she'd told him about this guy while they were on their way to Pigeon Forge.

Man, that felt like a lifetime ago even though it was only a few days.

He had cheated on Grace. She'd watched it on video. So why had she been holding hands with him?

Carl tried to focus on what he'd seen at the coffee shop. His brain had shut down as soon as he registered them holding hands. But was that what had he really seen?

Thinking back, he realized she hadn't been gazing lovingly into his eyes. She'd looked frustrated, maybe exasperated. He was holding her hand, but she hadn't been holding his.

Shoot!

Had he overreacted? Misread the whole situation?

But what about her calling him a hypocrite?

She was being unfair, and that comment was unjustified. It was certainly not something he could overlook...right? He could feel his heart beating faster, his hurt taking hold again.

She'd acted like a rich snob. Like Krisi. Lashing out at him for calling her out.

Except that really wasn't the Grace he knew. She wasn't one to take advantage of people, whether she had money or not.

And then his traitorous mind remembered the brief kiss at Stampede. And the much longer kiss in his backyard. Her kisses had completely rocked his world. Was he willing to give up on a relationship that might really be special?

Chapter 29

GRACE

"Love is like a butterfly, a rare and gentle thing."

Dolly Parton

GRACE AND BREENA WERE sprawled on the couch, wineglasses in hand, when the buzzer went off. Grace waved for Breena to stay seated and got up to answer it.

"Yes?"

"Good evening, ma'am. I have Miss Jillian here to see you. Would you like me to send her up?" Brian's voice came through the intercom.

Oh shoot! Grace had completely forgotten about their plans to go out that night and hadn't even mentioned it to Breena. And now Jilly was here.

And she'd just fought with Jilly's brother. How was that going to go over?

"Sure, send her up," she said into the intercom. "So, something I forgot to mention," Grace started as she walked back over to the couch. "We're supposed to go out with Jillian tonight. And now she's here. Oops."

Breena looked down at her loungewear, at Grace's black leggings and hot pink top, then laughed. "Hmm, maybe she won't mind staying in."

As the elevator doors opened, Grace stood up and smiled at Jillian. "Hey Jilly, go grab a wineglass. We have some catching up to do. And as you can see, we're nowhere near ready to go."

Jillian held up a wine bottle and laughed. "Yeah, I wanted to catch up before heading out too. I've got questions, girl."

Back in the living room with refilled wineglasses, the three women settled in for a good gab session.

"Okay. I want to hear about the meeting with the lawyer and tell me about that coffee date earlier today." Jillian was not one to shy away from asking questions.

"Soo..." Grace dragged the word out a bit, a little nervous to ask. "Have you spoken with your brother today?"

"No. Should I have?"

Breena laughed while Grace blew out a breath.

"Okay, this could get rocky. But let's start with the lawyer's visit. That was pretty crazy. Carl was there."

"Really?" Jillian's eyes opened wide.

"Well, he was before he got mad and walked out," Breena said.

"What? Why would he walk out?" Jillian raised her eyebrows almost to her hair and opened her eyes even wider.

"We learned at the lawyer's office that I inherited a lot of money, and Carl didn't take it well. He read a lot into it and decided I was another rich woman who couldn't be trusted," Grace said. "And then he saw me having coffee with Drake—my ex—and read a lot into that as well. So when I went to his house earlier today to talk with him about the lawyer's office...let's just say it didn't go very well."

Jillian sighed. "Yeah, I can imagine it didn't. I'm really sorry to hear that, Grace. You two were good together from what I saw."

Grace tried to smile, but she was still pretty raw about the whole situation. She thought they were good together too. The fact that he would so easily dismiss what they had started was both frustrating and sad.

They all took a drink of their wine, then Jilly asked, "So who is this Drake guy? You said he was your ex. What's the story there?"

"He was a mistake, for sure, but I didn't figure it out until it was right in front of my face, I suppose."

"She even has the pictures to prove it." Breena laughed.

"You have pictures? I wanna see."

Jillian jumped up and went over to the couch as Breena grabbed Grace's phone. Breena pulled up the offending pictures and held the phone out to Jillian.

"Oh. My. Gosh!" She looked from Grace to Breena and back again. "I need to hear this story."

After topping up their glasses again, Grace told the story with lots of interruptions and questions from Jillian and a lot of side commentary from Breena. She was curious to note that talking about Drake didn't bring up any pain, or even anger, this time around. It was just a story from her past.

Drake was her past and she had moved on.

"Holy guacamole!" Jillian was laughing now. "I would have loved to have been the cop picking those two up. So let me get this straight—he's in jail, trying to convince you he was just looking out for you and your townhouse. Really? Is he delusional?"

"Well, you met him. He gets by on charm and good looks but very little else. Once you press for details or information, he bolts."

"Tell me about this inheritance...you're rich now?"

Grace laughed at Jillian's ongoing stream of questions. She had no filter and, apparently, no qualms about asking personal questions.

"Hang on a sec. I think you need to read Mama's words for this one. Not sure I can do it justice yet." Grace ran to her bedroom and was back in a flash with the second letter. "This is the letter from my mother explaining the inheritance."

Jillian's eyes raced back and forth across the pages as she read the letter. A few times, she looked up at Grace with wide eyes, then back down to the page to continue tearing through the story.

"Wow, Grace. Just...wow. I had no idea Marilyn had all of that in her past."

"Yeah, me neither," Grace said softly.

"Your dad..." Jillian paused for a minute, uncharacteristically sensitive. "Did you know all of that?"

"Not at all. But honestly, it hasn't changed my feelings for him, and I don't blame Mama for not telling me. It was her story. Daddy was and is my father."

The door buzzed again, so Grace hopped up to answer it, thinking maybe it was Carl coming to make peace. "Yes?"

"Miss Grace." It was Brian's soft drawl on the intercom again. "Do you mind if I come up for a few minutes? I have something I need to share with you, and I think it's time."

Grace looked at Jillian and Breena, confused. "Sure, Brian, come on up."

"How mysterious," Jillian said as Grace walked back over to the couch.

"Yeah," Breena chimed in. "I wonder what that's all about."

"Well, it appears we're about to find out." Grace stood up again as the elevator dinged and the doors opened.

"Evenin', ladies." Brian walked in, looking comfortable in the space. They each said their *hellos* as he sat in a chair facing the couch. "I'm sure you're wondering what I've got to tell you."

Grace smiled and nodded. "You've definitely got our curiosity up."

"Yes, I imagine so. I won't keep you in suspense. Grace, I'm not sure how much of your mother's background you know, but she was a victim of spousal abuse when she was young."

"Yes. I just read a letter from Mama explaining all that."

"When your mother came back to Nashville a few years ago, she wanted to do something to help women whose situations were similar to hers so many years before."

"Oh?" Grace said, surprised.

"Marilyn had an understanding with a few of the local police officers and doctors. If they knew of a woman who needed to be hidden from an abusive situation, they could bring her here. I helped keep everything covert, so no one knew when a woman had been brought to the building. Marilyn took over from there."

Grace sat stunned.

But Breena had questions. "What about medical attention? Did the women get the help they needed after they came here?"

"I think I need to show you something." Brian stood up and walked toward Breena's bedroom. He stopped at the doorway and turned to her. "Do you mind if we go in?"

"Um, sure. No problem." Breena looked very confused now.

Brian walked in and went straight to the closet. He moved aside the few clothes Breena had hanging up before turning on the flashlight on his phone. He pointed it to the floor and showed them all a tiny button in the corner. "Go ahead and push that." He stepped back so Breena could get into the closet.

The space was cramped with four adults huddled around as Breena pushed the button. The back wall silently slid open to reveal a huge open space.

The three women stood there, stunned into silence.

Brian nodded and held his hand out, indicating they should walk through the opening. As soon as he came through, the secret door closed silently behind him. He hit a light switch on the wall to reveal another apartment.

The three women stood frozen, astonished at what was revealed to them.

"The three bedrooms in this apartment have been set up as a room for medical treatment, an exercise room for therapy if needed, and a bedroom. There is, of course, a living room, dining room, and kitchen as well."

They walked around the apartment in silence, looking at this whole secret world none of them knew existed.

"Girls, come in here." Jillian had wandered into the bedroom. Breena and Grace quickly joined her.

It was a massive bedroom with a queen-size bed as well as a bunk bed. There was a dresser on one wall, a comfy rocking chair next to the bunk beds, and a desk by a window. There was also a nice-sized bathroom with a tub and a shower.

But the closet was where Jillian was standing. Gaping.

It was huge, probably three or four times the size of a normal walk-in closet. It looked like a small clothing boutique, filled with a variety of clothes, sorted by size. Shoes were in racks along the floor. Again, lots of sizes and a variety of styles.

Something for any woman who might come through here, Grace thought. Along the back of the closet was a shelving unit filled with wigs on mannequin heads. Blond, red, brunette, gray, and black hair. Long, short, and medium lengths.

"Most of the women who came through showed up with nothing, so Marilyn built up this closet and let the women wear and take anything they wanted. And the women, once they were ready to go out into the world again, could do so in disguise if they needed to." Brian had followed them into the closet.

It was a lot to take in, and the three women wandered around.

Grace sat on the couch, not sure what to even think about all of this. "So how many women came through here?"

"I think Marilyn kept records somewhere, but my guess would be about a hundred over the course of the two years she was here. Some women were only here for a day or two, but others stayed for a month or more."

"The Hope Files," Breena said, looking at Grace. "We found a bunch of files in the filing cabinet. They were labeled Hope Files."

"That has to be what they are," Grace agreed. She shook her head. "I had no idea Mama did all this."

Brian walked back to the wall where the secret door was. "Shall we head back over? I'll answer any and all questions because I'm sure you have some."

He pushed another button, and they filed back through the door, through the closet, back into the living room in Grace's mother's apartment, where they had started.

They asked Brian question after question for thirty minutes before deciding they needed a break to let it all sink in. Brian headed back down the elevator.

"I think we should go out dancing," Jillian blurted out.

"What?" Breena looked at Jillian like she was crazy. Then she looked at Grace for support.

"We've just had a lot dumped into our brains, and Grace has had a rough day. I think we need to take a break. Dancing will take our minds off it all for a bit. And it will be fun."

"As crazy as that sounds, I think it's a good idea." Grace looked at Breena. "Please, Bree, let's go have some fun. I need something normal right now. After the day I've had. First Drake, then Carl, the letter from Mama, and now all this from Brian. I really want to go have some fun, to not think about anything. We can discuss it all on the drive back to Florida tomorrow."

"Okay. Let's go have fun. But I think we should Uber it since we've been drinking and will probably have more drinks."

Jillian called down to Brian to arrange a ride to her favorite honky-tonk while Grace and Breena rushed off to change.

An hour later, after being dropped off in front of a fairly nondescript building a little off the beaten path bearing the name Tyler's Honky Tonk on a small wooden sign, the women were already worn out from dancing.

Breena grabbed a table for them while Jillian headed to the bar to get some drinks.

Grace sat in her newly purchased jeans and one of her mother's shirts that seemed perfect for tonight's location. The turquoise fringe along the neckline matched her boots and she felt fun. She looked to the bar to see how Jillian was doing.

"Oh my gosh. Who's with Jilly?" Breena looked up just in time to see Jilly plant a big kiss on the man standing next to her, his arm around her shoulder. The couple, Jilly and the stranger, walked away from the bar loaded with drinks, heading toward their table.

They set the drinks down, then Jilly turned to him. "Thanks, Tex." She gave him a saucy wink and sent him on his way.

"Soo..." Breena looked at Jillian laughing, one eyebrow cocked. "Can't leave you alone for a minute, apparently."

Jillian looked back at the bar where three guys were looking at her. "Nah. He was just being a gentleman, and I let him. He didn't know I'm a cop and could have taken all three of those morons down without spilling my drink."

Seeing their confused looks, Jillian explained. "Those three guys at the bar there were trying to give me a hard time. Tex came up, put his arm around my shoulder, and said, 'Everything all right, darlin'?' So I played along and gave him a kiss for his troubles." She grinned. "And sexy Tex bought our drinks. So that was nice."

Grace and Breena picked up their drinks and toasted the stranger who had rescued their friend.

"So you two are going to Florida tomorrow?" Jillian almost had to yell to be heard over the noise in the bar.

"Yeah. We're going to drive Bree's car down to take care of Mama's townhouse. Well, Bree's house now."

Grace smiled at her friend. "We're going to get things packed up and put it on the market."

Grace could see something like relief cross Jillian's face. "Oh good. I was afraid you were going to move back down there. It's been a while since I've had girl-friends. I'm not ready to give you two up." Jillian grinned at them.

"Aw, thanks." Breena gave Jillian a side hug. "There's nothing for us in Florida anymore. And we really like Nashville, stupid men aside. It seems like a good a place to start over."

Jillian looked at Grace. "Speaking of stupid men. What about you and Carl?"

"I'm not sure there is a 'me and Carl' anymore. He didn't seem like he wanted anything to do with me when I went to see him today. It's disappointing." She took a deep breath. She had so many feelings but didn't want to get into it at the moment. "I really like him, but if he can't trust me and doesn't know who I am, then we've got nothing to work with."

The music changed and Jillian jumped up. "Come on, girls, we must dance again. I love this song."

Laughing, Grace and Breena followed Jillian back to the dance floor. The live band was loud and enter-taining. They found a small spot and started moving their hips. Grace found she didn't have space to move, but that was fine. It was nice to be out with girlfriends.

Jilly was right. It felt good to have fun and forget about her disastrous day for a little while. She couldn't even remember the last time she'd gone dancing with friends. She was glad Jillian talked them into it.

As the music got louder, the crowd got more rambunctious. One of the three morons from the bar was dancing with a woman who appeared to be very drunk. He kept twirling her out from him and then back in. There wasn't enough room on the dance floor for that kind of dancing, so every time he twirled her out, she bumped into other dancers. She didn't seem to be aware of what was happening, and the guy didn't seem to care.

Just as she was moving away from the couple to give them more space, Grace saw the woman twirling out toward her. She jumped out of the way, only to put Jillian in the line of fire. Jillian was talking to Breena while dancing and never saw the woman coming. The impact was hard. The drunk woman went down to the floor, while Jillian was thrown backward.

Before Jillian could hit the ground, though, arms came around her and kept her from falling completely. Grace saw the surprise followed by delight on Jillian's face as she was rescued yet again by the handsome stranger from earlier.

With her whole front plastered against the tall, dark, handsome Tex, Jillian looked up into his eyes. "My hero."

Grace heard her laugh, then Jillian leaned forward, and Grace could no longer hear what was being said, but she could see both Jillian and the stranger smiling.

"Ladies, let's get this young woman safely home." Jillian smiled at Tex, who was already helping the woman off the floor. Jillian and Breena put their arms around the woman and helped her out of the bar and into their Uber.

"Our work here is done. Let's go."

Chapter 30

CARL

"Money ain't everything."
Dolly Parton

C ARL WAS MISERABLE.

He hadn't slept well last night, and Grace was to blame for it. Miss Kitty had tripped him as he headed down the stairs, and he narrowly avoided breaking his neck.

And now he'd just discovered he was out of coffee.

After feeding Miss Kitty her breakfast, he noticed the letter from Marilyn still sitting on the kitchen counter. He'd put it there when he got home from the lawyer's office. He hadn't read it, and he wasn't sure he could handle doing so right now, with no coffee in his system.

For some reason, he was nervous to open it. He felt like Marilyn might have seen the way he acted at the lawyer's office and when Grace came by yesterday. He didn't want to disappoint Marilyn, even though she wasn't here anymore.

He sat on the couch holding the letter, wishing a cup of coffee would magically appear. When it didn't, he knew he couldn't stall any longer. So Miss Kitty followed him out to the front porch. Sitting on the steps, Carl was finally ready to read Marilyn's last words to him.

Just as he was opening his letter, he heard the unmistakable crunch of tires on his gravel drive. Hoping it might be Grace while at the same time scared it might be her, he looked up to see his sister's car pulling in.

Relief and disappointment in equal measure coursed through him. But when he saw two coffees in Jilly's hands, he almost wept in relief.

"My favorite sister ever," Carl greeted her.

"Geesh, you look like crap, Carl. And from what I hear, you certainly don't deserve this." She gave him a pointed look but handed him one of the cups.

Grateful, he inhaled deeply, enjoying the aroma of good coffee. Then he took a sip and let the caffeine do its magic.

"So who'd you get your intel from this time, Bean?"

Jillian sat down next to her brother and inhaled the scent of her own coffee. He heard her satisfied sigh as she took the first sip of her vanilla latte.

"Well, I went out dancing with Grace and Breena last night. And that's where I got my info."

Carl's head whipped around to look at her. "She went out dancing with you last night?" He was confused…and disappointed she hadn't had as miserable a night as he had. "Obviously our fight didn't affect her at all." He was pouting, and he knew it.

"First off, you have no idea how it affected her. You haven't asked her. And second, she had a pretty lousy day yesterday."

"Oh really? First, she has a coffee date with her boyfriend. Then she comes over here to give me an earful. And then, apparently, she ended the day dancing the night away with you. I guess I might do all that, too, if I'd inherited millions of dollars." He knew he was being snarky, but between the lack of sleep and low caffeine intake, he wasn't in the mood to hear how lousy *her* day was.

"You're being a jerk, Carl." Jillian was giving him what he thought of as her *cop look*. She took another sip of coffee. "Her coffee 'date' was with her *ex*-boyfriend, and I'm pretty sure you know that. He's a piece of work. And then, right after dealing with him, she comes by to make sure you're okay. It doesn't sound like that conversation was much fun for either one of you. Then she found out how her mother got her money, which was a hard story for her to hear. And finally, Brian sprung another surprise on her. So yes, we went out dancing last night to help her forget about a rough day. A rough day *you* contributed to, I might add."

Carl rubbed his hands over his face, then picked up his coffee again. Yesterday, he'd felt completely justified in his actions, but now...now he was feeling remorse. It wasn't sitting well.

"What was I supposed to think, Bean? When I saw her at the table with that guy, a sparkly necklace in her hand, I immediately thought of Krisi. It was like a punch to the gut." He took a drink of his coffee before continuing, "And then when she came by, I couldn't even listen to her. She called me a hypocrite, Bean. *Me*. A hypocrite."

He sounded so offended Jillian almost smiled, but instead, she just said, "Hmm. Were you being a hypocrite, Carl?"

Carl looked at her pointedly but didn't answer the question. "So what was the story about Marilyn's money?"

"Not my story to share, bro. You want to know, you'll have to ask Grace." With that, she got up off the step and started back to her car. After a couple of steps, she turned to look at her brother again. "She's the real deal, Carl. You screw this up, you'll regret it. I suggest you take some time today to think about what you really feel for her and what you're going to do about it."

Carl watched her pull out of his drive, then rested his elbows on his knees, hanging his head, wondering when life had become so complicated, when his little sister had become so smart. He knew he'd made some bad assumptions about Grace, but he wasn't sure what to do about it.

He decided now was as good a time as any to read Marilyn's letter. His hands were unsteady as he pulled the pale turquoise paper from the envelope. He was immediately engulfed by Marilyn's scent and memories of their coffee dates. He indulged himself, closed his eyes, and just let himself remember her for a few minutes before opening his eyes and looking at the letter.

Dear Carl,

First off, I want to apologize for leaving you so suddenly and not sharing what was going on. I know I kind of conned you into watching Miss Kitty for me, and again, I'm sorry, but I hope it has worked out okay for both of you.

Secondly, I want to say thank you. Thank you for being such a lovely friend to this old lady. I know our relationship was a bit unusual, and a few people wondered why we hung out so much. But I truly found joy in your company. Yes, at times you felt like a son to me, but I never considered our relationship as one of mother to son. It was just friend to friend.

I'm hoping by now you've met my daughter, Grace. Carl, that girl has been the absolute light of my life. I've pictured the two of you meeting for so long, and I hope you've gotten along well.

While I could write a whole letter about Grace, this letter, my dear Carl, is for you, and about you. My guess is you're feeling a little awkward about that, but that's okay. It's just a feeling, and it won't hurt you.

Carl laughed at that last line. It was so Marilyn. She'd always encouraged feeling your feelings.

When we met, you were just on the heels of a bad relationship. Over the years, I watched you morph into a man who avoided commitment. It made my heart hurt, but it was your life, and I never felt it was my place to tell you how to live. But obviously, things have changed. I have passed on from this world, and so I guess that makes me feel like it's okay to try to impart some wisdom to you, my friend.

Over the years, we've known each other pretty well, and I watched you put up walls between you and so many people. You got this notion in your head that rich people are the enemy, and while you will happily take them on as clients, you rarely deviate to a deeper friendship with any. I was the exception, but only because I wouldn't take no for an answer.

You are one of the best men I've had the pleasure of knowing. You are honorable, have a good work ethic, run your company above the board, and you're a lot of fun.

I know Krisi broke your heart, or at least your pride, but not every person who has money is like her. I feel certain you know that in your heart. I certainly wasn't out to take advantage of you in any way, and I had money.

And for crying out loud, Carl, you have money. Maybe you don't look at yourself that way, but I'm guessing you make a tidy profit each year. So lose the attitude about rich people before someone calls you out on that. Don't be a hypocrite.

Carl paused and stared at the page. He couldn't believe Marilyn had just called him a hypocrite too. *Like mother, like daughter.* Well, to be fair, she wasn't calling him a hypocrite. She was telling him not to be one. But the arrow hit pretty close to the target, and Carl was feeling uncomfortable.

And just in case you're wondering, Grace had no idea how wealthy I was. She is probably completely unprepared for it, so I hope you'll be a friend who helps her navigate this new path.

Now I want to make sure your life doesn't just revolve around your work. I know you love what you do, and that is great, but life needs to be about more than just work. So hopefully, my gift to you has arrived. Put it together and think of me every time you use it.

Grab a beer or a cup of coffee and take time to smell the roses, so to speak. Take time to think about what's important in life and then embrace it.

I love you very much and know I will miss you terribly when I leave Nashville.

Your friend,
Marilyn

Carl sat for a minute, thinking about the words from his friend. He rubbed his hands on his face and was surprised to find his cheeks wet. His heart ached missing Marilyn.

And now his heart hurt because of her daughter.

He realized he hadn't opened the box. He'd forgotten about it, truth be told. It was time to see what Marilyn thought he needed.

He headed back into the kitchen, plucked a knife from the block, then walked to the dining room. It was right where he and the delivery guy had put it, leaning against the wall. After pulling it into the living room where there was more space, Carl sliced the tape off each end.

He paused a moment before opening one end to see what her gift was. On the one hand, he felt like a kid at Christmas, waiting to see what Santa had brought. But on the other, he was nervous to find out what Marilyn thought he needed in his life.

With his heart beating faster than it should, curiosity won out, and he opened the flaps and pulled out the bulky frame he felt inside.

Carl let out a laugh. Apparently, Marilyn thought he needed a hammock. When he thought about it more, maybe she was right. She usually was. He was excited to try it out. He dragged the whole box to the backyard, to the spot he'd told Grace needed a hammock or a swing. And now he had a hammock.

It was easy enough to assemble, and it kept his mind and hands occupied for a little while. Standing under the trees, he smiled at the result of his efforts. The red hammock swung freely in the wind, just waiting for someone to climb in. It was wide enough to fit two. At the moment though, it would be just himself and Marilyn's letter. He ran back into the house to grab a blanket.

As he settled into the hammock with the blanket around him, Miss Kitty jumped up and settled herself right next to his body. Guess he wasn't going to have to do this alone. Feeling her small warm body nestled against his leg gave him the fortitude for another read-through.

The sound of tires on his gravel drive surprised him. Geesh, he'd had everybody and his sister come over in the last couple of days. Who was left? His heart clenched a little, thinking it might be Grace.

But then his mom walked around the corner.

"Well look at you, all sprawled out and relaxin'. Got room for your ol' mom in that thing?"

Carl smiled up at her and swatted Miss Kitty down to make room. It always amazed him at how youthful she still looked. "You look beautiful today, Mom. Come on in." He helped her down into the hammock, and they sat side by side for a minute, just enjoying the cold breeze blowing through the trees in his backyard.

"You look like you've had a rough morning. What's going on?"

"I think I screwed up, Mom. Royally." Carl blew out a long breath.

"Well, that certainly sounds dramatic. Tell me all about it."

For the next several minutes, Carl shared everything about the last few days with her. He liked that she didn't interrupt and let him finish talking.

"Why do you think you reacted so strongly at the lawyer's office?"

She didn't judge him, and he truly appreciated it.

"I'm not really sure. Initially, I was ticked off because she was excited about being rich. And then when I saw her with her boyfriend—"

"*Ex*-boyfriend, I thought you said," she interjected.

"Yes, ex-boyfriend. When I saw the two of them, it took me back to Krisi, and I just couldn't think straight."

His mom looked at him and took his hand in hers. "Are you sure, honey, that it's just Krisi you were thinking of?"

Carl looked down at their linked hands, his shoulders drooping. "What do you mean?"

"Honey, I think you know what I mean. Are you sure this isn't about your mother?"

He looked at her, his eyes hard. "*You* are my mother."

She rubbed his hand. "Okay, okay. Bio Mom, as you and Jillian call her."

He shrugged his shoulders, feeling like he had when he was a child and didn't want to answer her questions. "I don't know. Maybe."

"Honey, in all the years I've had the pleasure of being your mom, I've never said one word against her. But, Carl, that woman was self-absorbed and greedy. It's not fair for you to judge other women by her actions."

"Do you know what the last words she said to me were?" he asked softly. "She told me there were things in this world more important than love. Money is more important than love, she said. Then she ended with 'Remember that and you'll go far, kiddo.'"

"Do you believe that?"

"No, of course not," Carl huffed out.

"Honey, money is important, but it's certainly *not* more important than love. I'm sorry those are the words she chose to leave you with. Now about your young lady, does she think money is more important than love?"

Carl didn't have to think about it. "No. She seemed completely thrown off that she suddenly had money. Like I said, I screwed up. Big time."

"Yes, you did screw up. And probably big time." She patted his arm when his head whipped around to her. "Just because you messed up, doesn't mean you can't fix it. It just means it might take a lot of work and a lot of time. But if she's worth it, then you do the work."

He laid his head on his mom's shoulder. "Yes, she's worth it, Mom. So how do I fix this?"

"That, my darling boy, is up to you. You have to figure that one out on your own."

He hid his eye roll. "Yeah, I was afraid you would say that."

"It'll probably be super uncomfortable, and maybe even scary. But you still do it."

The steely look she gave him made him smile. It was the same one she'd given him so many times growing up.

"Well." He chuckled. "I've got that to look forward to."

"Just remember she's worth it, honey." She smiled at him as she pushed up from the hammock. "I like your hammock."

"Thanks, me too. It was a gift from Marilyn. I just opened it and read a letter from her. I hope she wouldn't be disappointed I messed things up with her daughter."

"She'll only be disappointed if you don't fix it, honey." And with that, she walked back around the house to her car.

Carl sat for a few more minutes, swinging in his new hammock, thinking about Grace and their last conversation. The energy coming off her had made him want to go to her. But at the same time, he'd been so stunned and hurt, and then angry, by the whole conversation.

He thought about her calling him a hypocrite. Had he been a hypocrite?

As hurtful as the thought was, he knew he needed to dig into it. His mom was right; this was going to be uncomfortable.

By most people's standards, he probably would be considered rich. At the very least, he had more than enough money for his needs and lifestyle.

She'd called him out on throwing money at the hotel problem in Pigeon Forge.

Dang it. She was right.

He *had* thrown money at that problem. He didn't even know how much the room had cost. He never even asked.

He paused the hammock and repeated that thought to himself. *He hadn't even asked the price.* He'd just thrown down his credit card to make the problem go away.

Crap!

He was definitely going to have to apologize to Grace.

Carl spent the rest of the morning lounging in the hammock with Miss Kitty, thinking about his life and future. What did he want it to look like? Was he happy with how it was now? What wasn't he happy with?

He loved his job. He loved bringing old buildings back to life. He loved exceeding the expectations of a client. He felt blessed to be able to do what he loved with men he respected, week after week.

But when he thought of his future, Grace kept sneaking into the picture. When he thought about making a life with someone, it was Grace who came to mind. When he thought about who he wanted to spend the next year with, it was Grace.

Heck, when he thought about what he wanted to do this coming weekend, it was her face that came to mind.

He wanted to spend time with her.

He put his foot on the ground to stop the hammock. Startled, Miss Kitty jumped off and headed back into the house. His heart was beating fast, and his hands were a little sweaty.

When, exactly, had he fallen in love with Grace?

He sat up and thought about that for a few minutes, waiting for the panic. He remembered trying to get behind the idea of a future with Krisi. The panic had always come swift and hard. He hadn't been able to talk about a future with her, much less think about it.

But now.

With Grace.

The panic didn't come.

Instead, a sense of peace and rightness settled into him. He knew it was too soon to talk about the future with her. But he also knew what he needed to do now.

He needed to make things right with Grace. His future—*their* future—depended on it.

He jumped up, ran into the house, and hopped in the shower. He was ready to make this future a reality. At least, he was ready to get it on the right track.

An hour later, Carl showed up at The Athenian with a huge bouquet from Mrs. Snowden's shop. This time, though, it was for Grace. The colors were soft and reminded him of her. Even the smell of these flowers made him think of her.

"Hey, Carl, how can I help you today?" Brian was manning the entryway as usual.

"I'd like to visit Grace. Do you mind calling up please?"

"No need for that. Grace isn't here anymore."

Carl felt the blood drain from his face. "Wh-what do you mean *she's not here anymore*? Where is she?"

"Oh, she and Miss Breena headed back to Florida late this morning. They were excited about it." Brian offered him a smile.

Now the panic started setting in.

Headed back to Florida? What was in Florida for her?

The boyfriend? That didn't feel right.

The panic was creeping in. He turned and headed back out the door, leaving a very confused Brian in his wake.

"Why didn't you tell me she was headed back to Florida?" Carl, standing on the sidewalk outside The Athenian, demanded as soon as his sister answered her phone.

"Well, hello to you too."

"Why didn't you tell me Grace went back to Florida?" Carl sounded panicky this time.

"Mostly because you didn't ask, Carl. You were a jerk to her. Why would I share her itinerary with you? And how do you know she's in Florida?"

"Brian just told me. I went by to apologize, and she's gone. *Gone.*" He knew he sounded pathetic, but he couldn't help himself.

"Did you try calling her?" Jillian asked.

"Yes, but it went straight to voicemail. Jilly, how can I make this right?"

"Carl, what are you talking about?"

"She's moving back to Florida, Bean. Back to *him.* I screwed up. Big time. And now, I can't even make it right." Carl's voice was shaking. "Maybe I should hop on a plane and head down there."

"Carl, take a deep breath. Because I love you, I'll tell you this. They are not *moving* back to Florida. And Grace is most certainly *not* getting back with her loser ex. I'm really glad to hear you've got your head on straight."

The vice around his heart loosened a bit. She wasn't moving back to Florida. She wasn't going back to her ex-boyfriend.

He took a deep breath before tentatively asking, "When will she be back?"

"I have no idea, Carl. You're going to have to figure that one out yourself. Or maybe just wait and see. I gotta go, bro. Hang in there. She'll be back."

The line disconnected.

Chapter 31

GRACE

*"Dreams don't just come true because you
want them, that's a wish or a fantasy. You
got to work for them."*
Dolly Parton

A FTER TWO DAYS OF sorting, packing, and toss-
ing a houseful of stuff, Grace and Breena were
exhausted. Not only was it physically taxing, but they
found it was emotionally draining to pack up their
childhood home.

They'd cleaned out the townhouse after her
mother moved out, and they were surprised at just
how much there was left to go through. Especially in
their own bedrooms. Grace came into the living room
with a huge pile of clothes in her arms.

"I don't know if I can wear these clothes any-more." She looked at the pile. For a lot of their time in Nashville, she'd been missing these clothes, but now, they didn't seem to fit her style anymore.

They had three boxes—keep, estate sale, and trash. Grace kept throwing shirts and dresses into the es-tate sale box. They were all nice quality and in good condition, but just so plain and boring. She cringed, realizing *plain and boring* summed up her earlier style.

Breena looked up from the pile she was sorting. "It's going to be fun to see what your new style is. I love that you're colorful again."

Grace smiled at her. "I'm looking forward to see-ing it too."

After finishing her pile, Breena walked into the kitchen and started working in there. A few minutes later, she came back out to the living room, holding a big purple ceramic dragon with cookie dragon written across its chest.

"I don't think I can get rid of this." She held the jar close.

"Of course not. I remember when Mama brought that home."

"Yeah, it was shortly after I moved in. I was do-ing a lot of stress baking. All she said was 'You can put all those lovely cookies in here, darlin'.' She never scolded me or told me to stop baking. She just made sure I always had flour and sugar. And she bought me a cookbook." Breena laughed. "They were pretty bad for a while."

Grace laughed with her. "Yeah, they kinda were."

Breena looked back down at the jar. "This will have to come to Nashville with us."

There was a lot of stuff that wouldn't make the trip with them, and it all brought back memories. Memories of their little family, now missing two members.

An estate sale company was coming next week to sell everything they didn't want to take to Nashville, and getting ready for that was their main focus. But at the moment, they still had a lot to go through.

"So how are you feeling about selling your house?" Grace asked Breena.

"It still feels very weird calling it *my* house. It feels like it should be yours. And after talking to the real estate agent today, I *really* feel weird saying it's mine. Grace, it's worth a *lot* of money. Are you sure you're okay with this?"

"Of course I am, Bree. You heard what Mama left me. I'm more than okay with this house being yours."

Breena smiled and gave her friend a hug. "Thanks, Grace."

"And I hope you'll stay in the penthouse as long as you want. I really love that place and would love to have you there with me." Grace said.

"Thanks. I have no idea what I want to do or where I want to be."

"Yeah. I've been wondering what I can do to honor Mama. I'd really like to start a foundation or something in her name. But at the moment, that feels kinda overwhelming."

"Ooh, I love the idea of you doing something in your mother's name. That would be brilliant. Maybe we could start small by getting the underground apartment up and running?"

"I like that. It doesn't feel so overwhelming. The secret apartment was a complete surprise. Do you want to start it back up?" Grace asked. After all, they would both be involved.

"I think it would be amazing. Hard to believe your mother had around a hundred women come through there. It's staggering. I would love to be a part of that legacy."

"I wonder how we'd go about it. Starting it back up, I mean." Grace thought out loud.

"I imagine Jilly and Brian could probably steer us in the right direction."

"Oh, of course." Grace laughed a little at the fact she hadn't thought of them. "I keep thinking about what Brian said, about some of the women needing to stay a month or more."

"Yeah. I've been thinking about that too. It seems like a big house in an out-of-the-way location would be useful, right? A secret apartment is fine for a night or two, but for a month or longer, it seems like you'd want more space and outdoors."

They sat thinking about that, drinking their wine.

"I wonder if a house in the mountains would work?" Grace asked.

"Ooh, yes. It would certainly be out of the way. I bet there are some big houses in those mountains that would be perfect."

"Mama's middle name was Hope. That's what Daddy used to call her, remember?" They smiled at each other, sharing the memory. "And she had the Hope Files. How about Hope's House?"

They spent the next hour dreaming up the perfect mountain house for the project. It was fun to dream again, Grace realized. It had been so long since she'd had the mental capacity to just let herself dream. She remembered a Dolly quote, something about dreams needing wings. They were going to give *this* dream big, beautiful wings. She touched her butterfly necklace. Big, beautiful wings.

Since they were dreaming, she realized she wanted Bree to be in charge of the medical aspect of things, Jilly in charge of the security, and Carl...

Oh. Right. Her heart clutched.

Carl.

Grace's heart hurt whenever she thought of him. He'd called a few times since they left Nashville. His messages were always short. He really wanted to talk with her. She couldn't tell if he sounded mad or sad. Disappointed? Frustrated? Hopeful?

She just couldn't tell.

As much as she wanted to talk with him, she wasn't eager to call him back. Geesh, she felt like she was in middle school again. She rolled her eyes at herself.

"So." Breena interrupted her thoughts. "What's going on with Carl? I've seen your phone blinking a lot. Have you spoken with him yet?"

"Funny. I was just thinking about him." Grace gave her a wry smile. "He wants to talk, but I'm not sure I'm ready. And since we've been so busy, it's been easy to avoid responding."

She wasn't sure she was ready for that conversation. She needed to figure out how she felt about him. At one point, she'd been thinking he might be *the one*, but how could he be if he only wanted her if she didn't have money?

Just then, she heard her phone chime with a new call. Carl. She held the screen up to Breena. "I'm not sure I'm ready for this," she said softly.

"Want me to tell him to stop calling?"

"No, no..." Grace paused for a moment. "Actually, yes. Tell him *I'll* call *him* when I'm ready."

Breena picked up the phone and hit answer. "Hi, Carl, it's Breena." She paused to listen. "Grace said she'd call you when she's ready to talk, so please don't call anymore or you'll just drag it out." She paused again. "No, I won't relay a message to her. You'll have a chance to talk to her and tell her whatever you want when *she's* ready. Until then, give her space, Carl." She set the phone down.

"Thank you," Grace whispered.

"You okay?" Breena rubbed her hand.

"Yeah, just have a lot of thinking to do." Grace rubbed her necklace but wished she had her journal.

Chapter 32

CARL

"I have surrounded myself with very smart people."

Dolly Parton

THE WAITING WAS KILLING Carl.

It had been a week since he spoke briefly with Breena. A long, grueling week. But Carl was honoring Grace's wishes by not calling her. It was probably the longest, hardest week of his life.

Which was ridiculous when he thought about it. He knew he was being dramatic and needed to snap out of it.

He jumped when the ringing phone startled him. He looked at the name while hitting answer. "Hey, Mom."

"Well, don't sound so excited." She laughed.

"Sorry. I was hoping it was someone else. No, no..." He sighed heavily. "I thought it might be someone else. I'm always happy to hear from you, Mom."

"Hmm, sounds like you haven't cleared things up with your girl yet," she said wisely before changing the subject. "Sunday dinner. Two o'clock. I expect you to be here."

Now it was his turn to laugh. "Yes, ma'am. I'll see you Sunday."

Sunday at two o'clock on the dot, Carl pulled into his parents' driveway. He noted the black Mazda Miata in the driveway signaling Jilly was already there. Hmm. He wasn't sure if this was good or bad. On the one hand, Jilly was great at keeping the conversation going. On the other hand, she could easily make Carl the topic of conversation, and he definitely wasn't interested in that.

Well, no reason to sit here and be late, then have to endure the wrath of his mother for his tardiness. Carl grabbed the bouquet of flowers off the passenger seat and headed to the house.

After a quick knock on the door, Carl opened it and walked into his childhood home. He always felt a sense of belonging and comfort in his parents' house. It hadn't changed a whole lot since his youth. The furniture had been updated after he and his sister moved out, but the scents and feelings were the same, and he felt good every time he walked through the front door.

He walked back to the kitchen where he knew everyone would be. He stood for a minute, unobserved, watching them all. His mom was at the stove, finishing up something that smelled amazing. His sister was sitting at the counter with a glass of sweet tea in front of her. And his dad was in the dining room, setting the table.

The whole scene made him smile. So familiar, this could be any Sunday for the past ten years.

"Hey, there you are." His mom noticed him and smiled.

"Hey, Mom, it smells amazing in here. Where can I put these flowers?"

She came over to him to give him a hug before taking the flowers from him and burying her face in them. Even though he brought her flowers regularly, she appreciated them every single time.

"Oh, these smell wonderful. Mrs. Snowden outdid herself with this bunch." She smiled up at Carl. Her eyes narrowed as she studied her son. "So did that girl ever call you?"

Jilly's head whipped around.

Carl looked at the two women in his life who he loved more than anything and sighed. "You know I love you, but there's no way I'm talking about that today."

He had zero desire to share anything about what was going on with Grace with any of them. Especially since nothing was actually going on. Only waiting.

The two women looked at each other knowingly and laughed.

He looked up to the ceiling. *Lord, help me!*

"Well, go find your seats, y'all. Lunch is served." His mom shooed them into the dining room.

She had made fried chicken, mashed potatoes, gravy, green beans, and dinner rolls instead of biscuits.

"Dad's been experimenting again," Mom commented. "You'll have to try the dinner rolls and let him know what you think."

For as long as Carl could remember, his father had experimented with baking. He'd pick what he was going to learn, then practice until he was satisfied. Remembering his father's last experiment—his first few attempts at sourdough bread had been brutal—Carl cringed, wondering how far along his father was in this experiment.

"Dinner rolls, Dad. Nice," Carl said diplomatically. "So how long have you been working on these?"

"Subtle, Carl." Jillian laughed, then looked at her father. "This is at least your third round, right, Dad?"

His dad laughed too. "I know you're thinking about the sourdough, but in my defense, sourdough is challenging for most people. Dinner rolls, on the other hand, aren't nearly as complicated." He took a bite from one of the rolls. "In fact, I'm almost done with this experiment. Maybe one or two more rounds, then they'll be perfect."

Carl loaded up his plate, including a dinner roll, content to just be with his family. As he was about to take his first bite, he felt his phone vibrate in his pocket. Knowing his mother's hard and fast rule of no phones at the dinner table, he stealthily sneaked a peek at the screen.

There was only one call he was hoping for.

The name on the screen read Grace.

Of course she'd call now. Right in the middle of Sunday dinner at his parents' house.

"Carl honey, you know the rule. Put your phone away."

Carl looked at his mother and back down at the phone, torn between wanting to follow his mother's rule and wanting to talk with Grace. He stood up from the table.

"Sorry, Mom, but I have to take this." He walked out of the room, knowing he'd pay the price with his mother later.

Going to the back porch for some privacy, Carl hit the answer button. "Grace, hi."

He was nervous but had been waiting on this call for days. His voice came out a little breathless, not only from the hurried walk to the back of the house but from the anticipation of finally talking to her.

"Hi, Carl."

Grace sounded tired. He wondered if she'd had a rough week, too.

"Thank you for honoring my wishes and not calling. I appreciate that."

"Grace, I'm so sorry about our last conversation." Carl had so much he wanted to say to her. So much he wanted her to understand.

"Listen, Carl, we both said things we regret." She paused for a second. "I've had a lot of fun with you since I came to Nashville. You're a great guy, and I really like you."

Carl was nervous. This was sounding like the kiss of death.

"But here's the thing. I can't be with someone who doesn't respect who and what I am. Or maybe I should say, I *won't* be with someone who doesn't trust me."

Carl's heart skipped a beat. It was painful to breathe, his lungs felt clogged. "Grace, I—"

But Grace interrupted him. She sounded like she wanted to finish what she had to say, so he listened, letting her say everything she needed to, even though he wasn't sure where this was going.

"I had been so hopeful for our relationship," Grace said softly, almost regretfully.

His heart pounded with dread, waiting to hear what came next. He didn't want to lose their relationship.

"What I'm willing to do, Carl, is be friends."

Carl waited to hear if more was coming, and when she didn't go on, he spoke. "Grace, I'm so sorry I was such a jerk. And you're right. When I saw you with your ex, I made all kinds of assumptions. My brain went straight back to Krisi with that man, and I shut down. I couldn't even think, to be honest. I didn't want to see or hear anything. And just like with Krisi, I wasn't willing to listen when you tried to explain."

"Sounds like maybe you need to have a conversation with Krisi, Carl. You might have been wrong about her, too."

"I—" That stopped him. Wrong about Krisi? Was that even possible? He hadn't even considered listening to her, letting her offer an explanation. "That never occurred to me. It's been so many years of me thinking I was right about what I saw..." He trailed off.

"As your friend, I think you should talk to her. It might free you to hear what she has to say. You might be right. She might have been cheating on you and your anger and distrust of her were deserved." Grace paused for a second. "But you might be wrong."

"That's a huge ask, Grace. One I've never even considered over the past six or so years." Carl took a deep breath before continuing. "But I will consider it."

"It was good to talk to you, Carl."

"Grace, wait." She was going already? Carl panicked. "Before you go, can we talk about what the rules of our friendship are? Am I allowed to call you?

I..." He spoke a little softer, much more vulnerable. "I would really enjoy talking with you again."

"I'd like that too, Carl."

He could hear the smile in her voice. At least he hoped that's what he was hearing.

"How about if I call you again soon?"

"I'd like that. Very much." He could breathe again. "Have a good day, Grace. I'll talk to you later."

He hoped it would be soon. She hadn't actually said *when* she'd call, but just the fact that she said she *would* call again made him hopeful.

He sat on the porch thinking about the conversation.

Friends.

She wanted to be friends.

Well, it certainly wasn't what he'd been hoping to hear, but it could have been much worse. He had broken her trust, and now he needed to figure out how to win that precious trust back. It wouldn't be easy, and it wouldn't be quick, but he was willing to figure it out.

Even if it meant talking to Krisi?

He walked back to the dining room, and all eyes were on him. He knew he needed to explain, but he wasn't sure what to say.

His mother helped him out. "So I'm guessing that was the girl you've been waiting for?"

"It was. I'm sorry I took a call at mealtime, but it was really important to me."

His mom smiled and looked over at his dad, who was smiling too. "Well, it's about darn time someone was important enough to break that rule. I look forward to meeting her one day."

Carl's mouth dropped open. Surprise didn't even cover what he was feeling. "So you're not mad I took the call?"

"Oh, honey, you're an adult. If someone is important enough for you to break a rule you've had all your life, then I'm thrilled for you."

Carl looked at his dad, who was still smiling.

"So when do we get to meet this mystery woman?" his dad asked.

"I, um. I have no idea. She's out of town right now, and I don't know when she'll be back. But I'm also not sure she'd want to meet the family, since she's just a friend."

"Hang in there, honey. If she's important to you, you'll figure out a way to let her know. We'll be here, ready to meet her when that happens."

"Thanks, Mom." Carl's voice was a little shaky. He looked down at his plate and started eating, even though swallowing would be tough with the lump in his throat.

Jillian set her glass down and glared at him. "I really like her, Carl. You better not screw this up any worse than you already have, or you'll have to deal with me."

He gave her a curt nod. Message received.

Chapter 33

GRACE

"I often get myself in love trouble because I'm so passionate; I love so much and so deep."

Dolly Parton

IT HAD BEEN TWO weeks since that phone call to Carl. They were back in Nashville and Grace was sitting in the living room with Breena, stealthily looking at her watch.

"You two have been talking a lot. What's going on?" Breena looked pointedly at her own watch, knowing Grace would disappear soon.

Grace blushed as she looked at Breena. Apparently, she hadn't been as sneaky as she thought. "Well, so far, nothing is going on. I told him I wanted to be friends, and he's respecting that."

"Hmm, but is that *really* all you want?"

Carl and Grace had gotten into a routine of talking every night, usually around nine o'clock or so. The first couple of calls had been a little awkward. Carl wasn't sure what the new rules were, and she understood that, but since then, they'd gotten into a really enjoyable habit of ending their days with one another.

They still hadn't seen each other. She hadn't told him she was back, even though they'd arrived a couple of days ago, and he hadn't asked. But once the moving truck picked up the things they wanted to keep, everything moved quickly. The estate sale had gone well, then the real estate agent had put the townhouse on the market, and Breena had an offer within two days.

The drive back to Nashville had been fun, and she was grateful to finally have her little Toyota there. It was a long drive, but going through the mountains was beautiful. They'd stopped in Chattanooga for a late lunch with Breena's friend. It felt good to stretch their legs a bit.

She hadn't expected to stay in Florida longer than a couple of days, but it worked out well and they'd accomplished so much.

Grace looked at her watch. Time to talk to Carl. "Well, I think I'm going to get ready for bed."

"Time to call lover boy?" Breena laughed.

Grace blushed. "First off, he's not *lover boy*. He's just a friend. And second, yes." She laughed as she walked away. "See you in the morning."

After changing into her pajamas and going through her evening bathroom routine, Grace grabbed her phone, ready to call. She wore her mother's long nightgown, even though she now had the means to buy something a little less Victorian. But she had gotten used to the nightgowns and liked them.

"Hey there," Carl answered on the first ring.

"Hey, Carl, how was your day?"

"It was great. I worked at the Kline house today. Mrs. Kline popped in to see how it was going. She's definitely getting bigger, and she's excited the room is almost finished, since she is too. Ha!"

Carl had updated her on the conversation he'd had with Mr. Kline. Since then, the project had been progressing nicely, and from the sound of it, Mrs. Kline's pregnancy was going well.

"Enough about my day, tell me how yours was," Carl said.

"I've been doing a lot of thinking about Hope's House. There's such a need for safe places for women in abusive situations."

Over the course of their phone calls, Grace had read her mother's second letter to Carl, about how she'd gotten the money. It had been nice to clear that air between them and to be able to talk about money without any weirdness.

"Have you started looking for a house yet?" Carl asked.

"No, but I think I'll contact a realtor tomorrow. Any suggestions?"

"I'll send you the name of someone I think might work well. So what do you want in the house? What're you looking for?"

"It's funny, Bree and I talked about this a lot while we were in Florida. I have such a clear idea of what I want, it might actually make it hard to find. I've even done a sketch of the house and a floor plan." She laughed a little.

"Really? I'd love to see what you have in mind. Do you mind sending me the pictures?"

She went to the home office next to her bedroom and snapped a couple of photos of the sketches she'd put up on her dream board.

"Okay, just sent them. I'm not a great artist, but I know what I want. Hopefully, it comes across in the pictures." Grace waited anxiously to hear Carl's thoughts on the house of her dreams. She'd put so much thought and passion, if not skill, into the designs, it was scary to share them. She'd not shown the pictures to anyone except Bree. And now Carl. It felt like baring her soul.

"Grace, wow!" Carl's voice was a little shaky. She wasn't sure what was going on in his mind. "That's, um...that's an amazing house."

"Wouldn't it be amazing to find something even kinda close to that? I know expecting to find *that* house is ridiculous, but I hope there's something close."

The house she had pictured was built from logs, with the bottom level as a garage. The middle level had a wraparound porch. There were also a couple of cabins next to the main house. They were much smaller but looked similar to the big house. Then there was a fence surrounding a huge property, protecting it all.

Though she didn't know how to draw the inside, she wanted it to be modern and to feel, if not luxurious, then special. The women who stayed there were coming to be safe, not to be pampered, but she wanted to take care of their mental state as well as their physical.

"I am confident you'll find your house, Grace. It's going to be amazing, just like you."

"Thank you. I feel so vulnerable sharing that with you. I appreciate your support. And yes, I think it will be amazing too."

After saying their good nights, Grace put her phone on the charger in her office and headed to bed, thinking of Carl and his comment—*it's going to be amazing, just like you.*

Chapter 34

CARL

"A great smile is a wonderful asset, but a good heart is pure gold."
Dolly Parton

CARL HAD BEEN STUNNED when he saw the picture Grace texted him. He was looking at Krisi's mountain cabin. Of course, it wasn't really her cabin. It was Grace's vision. But it looked almost exactly like the house he'd worked on for so many months. Even the floor plan she'd sent was scarily similar.

But the question was what to do about it? As far as he knew, Krisi wasn't selling. And geesh, it had been more than five years since he'd spoken with her. It would be miserable to talk to her. He'd managed to avoid it for this long.

But for Grace, he was willing to do it. He was willing to do pretty much anything for her, he realized. It took an hour to dig up Krisi's phone number from the papers in his desk. He'd deleted it from his phone years ago.

He knew Krisi was a night owl, but what he didn't know was if she were alone. He shot off a text before he could talk himself out of it.

CARL: Hey Krisi, it's Carl

KRISI: Um, wow?!

CARL: Yeah, I know. Is there any way we could meet one day soon?

KRISI: I'm available tomorrow

CARL: how about coffee at Music Row Joe's?

KRISI: See u at 11

Carl stared at his phone. He'd just made a coffee date with Krisi.

Krisi?

He was floored he'd just done that. But he knew this was what he needed to do.

Even if he and Grace's relationship never went past friendship, he needed to do this for her. But dang, this was going to be hard.

The next morning, Carl sat in his car outside Music Row Joe's, gathering his courage, thinking back to that afternoon so many years ago.

He was jolted out of the memory by his phone alarm alerting him it was time to go in. He walked into the coffee shop with a sense of dread and looked around.

She was sitting in a corner away from the other diners. Her blond hair was a little shorter than before, but she was still a very beautiful woman.

Rubbing his hands on the front of his jeans, he took a deep breath and headed toward her. "Morning, Krisi." He slid into the bench across the table from her.

She looked up and gave a tentative smile. "Hi, Carl."

He realized she looked as nervous as he felt. "I appreciate you meeting me today."

"Well, this is certainly unexpected. I can honestly say I never anticipated hearing from you again." She smiled at the waitress who dropped off her water with lemon and a cup of coffee before taking Carl's order.

"I guess I finally need to ask some questions. I want to know what happened. Why did you cheat on me? I thought we were doing well."

Krisi shifted in her seat and stared down at her coffee. "I was in a rough place during that time. Not an excuse..." She looked up at him. "Just an explanation. While I had a lot of fun with you, you were getting way too serious."

"I thought it was mutual?"

"You were an unfortunate casualty of my wasted youth. I'm sorry." She looked down into her coffee again.

"You came into a lot of money young, didn't you?"

"I did. I was twenty-one when my trust fund kicked in. All of a sudden, the whole world was my playground in a new, exciting way. My parents were off doing their own thing, so I kinda went off the rails a bit." She laughed. "Well, more than a bit. I was really sad when you left, but I convinced myself it was for the best. You were small-town, reliable, nice, and not at all what I was looking for. Probably what I needed, but not what I wanted."

Carl nodded. "Yeah, we were definitely in different places. I knew that, but seeing you leave with another man really hit me hard."

"You wouldn't even talk to me afterward." She sounded hurt.

Carl finished his coffee and nodded as the waitress refilled it. "What you did just flattened me, but not for the reasons you might think." He noticed Krisi's furrowed brow but kept going. "I came back up the mountain that weekend because Gabe had to cancel our weekend plans. Before I headed back up, I grabbed a bottle of wine and some flowers. I was excited to spend an unexpected, fun, romantic weekend with you. With my work schedule, we didn't get many spontaneous weekends. Before I could even get out of my car, I saw you two get in his sleek black Maserati and drive off together."

Krisi played with her coffee cup, then looked him in the eye. "I...I never realized you were there. That you saw us. I couldn't figure out how you knew."

"One of the things I never told you when we were dating was that my biological mother left us when I was about five years old." He proceeded to tell her the sordid tale of Bio Mom.

Krisi looked up at him, her eyes glistening. "Dang, Carl. Of course it hit you hard. I'm sorry to hear about your mom."

"She isn't my mom, just my biological mother." Carl's voice was harsher than he'd intended.

"Did you ever hear from her again?"

"I did, but I haven't told my family. She called last year. When a house I worked on was featured in Architectural Digest. She's so proud of me and the man I've become. She tells all her friends how proud she is of her son. Of course she wanted something from me. Money. She doesn't do love without strings attached."

Krisi's eyes widened. "Oh my gosh. What'd you do?"

"I told her she wasn't my mom, and there was no reason for her to ever contact me again."

"Has she left you alone?"

"So far. I never told anyone because I didn't want her to cause more pain in our family."

"Wow." Krisi looked at him for a minute. "Carl, I hope you can forgive me. It wasn't my goal to hurt you. I was thoughtless and careless with people and relationships."

Carl smiled at her. A genuine smile. "I do forgive you, Krisi. And I hope you find the person who makes you happy."

"Have you found your person?" she asked.

"Well, yes. But I screwed it up. She's part of why I'm here today." He could see confusion on Krisi's face. He took out the image Grace had texted him and laid it in front of her.

"My cabin? What? I'm confused."

"I bet." Carl laughed. He told her about Grace. He didn't tell her exactly what Grace wanted to use the cabin for—that was Grace's story to share—but he told her about their relationship and why he was talking to her. "She drew this picture without ever having seen your cabin. This is her dream house. Her vision."

"Wow. That's incredible." Krisi reached over and picked up the paper Carl had printed that morning.

"Yeah. I was stunned when she sent this to me." He looked Krisi in the eyes now. "So I thought I would see if you would ever consider selling your house. Or at least letting her look at it."

"Hmm, well. I haven't used the cabin in years, so I suppose it wouldn't be a big deal to have her look. Tell me what you've got in mind."

Chapter 35

GRACE

*"Being a star just means that you just
find your own special place, and that
you shine where you are."*
Dolly Parton

THE NEXT MORNING, GRACE and Breena were
traversing a narrow mountain road to meet
with a real estate agent. Grace had been surprised
when a Kristine St. Claire had called yesterday afternoon about a mountain cabin. She said Carl had
passed her name and number along, and she had a
home she thought Grace might like.

"Here. Right here." Grace pointed to the even
smaller road off to the right. A few yards later, they

came to an open wrought iron gate with a silver SUV parked in front of it.

A thin, blonde woman dressed in black wool pants and a yellow sweater hopped out of the SUV and came to the driver's window.

"Grace?" she asked after Breena rolled down the window.

Grace leaned over. "Yes, that's me. Are you Ms. St. Claire?"

"I am. I think the rest of the trip might be easier in my SUV." She looked at Breena. "Pull off to the side right inside the gate. That'll make it easier to get out when we're done."

After pulling the car off the path, they climbed into the SUV.

"Thank you for meeting me here. I would have picked you up but wanted to make sure the heat was on and it wasn't too musty in there. The house hasn't been used in several years."

Slowly, they went around a bend and the house came into view. Grace gasped, her hands going involuntarily to her mouth. In front of her was an exact, life-size replica of her sketch. A huge four-story log cabin, the bottom level a multicar garage. There were wonderful wraparound porches on the upper two levels. The area around the house had been cleared, but there were trees further out. She noticed a couple of smaller cabins off to the right.

After parking in front of the cabin, the three women hopped out of the vehicle and stood, looking up at the house.

"Why didn't this come up in my searches?" Grace asked.

"It's not on the market."

Now Grace was confused. "So why are we here if it's not for sale?"

"This is my house. I had coffee with Carl yesterday, and he showed me your sketch."

Understanding came gradually. "You're Krisi."

It wasn't a question. She heard Breena gasp softly.

Krisi nodded. "Carl said when you showed him the sketch, he knew he had to at least ask if my house was on the market."

"That must have been an awkward conversation," Breena ventured.

Krisi laughed. "It was, for sure. I never thought I'd hear from him again after what I'd done to him. He told me he'd really messed things up with you."

Grace looked up at her, surprised. "We're good. We're friends now."

"Oh, Grace, that man is so in love with you."

Grace started to protest, but Krisi kept going.

"Think about it. Why would he be willing to have that conversation with me—me who cheated on him and hurt him—if he didn't love you?"

Grace looked at Breena, who just lifted an eyebrow. This was a lot to take in.

Did Carl love her? If so, what was she willing to do about it?

"Well...want to look around?" Krisi asked.

"Oh yes, do I ever."

"So how do you want to do this? Inside or outside first?" Krisi waited to see what Grace preferred.

"Maybe we should do the outside first. Looks like it might snow," Grace said.

"Okay, let's walk around. I'll answer any questions I can."

The three of them walked around the house. Krisi hadn't brought the keys for the cabins, but they peeked in the windows and saw they both had three bedrooms—split plan, living room–dining room, and a nice kitchen in each.

There was a firepit with chairs circling it on the west side of the property. Off to one side was a large, covered chair swing overlooking the mountains to the east. Sunrises from that spot would be spectacular. Otherwise, it was mostly just open space surrounding the house. This was exactly the kind of property Grace and Breena had talked about.

The first few snowflakes started falling as they came back to the front of the house.

"Well, looks like it's time to head inside." Grace laughed as she ran up the stairs to the front door.

"Hopefully, it doesn't get much worse than this," Breena said. "Not sure my little car will make it back down the mountain if it's slippery."

Krisi pulled the key out of her pocket and opened the door. It was a little musty, but warm since she had already turned on the heat.

The front door opened into a small foyer with a short hallway, with a library to the left. Grace poked her head in but didn't explore the room. Across the hall was a large game room. Again, Grace poked her head in but didn't go in the room. She looked back at Krisi.

"Why don't you two take your time? I'll be upstairs in the living room." Krisi headed up the stairs while Grace and Breena explored downstairs.

There were a few unfinished rooms down the hallway where they, again, just poked their heads in. "This would be a great medical area. One could be made into an exam room and the others into recovery rooms."

"Yes. There's even enough room to have a sleeping room for a nurse or aide." Grace could see the vision. They finished poking around downstairs and headed up.

"Oh, I love how open this is. You feel like you're outside, even when you're not." Grace paused in front of the sliding glass doors leading to the wraparound deck. It was mostly a huge multipurpose room with a small sunroom to one side. Windows were everywhere, looking out on the mountains. Krisi had made a pot of coffee and was sitting in the living room on one of the couches.

"There are two bedrooms on this level and four more on the next level." Krisi smiled at them.

Breena checked out the kitchen while Grace went into a bedroom. It was large and open with lots of windows and a small balcony. The attached bathroom was large with both a tub and a shower. Her brain was working overtime, thinking of all the possibilities.

She met back up with Breena and they climbed the stairs to the top floor. The two angled rooms on either end were small, cozy sitting rooms.

"Any idea how many bedrooms you'd like?" Breena walked into one of the bedrooms.

"I was thinking around six to eight with space for kids, in case that was a need. Breena, this house is so perfect."

"I agree. The only potential sticky point is that it's owned by Carl's ex-girlfriend," Breena said softly.

Grace nodded, not sure how to respond. Breena wasn't wrong.

After checking out each of the remaining rooms, they headed back down to the living area. They found Krisi still sitting on the couch with a cup of coffee.

"So what do you think?" she asked.

"It would be so perfect for what we want to do," Grace said.

"If you don't mind me asking, what are your plans? Carl wouldn't tell me why you were interested in getting such a big house. He said it was your story to share if you wanted to."

Grace paused for a moment. Carl didn't share her story with Krisi.

"I just found out my mother had helped abused women. She'd help them get away from their dangerous situations, and then she'd protect them. She passed away recently, and I want to honor her and her mission. I'd like to set up a safe house for women, especially women who need time to recover or heal, or women who have children."

Grace watched a mix of emotions cross Krisi's face. "I love that mission," she finally said. "I've been looking for the right philanthropic opportunity to get involved in. I know I want to help women, but nothing has interested me thus far. I'm not sure if you're looking for investors or volunteers, or if you'd even want to let me help with my history with Carl, but I would really be interested in being part of your mission."

"Wow, um, I'm not even sure how to respond to that, but we could certainly use the help. Thank you."

They decided to leave Breena's car inside the gate, and Krisi gave them a ride back to the apartment downtown since her vehicle was built for the weather and she knew how to drive in snow. Grace's head was buzzing with so many ideas. Krisi had agreed to sell the house to her.

"So let's get back to Carl," Krisi said. "Why do you think he *isn't* in love with you?"

"He saw me having coffee with my ex-boyfriend and jumped to all kinds of conclusions. I won't be with someone who doesn't trust me, and how can Carl possibly love me if he doesn't trust me?"

Krisi glanced over. "You know his response didn't have anything to do with you, right?"

"What do you mean?"

"He told you about his past, about us, right?"

Grace nodded, remembering the ride to Pigeon Forge. It seemed like so long ago.

"His response to you was the same as his response to me. I mean, sure, I cheated on him, but he didn't even want to talk about it, right?"

Again, Grace nodded.

"Yeah, well, that's all down to his mother."

"What?" Grace was confused. How did Carl's mother fit into all this?

"When she left, it crushed him. He was only five, so obviously he was crushed."

"His mother left him? I thought his mom and dad were still married?" Grace looked at Breena, then over to Krisi. "I'm sorry, but I have no idea what you're talking about."

"Oh shoot. I'm sorry. I thought he'd told you. This is really his story, but I think you need to know." She went on to tell Grace about Carl's biological mother and how she'd left.

Now Grace had even more to think about. *Did Carl still love her?* The fact that he'd been willing to meet with Krisi, to talk about their past, to ask for a favor for her—for Grace—staggered her.

Had she been wrong about him? And how did she feel about him?

Krisi pulled up in front of The Athenian. "Oh my gosh, I almost forgot." She reached under her seat and pulled out a large brown envelope. "Carl asked me to give this back to you."

Confused, Grace took the envelope. "Thank you. And tell Carl...No, I'll tell him. Thank you, Krisi. For everything."

The three women hugged, and Grace and Breena headed up to the apartment.

Grace sat sat in front of the fireplace and opened the envelope. "My journal!" She immediately recognized the book, and a smile crossed her face. She'd missed having her journal to write in at the end of the day. It felt like an old friend had returned. She flipped through the pages, remembering.

She smiled as she read through her journey to find Dolly. Reading through her journey with Carl made her confused.

She came to her final entry, at Dollywood, and read the letter she'd written to Dolly—a letter she would never send, of course—and the entry she'd written in the car so she could remember what the woman said to her.

Thinking she'd like to write a new entry, maybe catch her journal up on all that had happened in the past few weeks, Grace flipped to a new page. A breeze blew through the room and fluttered a couple of pages over. How odd. Why was there writing past her last entry? What was this?

Confused, she grabbed the journal and held it closer so she could read the flowy script.

Find out who you are and do it on purpose.

She'd heard that before. Thinking back, she remembered her mother had written it in her letter. She also remembered that's what the woman sitting next to her at Dollywood had said. Her eyes moved down to the signature.

Dolly.

Grace sat stunned. Her heart was beating loudly and her hands, still holding the journal, were shaking.

Then she let out a loud shout. "Breena!"

She hopped off the couch and ran toward Breena's bedroom. She reached the dining room at the same moment Breena did, and they almost collided.

"What? Are you okay?" Breena was breathless.

"No. I mean yes. But I need to show you something." Grace dragged her into the living room and grabbed the journal. "I found Dolly!"

She put the open journal into Breena's hands and watched as she read.

Breena looked up, her eyes wide. "Dolly wrote in your journal? How is that even possible?"

"Remember the woman I told you I met at Dollywood? It had to have been her. She watched over my stuff while I was talking to Carl. I had just written a letter to her." Grace flipped back a few pages and showed the letter to Breena. "Of course I was never going to send it, but it felt good to write it down. Kind of like closure, I guess. She must have seen it. Read it."

"Oh my gosh, Grace. Dolly Parton wrote in your journal. You found Dolly!" Breena pulled Grace up to dance around the living room with her.

Tucked into her mother's bed, Grace picked up the journal sitting on the nightstand. She wanted to look at it one more time. It felt like a miracle. Like her mother had reached down to give her a hug.

She opened the journal from the back and flipped forward, looking for the last page with writing on it. Finding the writing, she opened the page to savor the words again.

But this wasn't Dolly's writing. This was something different. She held the book a little closer to read the words.

Every moment I've spent with you is a precious gift I cherish.

Your smile, your laugh, the way you look at me - you fill my heart with joy and happiness.

I will always be here for you, no matter what.

You will always hold my heart

Carl

A tear dripped onto the page and Grace hastily wiped her eyes, not wanting to mess up this page.

Before she could talk herself out of it, she threw on a pair of jeans and a sweater and grabbed her coat. She left a note for Breena in the kitchen, near the coffee pot, and headed down the elevator.

She had to find out if he meant those words. If he really did love her.

Krisi seemed to think he did, but what if he didn't mean them anymore? She didn't know when he wrote it.

She pulled into his driveway, gravel crunching under her tires. She glanced at the clock and was surprised to see it was midnight. *Crap.* She probably should have looked at the clock before she left.

But then she wouldn't have come. As she was debating whether to get out or head back home, lights came on in the living room and the front door opened.

Carl stood in the doorway, staring out at her. He was wearing jeans and buttoning a flannel shirt. She couldn't see his face because the light was behind him.

But she knew she needed to go to him. *God, it was scary.* Her whole future was in his hands.

She opened the car door and walked to him, journal in her hand.

He met her at the bottom of the stairs. His face was unreadable.

"You will always hold my heart too." Her voice wavered, but she had to know. She had to let him know.

Carl closed his eyes. He still hadn't said anything.

He took a step forward until he was a breath away. He looked down at her, his hands going to her face. His gaze roamed her face, seeming to memorize it before meeting her eyes.

"Welcome home."

And his lips came down on hers, and she knew she *was* home.

Epilogue

EPILOGUE

EPILOGUE

*"Don't let anyone, even me, steal your
sense of fun or the kindness that has
always been in you."*
Marilyn Parson

I T HAD BEEN YEARS since Grace experienced a
Christmas as noisy and chaotic as this one. The
remnants of the morning were all around them. It
was wonderful.

Seated next to Carl in his living room, she looked
at the group of people she had in her life now. Carl's
mom was in the kitchen, taking casseroles out of the
oven for brunch. His dad was leafing through the copy
of *Baking with Julia* Grace had given him that morn-

ing. Jilly and Breena were making a new pot of coffee and setting the table.

And even though her mother wasn't physically here anymore, she could feel her presence. It brought her a lot of comfort.

Outside, it was cold and snowing lightly; inside, the fire kept them cozy and comfortable. The stockings, waiting to be opened after brunch, hung from the mantle. Life looked so different from last Christmas.

Carl nudged her and leaned over. "I've got your present in the basement. Let's head down while everyone is busy."

She wrinkled her brow. "But you gave me that wonderful purple scarf."

"Come on." He stood, pulling her up with him. He gave his mom a kiss on the cheek as they passed through the kitchen. "We'll be right back."

His mom smiled and went back to stirring. Carl grabbed Grace's hand and led her through the kitchen to the stairs to the basement. He hit the lights when they reached the bottom and a smile split across Grace's face.

"You put the dancing pole down here?"

Carl had taken down the pole from the penthouse living room, but she'd had no idea he had installed it in his house. "Well, I couldn't get rid of it. There's a lot of sentiment attached to that pole. After all, it was the pole that brought us together."

Grace laughed and threw her arms around his neck. "Thank you, Carl. I love it!"

She loved the idea of spending more time at Carl's house. It was beginning to feel more like home than the penthouse. She resonated with being surrounded by nature.

Carl gave her a slow smile. "I think you misunderstood the gift."

At her confused look, he pointed up. Attached to the very top of the pole, almost touching the ceiling, was a small box. It looked to be about four or five inches square, wrapped in gold with a red bow on it.

"I—" She looked from Carl to the box and back again. "So you want me to climb the pole to get my Christmas present?"

"Exactly." Carl looked entirely too pleased with himself. His twinkling eyes crinkled at the corners, and his dimples stood out.

She rolled her eyes, then sat down on the floor to take off her boots and socks. Good thing she'd worn jeans this morning rather than the skirt she'd been contemplating. Grabbing hold of the pole, she pulled herself off the floor, then set her hands higher up. She got a foothold several inches off the ground and steadily worked her way up the pole.

When she reached the top, she took one hand off the pole to grab the present. But the box wouldn't move. It was stuck there securely. She looked down at Carl, but he offered no help, just shrugged up at her.

Rethinking her approach, she wiggled the top of the box and realized she could take the top off and pull out what was inside. Resetting her hands and feet, she reached up with one hand and eased the top of the box off. Once it was free, she threw it at Carl. She smiled as it glanced off the side of his head. With the top off, she was able to fit her fingers inside the box. Feeling around, she found another, smaller box.

She could feel her palms getting sweaty. She needed to wrap this up before she slid down the pole. She wiped her hands on her jeans, one at a time, set herself again, and slipped her fingers into the box to work the smaller box to the top and out.

She gave a sharp tug, and the smaller box popped out. As if in slow motion, she watched the small black box arc up before slowly making its way down. She stretched out her free hand to grab it, but it was a little too far away and her hand on the pole lost its grip. As she felt her fingers close around the box, she found herself soaring through the air toward the floor.

Before she could even sort out what was happening, strong arms wrapped around her, stopping her descent.

Carl grinned at her. "Thank you for not breaking my nose this time."

Smiling, she looked from him to the small box still clutched in her hand. Her eyes widened and her blood pumped quicker as she looked more closely at the small black velvet box.

Carl shifted her body and set her gently on her feet while keeping his arms around her. "May I?" He took the box from her hand, opening it to reveal a sparkling heart-cut diamond ring.

"Oh!" Her hands flew to her mouth as she watched him lower to one knee.

She could feel the tears threatening. She felt so much love for this man.

He looked at her with such tenderness. "I fell for you the moment I met you."

Her laugh caught in a sob. Her hand pressed to her heart.

"I told you before, you hold my heart. I love you with everything in me, and I want, more than anything, to spend the rest of my life loving you. Dolly Grace Parson, will you do me the honor of marrying me?"

Grace's knees couldn't hold her up any longer, and she lowered herself in front of him. "Carl James Montgomery, I will take your heart and treasure it. Just like you've done with mine."

She leaned over and pressed her lips to his.

"Wait." Carl pulled back from the kiss and looked at her with concern in his eyes. "Is that a yes?"

She could see what she couldn't before, just how nervous he was.

"You bet it's a yes! Now put that gorgeous ring on my finger and kiss me properly."

Want to read Breena's story?

"Love is just a bid away in Nashville"

When spunky and independent Breena wins Gabriel (not Gabe) at a bachelor auction, neither of them is looking for romance. But they both have their own reasons for needing this fake relationship to appear real.

As they navigate the complexities of their fake relationshipand the social obligations that come with it, Breena and Gabefind themselves growing closer and developing genuine feelings for each other.

And sometimes, just sometimes, it's hard to remember that it's fake.

Go to

https://www.amazon.com/dp/1960969064

If you enjoyed this book, please take a few minutes to leave a review. Authors really appreciate this, and it helps let other readers know this is a book they might like. Thank you!

https://www.amazon.com/dp/1960969013/

Are you curious about Grace's mother's story? Read all about Marilyn and Martin and how they met and fell in love for FREE in Rescuing Hope.

This was such a fun book to write. Marilyn is a free spirit, Martin is a buttoned-up college professor. Their worlds unexpectedly clash on a road trip from Las Vegas to Nashville.

Grab the Prequel to Finding Dolly at
https://dl.bookfunnel.com/t9znmph6n8

Acknowledgments

THERE ARE SO MANY people to say thank you to. It truly takes a village. While writing might be a solitary endeavor, getting a book out into the world is not!

Thank you to Kerry Evelyn for encouraging me to write the story that came to me and helping me every step of the way. Thank you to my accountability partners, Nicole and Sarah, and my Writing Sprint partners for helping me stay on track. Thank you to my walking partner, partner in crime, and sister, Patti for listening to *everything* for the last eighteen months. I am very grateful to be part of FSFW writing group and the education and encouragement that community provides. The book wouldn't have turned out nearly as well without my Beta readers who gave such amazing feedback and helped Grace and Carl's story turn out even better. I certainly couldn't have put out such a professional, polished book without the help of editors and a fantastic cover designer.

Thank you to God for entrusting me with the idea for Grace's story and the endurance and patience to see it through.

And for my wonderfully patient husband who loves me through all my crazy ideas and trips.

And a huge thank you to you, dear reader, for coming along for the ride. I hope you stick around and read Marilyn, Breena, and Jillian's stories as well.

Also by Becki Lee

Nashville Hearts series

Rescuing Hope (prequel)
Finding Dolly
Dating Breena
Discovering Jillian
Marrying Grace

Nashville Billionaire series

Betting on Brian
Remembering Beau
Always Alex

About Becki

ABOUT BECKI

B ECKI LEE IS A sweet contemporary romance author that loves to throw in a dash of humor, good friends, and good looking heroes. She loves reading and writing stories that give you an escape and glimpse into other parts of the world.

You can read more about future books on her website:

beckileeauthor.com

www.ingramcontent.com/pod-product-compliance
Lightning Source LLC
Chambersburg PA
CBHW060223030726
47499CB00004B/1170